Stepwives

Stepwives

A Novel by
Phillis Stevens

Crown Publishers, Inc. New York

Published by Crown Publishers, Inc., 201 East 50th Street, New York, New York 10022. Member of the Crown Publishing Group.

CROWN is a trademark of Crown Publishers, Inc.

Manufactured in the United States of America

Library of Congress Cataloging-in-Publication Data

Stevens, Phillis.
    Stepwives : a novel / by Phillis Stevens. — 1st ed.
        p.   cm.
    I. Title.   II. Title: Stepwives.
PS3569.T4519S74   1990
813'.54—dc20
                                                89-20988
                                                    CIP

ISBN 0-517-57678-3

10 9 8 7 6 5 4 3 2 1

First Edition

THIS IS DEDICATED TO
THE MEMORY OF JONNY JASPER
(FEBRUARY 13, 1963—MAY 27, 1982)

She dreamed, she endured, and she never gave up.

Stepwives

1

Killing Mac Carpenter should have been easy. After all, he'd already had three heart attacks; he worked too hard, drank too much, smoked constantly, and in spite of his doctor's repeated admonitions, his only form of exercise was lumbering from the dining-room table every evening to the couch where he vegetated through prime-time TV until bedtime.

"It'd be easy to give him another heart attack," Marilee Smith Carpenter Finch Sommerfrught Wallace had told me. "Easy as taking candy from a baby. Easy as pie."

I was not the killer type—at least not then. I had never done anything more criminal than steal a dime from a pay phone years ago, something that, for a long time, could activate my guilt in the middle of the night when I had nothing better to worry about.

As it happened, I hadn't worried about that dime for several months before I met Marilee. I'd certainly had much better things to worry about than a lousy dime, pilfered from Ma Bell or more likely, some uncaring caller to whom dimes meant nothing. I'd ended a twenty-five-year marriage in a burst of uncharacteristic anger and vindictiveness when I'd caught Jack Travis, my ex-husband, in bed with another woman—in my house, in my bed—with my friend.

"Stop and think, Karen," another friend had counseled urgently. "This happens all the time. Don't let it make you do something you'll regret later. Stay with him. Make his life hell for a few weeks. You'll get another fur out of it, or maybe even a new car."

I'd been too hurt, however, too outraged, too crazy, and divorced him forthwith, unable to reconcile myself to what, in my abject in-

nocence and naïveté at the time, I'd dubbed "the ultimate betrayal."
What a joke.

She'd been right. I did regret it later. Jack was an astute businessman
and had an even more astute lawyer, who'd bought off my lawyer,
something that happens all the time, I came to learn. Since we'd
divorced in Oklahoma, where we lived at the time and which is not
a community-property state, I found myself suddenly alone, forty-five,
nearly broke, and helpless to know how to support myself.

I'd moved to Santa Fe, New Mexico, to get away from memories
and old friends who, still married, had no time for a divorced sister
who was suddenly a rival. Santa Fe suited me. It was laid-back, slightly
skewed with the real world, culturally adept, and small-town friendly.
Best of all, no one there knew I had been wealthy and was now poor,
new poor. To every one of my new acquaintances, I was just another
single woman living in Santa Fe, making do, experiencing life's lessons, existing, and managing to make it palpable and sometimes,
rarely, even fun.

I'd seen the pink Cadillac around town; everyone knew it. It was
an insider's joke on the plaza that if you caught a flash of titty-pink,
you ran like hell for a building because you weren't even safe on the
sidewalk. It was a '59 DeVille convertible, the model with the wildly
rearing tail fins, chromed and fender-skirted, complete down to the
little curb feelers that had gone out with the other motorized dinosaurs
of that time. All the young Hispanics who drove custom-lowered,
older-model domestic cars, the "lowriders," loved it and sometimes
would follow it around the plaza and down the Paseo, honking and
waving, trying to keep up with the flame-haired maniac as she drove
it through the narrow streets, scattering tourists like chickens, causing
old people and busted-up skiers to leap spryly for safety, leaving their
crutches, canes, and walkers in the street to become short-term grill
ornaments for the Cadillac.

I came to learn later that the only thing that saved the citizens of
the town from any worse was the fact the car got only eight miles to
the gallon. The woman who owned it was in even direr straits financially than I was and couldn't afford the gasoline for more than a few
minutes each week.

I'd sold my Jaguar, along with most of my other liquefiable assets, piece by piece, living off the proceeds before I came fully to the terrifying realization that there was no inexhaustible supply of money being regularly deposited into my account anymore, that there would be no one to stand between me and the horrors of the world, and that I would have to support myself, something that I had never done in my life, had no training in. Through a series of flukes and sheer luck, I managed to get a job and rent a house. I'd bought a used Volkswagen Bug, and even if it had seen better days, it somehow suited me, and as I'd done with Santa Fe, I developed a love for it that bordered on fierceness. It was easier to love things than people then, and my VW turned out to be more dependable than its low initial cost had suggested it would be—and certainly more dependable than the people in my life had been.

I'd left the Museum Shop in the Palace of the Governors where I worked to run to the post office. The November sky was pewter colored and heavy looking, suggesting an early snow or worse, chilling rain. The mountains surrounding the city were cut off halfway up by the clouds, making them seem somehow foreign, as if someone or something had toted off the Sangre de Cristos and the Jemez and replaced them with defective mountains, seconds, ones with no tops.

I could have walked to the post office—everything in downtown Santa Fe is accessible by foot—but it was dreary that day and I was coming down with a cold, a cold that I'd had no time to baby as I'd always done before by staying in bed and reading murder mysteries and sipping brandy. I was expected to be at work now, cold or no cold, and jobs for untrained, destitute, fortyish women in Santa Fe weren't so easy to come by that I could luxuriate in bed anymore, treating myself with books and irresponsibility as I'd done B.D., before divorce.

I started my Bug and eased out of the postage-stamp parking lot behind the museum, carefully working my way through the cars wadded into it until I reached the street. At that precise moment, several things happened. The load of invitations that I'd been going to mail slid onto the floor of the VW; a pedestrian, an authoritative-looking Hispanic male, gestured irritably for me to proceed in front of him, and distracted by that and the fear that the invitations might have gotten dirty on the floorboard of my car, I missed the fearful flash of pink that would have signaled, at the very least, extreme caution. I pulled onto Lincoln Street just as the Cadillac veered for the sidewalk, and we met in a crunch that sounded exactly like a gravel truck unloading pebbles onto a tin surface. The Caddy stopped with one wheel on my trunk, the forward part of my VW, and lodged there like some monstrous behemoth who'd succeeded in establishing dominance over a mouse. Shocked, I sat there for a few seconds, staring at the front tire against my windshield, and then, suddenly and untypically furious, I boiled out of my violated car, ran around the back of it, and confronted the woman who'd gotten out and was standing, arms akimbo, staring at the melded mess.

"You utter and complete idiot," I hissed, remembering even in the stress of the moment that refined ladies didn't shriek on the street as I wanted to do, adding needlessly, "See what you've done to my car!"

"Look, asshole! What's the idea of pulling out in front of me like that?"

I stared at her, too outraged by the injustice of the accusation to reply instantly, and she took my hesitation for weakness and pressed her point.

"I'm going to sue the shit out of you for this! This car is a classic and you've destroyed it. Do you know how much this car costs? Or would have if you hadn't torn it up like that? Try twenty thousand dollars, you asshole! Try twenty-five! There's only a few of these things left in existence and you've absolutely destroyed a relic."

By this time a crowd was gathering, ambling up, Santa Fe style, curious but not curious enough to hurry. They would gather the same way for a bomb explosion in the middle of the plaza. Ordinarily, I would have found the idea of making a public spectacle of myself abhorrent and would have backed down a little, tried to reason with her, or perhaps even ignored her unladylike tirade while I summoned, as gracefully as possible, the policeman on the plaza beat halfway down the block. The sight of that huge, disgracefully obscene monster squatting on my defenseless little Bug completely undid me, however, and I shoved my face up into hers and yelled, "You mindless harridan! How *dare* you suggest to me I'm at fault here! There's witnesses right here, on this sidewalk, who saw you deliberately aim for me, and if you want to sue, then you just go ahead! I know several mean and competent attorneys who'll make your case look like hash. Just do it! Go ahead, I dare you!" I added for good measure, "Asshole!"

I'd backed her up a little, but just as I was beginning to get into the excitement of the thing, relishing my anger and its outpouring, she did a strange thing. Putting her arm around me, she laughed. I'd flinched at the sudden move toward me, thinking she meant to strike me, but she persisted, hugging me to her, motherly, and turned me to face the wreck again.

"It looks like a Scarborough, doesn't it?" she asked, naming a local sculptor who did massive, crumpled things and titled them with names like *Flowersong*, *Nightlaughers*, *Cost-Effective Lovers*, and who held his showings in the Santa Fe Auto Park, graciously guaranteeing delivery and setup for the six-figure price tag. Once I could have afforded his preposterous pieces on my lawns, but no more—fortunately, perhaps.

"What do you think?" she said. "It looks like Beauty and the Beast, doesn't it? We could call it *Detroit and Berlin, Fucking Each Other.*"

The word "fucking" put me off a little, doing more to diffuse my anger than anything else she could have done. I was no prude. I'd heard the word before, of course, had even used it myself fairly often, but not, never, in public, amid a crowd of strangers and on a street. My mother would have fainted dead away at the news that I had done so and then, in the soft, sweet drawl that characterized the steel-cored women in my family, made my life hell for weeks afterward.

I looked at the woman with some astonishment, and interest.

She was a good deal shorter than I and was built much like the Russian women who are always in any documentary of the Soviet Union, the kind of women who wear babushkas tied around their heads and are apt to say things like, "Let's climb on our tractors and make the earth strong for the motherland," or something. She had that fiercely red hair, an unusual shade suggesting carrots or a healthy portfolio of Miss Clairol stock. Her eyes were a warm brown, and though lined and wrinkled a little her skin was healthy and glowing with a slightly yellow cast that was overlaid with enough tan so that it suggested apricots and peaches. The combination was pleasing, attractive even, and I guessed her age to be around fifty. It was not the kind of beauty that I would have chosen for myself, but on her, it fitted and was striking.

I, on the other hand, had what had been described to me by an unfortunate choice of dates as the rich-bitch look, intensely intimidating apparently, the kind of looks that catch the eye but don't

encourage any sort of frivolous flirtations. I was tall, thin, still blond—
thanks to my own share of Miss Clairol—and to my credit, my light-
olive skin tanned instantly and stayed that way without effort. I had
a long nose, however, that missed being beaked by a hairbreadth, and
my eyes were brown, too, but a dark brown, almost black, obsidian,
icy. When I'd had money—most of my life—I could use those eyes
like a weapon and freeze someone into instant submission with them,
but the constant realities of poverty had made them flat and blank
most of the time, and whatever it was that made the other woman's
brown eyes sparkle with life, mine lacked.

I stood next to her on the street in my coordinated wool suit and
silk blouse from Neiman's, B.D. clothes, feeling like nothing more
than a stick that's been left in the sun too long, dried-up, bleached,
withered. She, by way of contrast, had on a long jeans skirt over
cowboy boots and a pullover, burnt-orange, velveteen overblouse
caught at the waist by a belt of linked conches, each nearly as big as
my hand. She should have looked frumpy, silly even, but strangely
did not. She looked Santa Fe smart, moneyed, artsy without being
bizarre. She looked like I wanted to feel but lacked the courage for
it.

By this time, the plaza policeman had ambled up, greeted several
of the Hispanics in the crowd by name, among them the man who
had gestured for me to pass, and walked around the back of my car
to stare at the joining of the two.

"Who-ee," he said, accurately appraising the situation.

"Young man, what's your name?"

She'd said it with a good deal of asperity, and obeying that imperious
teacherlike tone, he answered, "Ernesto Baca."

"Well, Officer Baca . . . or is it Sergeant Baca?"

She smiled at him suddenly and fluttered her impossibly long eyelashes, both sets of which had come unstuck at the ends of the bands,
curling up at all four corners of her eyes, giving her a slightly *Star
Wars* look. Amazingly, he responded to the flattery and grinned back,
saying, "Officer Baca. You have a wreck here?"

"Well, you know," she said, "just a little fender-bender thing. What
do you think? Do you suppose they can be fixed?" she asked, peering
up at him anxiously.

I knew what she was doing. She was trading on that love of au-
tomobiles that, stereotypical or not, was part of nearly every male

Hispanic and topping that off with the sugar-coated, oh-how-wonderful-you-are crap that was sure to make him warm Silly Putty in her hands. I'd grown up in Texas. It was something that all Southern girls learned on the playground, and I suddenly realized if I didn't get back into the conversation very fast, I would have lost out.

Sweetly, sadly, I said, "I just don't know what I'm going to tell my husband. He'll just be furious with me. He gets so mad and sometimes, he just blows up and . . . Well, you know."

I rolled my eyes up at him anxiously. I hated myself for the dissembling, but I couldn't afford a ticket and I didn't have the kind of clout anymore that would handle the situation any other way.

He certainly did know, or could imagine, having had more experience with brutal husbands than with other kinds, and I furtively twisted my pearl ring around on my ring finger so the stone wouldn't make a liar out of me. My efforts were rewarded by an amused and approving glance from the Caddy's owner, and she said to him, winking surreptitiously at me, "I'll bet if you backed my car off hers, honey, we could just run on and our husbands would never have to know."

"Well . . ." he said. "I don't know. It might have done something to her car. The axle looks broke to me."

It looked broken to me, too, and I suddenly realized I had no money to fix it and was, in effect, carless for the first time since I was sixteen years old. Overwhelmed by the fact I had no wheels in a society where a car was a necessity, not a luxury, I began to cry in spite of myself, real tears, the kind that sting the eyelids and make the nose run. The Caddy's owner, noticing it and realizing it was genuine, put her arm around me again and whispered to me, "Hey, fut the whuck, honey! It's not that bad."

"Yes, it is," I sniveled. "I'm broke and there isn't any way I can pay for this. I don't need this! Why is this happening to me now, of all times?"

The policeman had walked over to the crowd and was talking to my witness in rapid-fire Spanish. I caught *"gringas locas"* and *"brujas blancas"* several times, but upset as I was, I couldn't invest the attention I needed to follow the conversation.

"Yeah, I know the feeling," she said, staring again at our melded cars. "This is probably going to be the absolute end of my life, too. Well, shit," she said, throwing her hands up into the air—histrionically, I thought—"let's us just go get a drink and straighten this thing out ourselves. This asshole cop is just going to piddle around until one of us dies of old age, and with my lousy luck, it'll be you."

"I don't know..." I began doubtfully. It seemed to me I'd read somewhere that one should always get a policeman's report or something for the insurance people, but lacking any real experience with traffic accidents, I wasn't sure. Jack, my ex, or his assistant, had always handled things like this, but now I would have to. Frantically, I searched my mind, trying to decide the logical thing to do.

"Yeah, let's get outta here," she said. "If we hang around, he's gonna have to give one of us a ticket."

"But what about my car?"

"Tell you what. We'll tie your car to the back of mine and haul it down to the shop where my ex-husband has all his work done. We'll leave it there and get José, the guy who runs the place, to fix it and put it on my bill, and that way, my ex'll think it was all stuff for my car. He'll pay it and bitch for three weeks and then everybody'll be happy. How's that sound?"

"Well, I don't know... Will the garage do that?"

"Sure. José will do anything for me. I let him drive my car sometimes, practically on demand. He calls up, tells me it needs something fixed, and then drives it around for a couple of days. He thinks it's real statusy or something."

"You let a mechanic drive your car around whenever he wants to?"

"Sure. It's nothing to me and it always has a full tank when I get it back—and that's a big gas tank. I don't know about you, but I can't afford to fill that thing up myself, the price of gas being what it is. And whenever I need a little favor, José's right there to take care of it for me."

"It doesn't sound very fair for your ex-husband," I said, reverting back to the original discussion.

"No, it'll be great for him. It'll give him something to needle me about for a few weeks. He'll be like a pig in a mud puddle, believe me."

"I don't think I'd better do that. It doesn't seem right to me somehow."

"And gettin' a ticket from Officer Baca over there does? I don't know about you, but I don't need another ticket. You! Young man..."

She waved imperiously at a tattered young man with a backpack and about a year's growth of beard and extremely bad teeth who'd wandered up to view the excitement.

"Yeah, you! Com'ere, darlin'. Hop in there, sweetheart, and back my car off hers and then pull it around so we can tie them together."

"Lady, I don't think you want to do that," he said in a California accent. He seemed amused and looked worse, a little wild-eyed.

"Sure, we do, darlin'. Now, hurry."

"Look, lady. I don't think the Bug's gonna roll down the street too good. It looks to me like the axle's broken. See how those wheels are splayed out? It ain't gonna roll anywhere—at least, the front end ain't."

"Are you sure the axle's broken?" I asked, this new anxiety growing until there was a very real chance I might throw up in the street. "Maybe it's just bent."

"Doesn't matter. It's gonna have to be replaced. You're gonna hafta get a wrecker in here to haul it off."

"A *wrecker!* How much will *that* cost?"

"Oh, twenny-five dollars or so. Yeah, I know," he added, seeing the horror on my face. "It's a major bummer, but that's the way it is."

The driver of the pink Caddy put her arm around me again, literally holding me up against her. It was a good thing she did; my knees were giving out and there was a good chance I would have to sit down in the middle of the street, if only to cry. She turned back to the young man.

"Tell you what, sugar, how about if we pop my trunk and put the front end of her car in it and then we can drive it to the garage that way. How about that?"

"Well, it might work, but you're still gonna need a wrecker to hoist it up and set it in. And I sure wouldn't wanna be the one who drove it down the street."

As it turned out, he was. I stood by and watched as the redheaded woman talked him into backing her car off mine, turning it around, and then, amazed, watched her marshal a half dozen men out of the crowd, including Officer Baca and the old man who'd waved me out into the street in the first place, and had them pick up the front of my car and wedge it into the open trunk of hers. The Caddy dipped less than two inches as they released the weight of my car onto it.

She put me into the front seat of the Cadillac and went back to where the cop was dusting off the legs of his uniform. I watched as she talked to him for a few minutes, smiling up at him and patting his arm, and then, as he turned away, she said something to the young hippie. Whatever it was caused him to shake his head back and forth, at first slightly, and then, as she continued to talk, with a great deal of violence. The next thing I knew he was crawling into the Caddy under the wheel, grinning over at me, and just as I was trying to assimilate that, the Cadillac's owner opened my door and she scooted me over next to him, crawling in beside me. I tried to hold my breath as unobtrusively as possible at the smell of him.

We made the trip to the garage without much difficulty except for the horn blowing that seemed to follow us all the way, and the fact that I had to keep moving the hippie's hand off my legs. I tried giving him my best affronted look, then the imperious stare that I'd learned from my mother, which was guaranteed to whip the most unruly serviceperson into line, but he was impervious to them both, grinning at me.

When we pulled up in front of the bays of the garage, a Hispanic man came out, wiping his hands on a grease rag, beaming. I'd had men look at me the same way he looked that Caddy over, but not for a long time, not since before I was forty anyway.

"Hey, Miz Wallace!" he yelled. "How you doin', man?"

The woman next to me slid out, dragging me with her, and said, smiling, "Just fine, José. How's María and the kids?"

"Doin' okay, man. Wha's'appenin'?"

"Now, José, we have a special little job for you. And we brought it to you because we knew you were the only one who could do it right. You know I wouldn't let anyone else in Santa Fe touch my car."

Quickly, she outlined what she wanted, doing a lot of arm patting and eyelash waving. I could almost feel the breeze from them from where I was standing, but I couldn't give it too much attention. For some reason, the young hippie who'd driven us to the shop was standing close beside me, too close, still grinning at me. He'd grinned at me all the way to the garage, and it was beginning to get on my nerves. What he was doing was worse than a grin, actually. It was more like a leer.

Finally, Mrs. Wallace and José finished their dickering, and José turned to go back into the shop office. The hippie took my arm.

"Now?" he asked, looking at Mrs. Wallace hopefully.

"Now, what?" I asked, jerking at my arm, trying to free it from his grip, which had tightened until it was almost painful. Mrs. Wallace took my arm away from him, gently, and leading me a little distance away, she called back to him, "Just a minute, sugar. We'll be right with you."

"What's going on?" I asked. "What's the matter with that guy? Is he on something? What—"

"Look," she whispered urgently. "I had to make the best deal I could. I needed to get him to drive us over here. You weren't in any shape to do it and I knew I couldn't. Somebody had to."

"What are you talking about?"

"Look . . ." She looked back over her shoulder at the leering hippie and smiled at him. When I looked, too, he waved at me, winking. I turned back to her, suddenly very uneasy.

"What kind of deal did you make?"

"Well, I told him if he drove us over here, you'd fuck him."

"What!"

"Hey, I had to tell him something. You know how these cookie bandits are. All they ever think about is sex and—"

"Listen! I am *not* sleeping with that guy!"

"I don't know," she said judiciously, looking over my shoulder at him. "Give him a bath and he might be all right."

"Then you fuck him!"

"I don't think it's me he wants."

"Well, he isn't getting me!"

"What am I going to tell him?"

"I'm sure you'll think of something. I'm going to the ladies' room!"

I stalked off with as much dignity as possible and prowled around the back of the garage, looking for the women's room. When I found it, I went in, ignoring the filth and shutting the door. I locked it and leaned against it, closing out Mrs. Wallace, the hippie, José, and the pink Cadillac.

"Jesus God," I whispered. "Please let this day be over with real soon."

I realized my cold, instead of going away, was getting worse, that I probably had, not just a cold, but the flu that was going around. God damn Jack, I thought, adding another curse to the countless ones I'd already heaped on him. It had become a habit, this calling down the evils of heaven on my hapless and uncaring ex-husband whenever I was faced with something that was painful. God damn him, I thought, this is all his fault and I hope he gets some incredibly debilitating disease, something that deforms his dingle. Only that would pay him back for what he's done to me.

Someone began pounding on the door behind me. Without moving from it, I asked, "Who is it?"

"It's me, honey, Marilee. Open the door."

"No."

"You can open the door. He's gone now."

Cautiously, I cracked the door, peering out at her.

"Come on out," she said, grinning. "I wouldn't lie to a girlfriend."

"What did you tell him?"

"I made José give him a twenty and he went on down Cerrillos. Turns out he was going to the youth hostel anyway and he got a free ride more than half the way—plus the twenty. He was happy."

"What about the twenty?"

"José is going to add twenty-five to the bill. Come on out and let's go get a drink. José is gonna run us over to the Pink."

I opened the door and left the stinking bathroom.

"By the way," she said, "I'm Marilee Wallace."

I told her my name and said, "I'm supposed to be at work. I was supposed to mail all those invitations, too. I'm going to lose my job."

She patted my back, reaching up to do so.

"No, you're not, darlin'. It's lunchtime anyway. A girl's gotta eat. And besides, if there's any trouble, I'll go in and talk to your boss for you."

"No! Absolutely not! Don't even suggest it!"

"Well, you seem kinda meek." More patting. "You need to learn to stand up for yourself more. Now come on, go get your invitations outta your car. We'll get José to drive us by the post office on the way to the Pink."

I got my invitations and we loaded ourselves into José's "Chebby trock," an amalgamation of ancient pickup parts loosely held together by God knew what, that had, at one time, probably been blue. I tried not to be obvious about hiding my face, but the truth of the thing was that I would have died if I saw anyone I knew. Marilee had no such compunctions. She and José kept up a running conversation of questions from her and answers from him about people I had never heard of and probably didn't want to know while I examined the floorboard of the car from behind my right hand. In true lowrider fashion, José inched down the streets at fifteen miles per hour, talking all the time and causing the yuppie four-by-fours to wad up alarmingly behind us. José cheerfully ignored their honking, slowing down even further to ease over each of the dozens of potholes that scarred the streets.

"You can't be too careful, man," he explained. "These damn streets can ruin a good trock."

"I know it!" Marilee agreed vehemently, but when I looked at her in surprise, she turned her head and grinned at me, a flat-lipped grin that caused me to turn away quickly so that José couldn't see my face.

José deposited us in front of the Pink Adobe, which, as it turned out, was Marilee's favorite watering hole. He completely blocked both lanes of the Old Santa Fe Trail while we slid down, out of the pickup, onto the pavement. I scurried into the lane, heading for the door of the bar, my head averted from the passengers of the cars who waited patiently, Santa Fe resigned, in front and behind him, but Marilee stood for some seconds in the middle of the street, at the open door of the pickup, thanking José. Finally, she shut the door carefully and joined me in the lane.

"You know," she said mildly, "if somebody gives you a ride, you ought to at least tell them you appreciated it, whether you did or not."

I had no answer to that—she was right. I had been an asshole— and so I followed her, meekly, into the bar.

It was something I was to get a great deal of experience at over the next few months, following her meekly. I got really good at it eventually.

The summer tourists had all left and the skiers hadn't begun to arrive in Santa Fe yet, nor was the state legislature in session, so the Pink Adobe was fairly quiet. Marilee headed for a corner table, detouring past the popcorn machine to scoop up a basketful.

"Lunch," she said, waggling the basket at me and grinning.

When we were seated, she asked me, "How much money do you have on you?"

That question, coming from anyone else, would have been tacky, offensive even. Without thinking about it, I dug my coin purse out of my bag and counted out my cash. I had five dollars and twenty-three cents, and payday was three days away. Once again I felt the sudden shock that came when I realized that all the money I owned was in my hand. It had been brutal, at first, the onset of those spasms of sudden understanding that there was a finite limit to my financial resources, and even though it had faded a little with each repetition, it was still severe enough to panic me. Frantically, I wondered what I would do for three days without any money. I still didn't consider five dollars and twenty-three cents real money, even then, even after all that had happened to me.

"Well, I have nine dollars and something," Marilee said. She took the money out of my hand and piled it with hers in the middle of the table. "Good. That's enough for two drinks apiece and a decent tip for the waitress."

I started to protest, but realizing that five dollars wouldn't even buy cab fare to and from work for one day, let alone three, I gave in. If I couldn't have cab fare, then I could better spend the money on a drink. I could use the drink.

"What you need is something with a lot of vitamin C in it," Marilee told me, eating the popcorn one kernel at a time from the fistful she'd picked up from the basket. "You're coming down with a terrible cold."

"Yes," I said morosely, dismembering a paper napkin.

"What you should do is go home and get into bed."

"I can't. I've got too much to do at the shop."

"What shop?"

"The place where I work. The Museum Gift Shop at the Palace of the Governors."

"What do you do there?"

"I'm the cashier."

"You look like the type that would own a shop."

"No."

"Well, that surprises me. What's a nice lady like you doing, working for the State of New Mexico?"

"The Museum Foundation."

"Whatever."

Briefly, I told her my story, too miserable to even work up any self-pity over my downfall.

"You've heard of new rich," I said when I'd finished. "Well, I'm new poor."

"Yeah, I know the feeling. My ex and I were married for twenty years and I left him for a cop. That's right," she added, seeing my surprise, "one of Santa Fe's finest. That's why Officer Baca let us off like he did. He knows me, and like the others, he thinks I'm the world's worst dingbat. They'll do damn near anything to keep from having to mess with me. It makes them crazy or something."

"Really?" I asked.

Either missing, or choosing to ignore, the sarcasm, she continued, "That didn't last very long, and then, let's see, I married that decorator. He was a sweet little thing, great in bed but a real bore otherwise. All he wanted to talk about was colors and textures and shit like that. Then I married that psychiatrist—how many's that?"

"Four," I said, surprised. "Counting your first one."

"Then that's all of them. Sometimes I lose count."

She picked up the drink the waitress set in front of her. "Thanks, honey." She smiled at the waitress. "Cheers," she said to me, and took a mouthful. "God, I *needed* that. What a day!"

"Were all your husbands from Santa Fe?"

"All but Mac, my first."

I looked at her with some respect.

It was an absolute truism that a single, straight, nonaddicted man who was even halfway mature was rarer in Santa Fe than well-paid jobs, which were almost nonexistent, and this woman sitting at the table with me had managed to find three of those men and not only got them interested in her but managed to marry them as well.

Remembering her interactions with José, the young hippie, and Officer Baca, as well as the diverse men in the crowd, I could suddenly see why she'd been married four times, even in Santa Fe, the purgatory for single women.

"Look, honey," she said, patting my hand. "It isn't that bad. José will get your car fixed up fine and then you'll be all set again."

"Are you sure your ex won't mind paying for it?"

"He'll never know about it. Fut the whuck! I'll fix him a good meal and he'll be too sleepy to complain until the next morning. I'll still be asleep then, and when he gets home from the office . . . Well, I'll have another good meal ready for him."

"You live with your ex-husband?"

"Sure. Where else would I live between husbands?"

"Well, I don't know. . . ." It seemed a little sinful to me, somehow, more so than living with a strange man would have done.

"It's purely platonic, believe me. After being married to Ricky, the decorator, there's no way in hell I'd let Mac touch me, even if he wanted to. We didn't sleep together too much before we were divorced, anyway. Now, I function as his housekeeper and let him take his irritations out on me, and everybody's happy."

"Doesn't that bother you?"

"Why should it? I put up with it for twenty years as his wife. I'm used to it. I don't even hear it anymore."

Suddenly, my bleak and lonely life lost a small measure of its unhappiness.

"It's really not a bad life," Marilee continued. "I manage to wheedle a little spending money out of him every week and I have a roof over my head. I live in deadly fear, though, he's gonna find somebody else, marry her, and then where will I be?"

"I can certainly imagine that the second Mrs. Mac might be a little anxious to have you move out."

"Well, yeah. And the bastard knows it, too. He's always hinting he might marry whatever girl he's going with. I know it's just bullshit. If he did, he wouldn't have me to pick at anymore, but maybe he could find somebody just like me, only younger."

For the first time, I realized there were cracks in her ego, and that, more than anything else she'd done that day, caused me to warm toward her. I was tempted to reach out my hand, to pat hers as she'd done mine several times, but not being accustomed to making any effort toward physical contact with someone else, I hesitated and caught myself in time.

"Why do you put up with that?" I asked instead.

"Well, what else am I going to do? I've never worked a day in my life. I have no skills at all, just being a housewife and giving little dinner parties and stuff like that. Who'd hire me? And what could I do? I'm not competent like you are."

I stared at her, astounded.

"Are you serious?" I asked. I pointed out that she'd single-handedly masterminded the cleaning up of the wreck while I'd stood around, wailing and wringing my hands.

"Well, sure," she said. "But that's just talking to people. That's not working at a job for a boss. I wouldn't last a day at a real job."

"Your ex tell you that?"

She smiled ruefully and said, "Several times a day."

"And let me guess," I added. "He makes it very easy for you to come back after each one of your marriages is over. Right?"

"Yeah, that's really the only time he's ever sweet to me."

"You realize it's a game the two of you are playing, don't you?"

"Maybe so, but I know the rules to this game. I don't know the rules to anything else."

"Well, I certainly know *that* feeling."

She picked up her drink and took a large mouthful of it, holding the ice back with her tongue to do so.

"Besides, the main reason I keep waiting around is for him to die."

"What?"

"He's had three heart attacks, Karen. He works too hard, that's all he lives for. He eats too much, drinks too much, smokes all the time. The doctors keep telling him it's only a matter of time unless he changes his ways. I've got too many years invested in him to leave him now. I think something comes to me when he dies, but if he gets married again, he'll change his will and I won't get diddly-squat. After twenty years being married to him and another ten off and on, mostly on, I've lived with him, I sure as hell deserve *something* out of it."

I didn't know what to say. Jack, at his very worst, had been a far better husband than this Mac Carpenter obviously had been, and I'd left him in a flash over another woman without even thinking of any ramifications of my leaving. Marilee, obviously, was not the sort to do something willy-nilly like that and regret it later. I wasn't sure which had interested me the most—the idiocy of her taking his constant punishment, betting on the come (to use a crapshooters' phrase), or the level of deep planning that apparently frivolous head was capable of. Anyone else, looking at the two of us, would have thought the opposite, taking Marilee for the impulsive, feckless idiot and me for the calm, resourceful one.

From somewhere, I felt a shard of admiration for her, a tiny sliver that, in spite of myself, I allowed to grow. How much better off would I have been, I asked myself, had I stopped to think before I careened off, mindlessly responding to the painful stimulus of Jack's infidelity?

Marilee grimaced, staring at her drink, which she rotated carefully.

"I wish he'd find himself a hot little bimbo and fuck himself to death."

"You really don't like him, do you?"

"Does it show?" She laughed, her light mood instantly restored.

"Why did you marry him in the first place?"

"He was different then, Karen. He was young and handsome and I saw something in him nobody else saw. He had potential, I thought, and I was right. When I married him, Daddy cut me off and I haven't talked to him since, the fucker. Mac's made more money than Daddy ever thought about making."

"With your help," I prodded.

"I guess. Anyway, I really loved him then. I didn't know he'd turn into a workaholic, that he'd get fat or fry his brain cells and get stupid with booze. I think that's why I keep getting married, hoping to find another young Mac. Shit! What a bummer!"

Her use of the word "bummer" made me think of the young hippie. In spite of myself, I laughed, and when she looked up at me, I asked her, "Did you really tell that kid that I'd sleep with him if he drove us to the garage?"

"Sure. It was obvious he had the hots for you, and fut the whuck, how did I know but whether or not you really might *want* a little roll in the hay? Who knows? I might have been doing my good deed of the day by putting the two of you together like that."

"He had the hots for me?"

"Sure! Didn't you notice that? Old José looked you over pretty good, too, or didn't you even see that?"

I really hadn't. I looked at her with some suspicion. I wasn't accustomed to such flattery, and certainly not from another woman, and I quickly went through any reasons she might have to butter me up. None of them seemed very plausible, however. That was one good thing about being broke, I realized; I didn't have to worry anymore about someone's buttering me up for a possible favor. I couldn't help but smile at her when she said, "Look, toots, I wouldn't lie to a girlfriend. Don't tell me you aren't used to having men stare at you?"

To change the train of the conversation, which had become uncomfortable, I asked instead, "I'm not going to have to sleep with José, too, am I?"

"No, God, he's a good Catholic and he's more interested in my car and Mac's money. Besides, he's scared to death of blond *brujas*. You're safe with him. By the way, I'm glad to see you have a sense of humor. I was beginning to wonder."

"Well, you try having a cold and then let some idiot run into your little car and then take all your cab fare away from you. See how much humor you can see in that!"

"This hasn't been a good day, has it? Well, cheer up. It could have been worse."

"How?"

"One of us could have been hurt."

"I guess. Or we could have gotten tickets."

"No chance of that," she said. "Listen, how are you going to get home tonight from work if you don't have cab fare? Where do you live?"

"On Garcia."

"Well, that's too far to walk at night. Do you have a friend you could ride with?"

Thinking about it, I was slightly surprised to realize I really had no one, that among all of my numerous acquaintances, none of them were close enough that I felt I could ask a favor. And then I realized I had never really had a close friend. I hadn't allowed that, and thinking about it, I suddenly found that sad behavior, indeed. In any case, it would have been difficult for me to have asked even a close friend for help, even if I'd had one. I wasn't accustomed to begging for anything.

"That's all right," I said. "I can get home okay."

She squinted up at me and then said, "Bullshit! Quit being Miss Tough Lady. I'll send somebody after you. What time do you get off?"

"No, really, I—"

"What time do you get off?"

So I told her and she said, "There'll be someone there to pick you up. I'll send Ricky; you'll like him."

"Ricky? The decorator? Your ex-husband?"

"One of them. Ricky will like you, too. Just be sure and talk to him about his work. He's very driven that way. Who knows? Something nice might come out of this day, after all. Stranger things have happened."

"Are you trying to set me up with one of your exes? Because if you are—"

"Don't get all upset, honey." More hand patting. "I'm just getting you a free ride home, that's all."

After work, I left the shop, and when I'd locked the door behind me and stepped out onto the street, I saw that a cream 924 Porsche was double-parked at the curb. The passenger's window went down and a man's face leaned toward it.

"You Karen Travis?"

I was unaccustomed to a man's hailing me on the street like that, but I swallowed my pride and walked warily to the car.

"Yes. I am. Are you Ricky?"

He laughed.

"Richard. I only allow Marilee to call me Ricky, and that's because, short of murder, I can't stop her, and really, I don't want to. On her, it sounds good. But only on her. Hop in."

I got into the car and ran my hand surreptitiously over the leather upholstery, relishing the rare and wonderful feel of richness again. He put the car in gear and pulled smoothly away from the curb, making a left on Palace in front of a Bronco with California plates who honked fiercely at the outrage. Ignoring it, he said, "I'm supposed to take you to dinner before I take you home."

"Oh, no! I don't think—"

"Marilee said you'd be prissy about it. She also said you'd be a good dinner companion. She knows how bored I am with the New Age women who have hair under their arms."

"Really! I—"

"She said to be forceful with you. I've learned to listen to Marilee so, like it or not, you're going to dinner. Ernie's okay?"

"Well, yes, but . . . Are you sure? Don't do this just because Marilee asked you to. I know how she can be."

"Then you know she only talks people into doing what they really want to do in the first place. She just gives people permission, in a manner of speaking, to do what they wanted to do all along. How did you meet her?"

"She ran into me today."

He didn't even ask me what I meant. "Oh, the pink Cadillac.

Somebody ought to blow that thing up." He glanced at me, grinning. "That's how I met her, too."

He was a good deal younger than I, and much younger than Marilee, and had a rugged face that I would have associated with a rancher, rather than a decorator. He was brown haired and blue eyed and had an energy about him I found somehow exciting. Only partially playing the role of the Good Date, I asked him about his work, and once started, he needed very little further prompting. He was interesting, obviously excited about his work, and in spite of myself, I found myself responding to this enthusiasm, a rare treat for me. After a lengthy dinner, we went to Vanessie's for the music, dancing a little, and finally he said, "I always expect Marilee to be wrong, but she never is."

"What do you mean?"

"She said if I could get past your prickliness, you and I would have a lot in common."

"Did she?"

"Did I offend you? I'm sorry. I was trying to think of a clever way to wrangle an invitation to stay the night with you and I bumbled it, didn't I?"

"Yes, you certainly did!"

I turned and left him standing on the dance floor.

"Hey! Wait! Where are you going?"

"Home!"

I stalked past our table and picked up my coat and bag. He caught up with me at the door and said, catching my elbow, detaining me, "Look, I'll drive you home."

"You needn't bother! Thank you very much for a lovely, *lovely* evening!"

"I'll drive you home, Karen. I know you don't have cab fare, and I won't have you walking home in the darkness and this weather. You don't have to sleep with me, for Christ's sake. It was just an idea."

Reluctantly, I allowed him to insert me into the Porsche, but driving past the plaza, he said, "It's almost worth this to show Marilee up."

Stunned at what I took to be a new display of utter and complete bad manners, I stared at him and then said furiously, "I don't suppose I'll ever get over the cavalier attitude of the single men in Santa Fe."

"What are you so excited about? I merely asked to spend the night with you. What the hell, you act as if I'd tried to rip off the crown jewels or something. I don't need this!"

"And I don't need your patronization, either! Won't this thing go any faster?"

He slammed into a downshift and swerved around the cathedral. His jaw muscles were bunched and the grip on the shift knob was white fingered. I didn't care if I'd made him mad. I was too upset myself to worry about some little hot-shot "cookie bandit" Marilee had tried to pass on to me, having used and discarded him herself.

Tersely, I directed him to my rented house, writhing with agony at its derelict appearance, knowing how a decorator must appraise it. When I got out, I did so without speaking, slamming the door viciously. The car spun a tight U-turn in the dirt of the yard and sped out of the driveway, spewing gravel on my legs as it went.

When I got inside, I locked the door, and jerking off my shoes, I threw one at the far wall of the little living room, and without thinking, obeying another naughty impulse, I threw the other. It bounced off the wall and hit a bust, a Houser, one of the last of my B.D. possessions of any worth. Horrified, I stared at the chip that popped off and then burst into tears. In the excitement of my little shoe-throwing fit, I didn't hear the growl of the Porsche's engine again, and so great was my consternation over the Houser that, when he knocked on the door, I opened it without the preamble of finding out first who was knocking.

"Hey! What's the matter," Richard said, taking me in his arms.

"I broke my Houser," I sobbed, leaning against him, utterly defeated.

"*What!* Where?"

He examined it and then said, "Look, Karen, it's merely chipped and the piece is out of the back. I know a woman who can repair it so it won't even show. You'd have to tell a prospective buyer about it, but except for that, it'll be as good as new."

His kindness on top of all the other things that had happened to me that day completely undid me, and I realized I couldn't stop my crying.

Taking me in his arms again, he said, "Look, I'm sorry. I was rude and I shouldn't have been. Okay? All right?"

"I have a cold," I sobbed.

"I don't care," he said, kissing me.

Marilee was right. He was very good in bed.

Thanks to Marilee, I had a ride to and from work every day that my car was in the shop. Richard was always waiting for me as I got off work, and without really measuring any escalation of my emotions, I found I looked forward to five o'clock more and more every day. He almost always took me to dinner, and once I even thawed out my rule against feeding men and did a little supper for him. It was something I seldom did since it had been my experience that, even though single men said they wanted a home-cooked meal, when it was offered, they ran like jackrabbits, fearing they were treading on dangerous ground, commitment-wise. In any case, cooking was not something I was really competent with anyway, having had no real experience with it myself, and I counted one of my meals to be successful when everything was ready at the same time.

Richard's insistence that we go out to dinner each night had nothing to do with my lackluster cooking skills nor even his fear of a commitment, I came to realize. It became obvious to me that he enjoyed showing me off, but since I was accustomed to being an arm decoration, had been trained for it, it didn't concern me very much. I didn't bother to analyze his interest in me at first, however. It was so easy to give in and let him take me to dinner every night, knowing it was a nice meal I didn't have to scrimp pennies for, that I could dress up in my B.D. clothes and what jewelry I had left, pretending, for a couple of hours at least, that I was once again moneyed, powerful, protected, secure.

I did realize, however, how much I had missed that feeling of having some man in my life who would pay the check, order the wine, leaving me to relax in my chair, knowing someone more competent than me was in charge, that I wouldn't have to make any decisions that might or might not be right.

Marilee and I did lunch together a couple of times over the next week, and in spite of my preliminary reticence, I found I rather looked forward to her phone calls, which usually started off breathlessly with something like, "If I don't get out of this house, I'm going to slap the *shit* out of someone. You'd be doing the world a favor by going to lunch with me." It was definitely blatant, of course, but even though I might feel I had too much to do to take off for lunch, somehow I usually wound up going anyway and enjoying the meal in spite of myself. It was hard, eating lunch with her. She knew almost everyone in town, and our meals were often interrupted by people stopping by our table to chat with her. It was impossible for her to be irritated by their doing so, she seemed genuinely glad to see each and every one of them, and no matter how often we were interrupted, she always gave the impression that she'd been waiting for just that person to come by and say hello to her.

I knew Mother would have died, had she realized the kind of company I was keeping. Marilee Wallace was not what Mother would have considered acceptable—she was flashy and earthy, and worse and unforgivable, she was new rich, her money (or her husband's, in this case) having been made in her lifetime, and in the latter half of it, at that. But then, there were so many things in my current life that Mother might have died over, had she known about them. Like Marilee, I'd had words with my family about the unacceptability of Jack Travis as a husband, and also like her, I'd defied them and was too proud to admit I'd been wrong. Mother, doddering away in the first stages of Alzheimer's disease (which Marilee called "old-timer's disease"), had the impression I was living a life of ease and luxury in Santa Fe, doing the artsy things, being as overtly bohemian as anyone in our family could possibly be, by choice, not by necessity, and that, when I got tired of my foolishness, I'd go home to Austin, get married again to a respectable man, and be normal once more.

I discussed all these things with Marilee over lunch at Oglevie's one day the week after our accident, surprised I was doing so but relieved, too, in a way. It was almost as if I'd been mute for a long time, or stranded alone on an island, unable to talk with anyone else, and then been reprieved suddenly. Marilee was sympathetic, and when, realizing I ought not to divulge such private information to a stranger, I might begin to lag, she would prompt me with gentle questions, drawing me out, draining my soul of all the toxins that had been stored there.

"Why don't you just call your mother and have her send you some money every month?" she asked.

"Sometimes I get fed up with everything and I think I will, but then I see her face in my mind, sneering at me, saying, 'I told you so,' and I just can't, Marilee. It's kind of a whip I use on myself to give myself the energy to plow on. You know?"

"Maybe. I tell you what, I sure as hell would call mine if she had any money. But then my mom wouldn't be into sneering. Anyway, she doesn't have the money and so I'm better off with Mac. Besides, it's too much trouble to pack up my stuff and move it, and I just don't want to fool with it right now."

"Well, Mother's been waiting all these years to say it, and her incipient senility isn't so far advanced that she wouldn't do it and get a lot of pleasure out of it."

"So what are you going to do for the rest of your life? Live on your pride?"

She'd shown up for lunch wading through the first snowfall of the year in a curly lamb coat that made her look like a teddy bear. She had surprisingly good legs, given her Earth Mother figure, and had worn extremely tight pants over them, dark green, tucked into knee-high boots, and a dark-red oversize sweater that almost, but not quite, clashed with her hair. Her jewelry looked like something that had come off a Kenyan safari, and her red hair swirled wildly around her face, illuminating it with reflected light. The effect was stunning, and sitting across from her in a tailored gray dress, I felt like a washed-out piano teacher, a frump, a used-up and discarded housewife.

I sighed, thinking that I ought to look through my clothes for something with a little more color, and answered her.

"I don't know, Marilee. I can't think about that right now. Maybe someday, when I'm stronger, I can make some decisions, but right now, it's all I can do to put one foot in front of the other."

"That divorce really racked you, didn't it?"

"Yes, I guess it did."

"Do you still love him?"

"I don't know. I'm not sure I know what love really is, Marilee."

"Would you go back to him?"

"No!"

"Wow! So much for indecision!"

I took a sip of my water and putting the glass back down carefully, said, "It would be the same thing as with Mother, Marilee. He told me I couldn't make it without him. Besides, he's remarried."

"How do you do that?"

"Do what?"

"Control yourself like that? I wish I could close myself off like that; it would save me a lot of trouble. It must be in the breeding or something."

"I don't know what you mean."

"Well, it's not important. By the way, you can pick your car up this afternoon. José is all finished with them and I'm going to get mine after lunch. Then I gotta take the bill to Mac. Hold good thoughts for me. I'm gonna need 'em."

"Do you want some help?" I asked doubtfully. I certainly didn't want to meet Mac, angry and ranting as she'd described him, but I felt that fair play insisted that I offer.

"No. It's better if I handle it alone. I know how to do it, and if he doesn't have an audience to play for, he's not as bad. Cheer up, maybe he'll have another heart attack when he sees the bill and die."

"Marilee, you really shouldn't say things like that, you know."

"Oh, piffle! He's going to have another one sooner or later, Karen. He's programming himself for it and he's not doing a thing to prevent it. He's always saying, 'I'd rather die sooner, living like I always have, than live longer in misery.'"

"I can understand that, you know."

"Well, I'm sweating blood again. He picked up some little chick at Mr. R's the other night and he's been seeing her every spare moment since."

"Why does that bother you?"

"What if she angles him into marriage? You know where that will leave me. Out on the street, without anything. I haven't put up with Miserable Mac all these years to wind up in the gutter."

"Surely, he won't marry her, Marilee. Surely, he has better sense than that."

"She's already told him she doesn't think it's right that we live in the same house."

"Indeed? And he generously passed that little bit of information on to you, right?"

"Well, I tell myself he'd be cutting off his nose to spite his face if he did. He wouldn't have me to pick on anymore, but you know how these old fools can be. Sooner or later, some little fluffy thing with firm tits and a tight ass is gonna catch him in a weak moment, and then, it's good-bye, Marilee. I just hope she fucks him to death. He'd like that—going out in style that way."

In spite of myself, I was fascinated by the relationship between the two of them. According to what I'd heard from Marilee, it was something that had developed into a love-hate friendship, much as two old enemies might build, falling further and further into that comfortable and predictable irritation until, I thought, should one of them actually die, the other would certainly feel a large part of him was gone, leaving him somehow empty or broken.

"What would you do if she did?" I ventured, hating myself for showing such tasteless curiosity and yet unable to restrain it. "Before she got him legally committed, I mean?"

"Oh, I don't know. Probably find some investment broker and put all the money in some kind of absolutely steel-trap kind of thing so I couldn't get to it and live off the income for the rest of my life. I know how I am."

"Somewhere there's an investment broker that's living on borrowed time."

She grinned. "He'll just love doing business with me."

I laughed, a short laugh that was almost a cough in its brevity. "Yeah, I'll bet," I answered.

"Well, anyway, there's no sense in talking about it. Mac is living a charmed life now. It's like he's staying alive just to spite me. How are you and Ricky doing?"

Instantly, I was on guard. As nonchalantly as possible, I said, "Fine. We've gone to dinner a few times."

"He's the perfect man for you."

"I don't think so, Marilee. He's at least ten years younger than I am."

"Well, he was more than that younger than me and I married him. I'm telling you, Karen, you don't want some old geezer. They're cranky and sick all the time and they don't do anything but get older and sicker and you have to take care of them. They're set in their ways and they have denture breath. Trust me. I wouldn't lie to a girlfriend. Give me a cookie bandit anytime."

"To sleep with, maybe, but not to marry."

"Who's talking about marriage?"

"You were."

She began digging through her voluminous bag and finding what she was looking for, pulled it out. I saw it was a small vial of Super Glue and I watched, fascinated, as, with her thumb, she tipped one of her fake Dragon Lady nails forward off the bed, rotating it where it was still stuck at the end of the nail, and holding it six inches from her face and squinting fiercely, she squirted a drop between the fake nail and her own, ignoring completely the fact that she was in a public place. She'd been talking all that time, and now that the operation was successfully completed, I tuned into her again.

"Maybe if you wore some oranges," she was saying. "That would certainly be pretty with your complexion, and you might also think of something in magenta."

I shook myself slightly, exactly as one who was coming out of a trance would do.

"I don't think magenta is my color," I said with a good deal of firmness.

"Well, those beiges and grays certainly don't do anything for you. You need some excitement in your wardrobe."

"I'll keep that in mind."

"A friend would tell you," she said, and while I was trying to decipher that, she dug through her voluminous bag again and pulled out a handful of wadded-up bills. Instantly, I reached for the check, determined to pay my share. She beat me to it, however, and holding the check almost against her face, she peered at it and said, "Let me get this. I got money from Mac to go to the market this morning and I had some left over. He doesn't know the difference between ground round and ground chuck anyway."

"Are you sure?" I asked doubtfully, meaning the bill.

"Right. He thinks he's died and gone to heaven if I serve him meat loaf, and the greasier, the better."

Imperiously, she waved at a busboy, a young man who had the pitiful look of a calf lost in the snow. I knew without having to think about it that he was an artist of some kind, someone prostituting himself by service work so he could feed his true vocation and keep himself alive while he waited for his big break. Santa Fe was full of them.

He wafted over.

"Darlin'," she said, smiling up at him, "look at this check for me. Those little computer numbers are too small for me to read. Here's some money. Take what you need and put some money on it for our waiter, okay? And tell him to bring us another round of drinks."

She piled her wadded-up bills on the table and he sifted through them. If he was surprised by her directions, he didn't show it, acting as if he waited on blind, crazy women all the time. I pushed my chair back decisively and got to my feet.

"No, Marilee. I have to get back to work and I won't be able to deal with that idiotic cash register if I drink anything else."

"What you should do," she said, rising and following me out of the dining room, leaving the rest of her change on the table, having already forgotten it, "what you should do is take this afternoon off and let's you and me go to your house and look through your wardrobe. Maybe we can put together some looks that will knock people's eyes out, give you some pizzazz."

"I can't, Marilee. I have to work," I said, thankful for my job for the first time since I'd had to get it.

"Well, all right, but that's something we don't want to put off too long."

I started to give her a withering stare, but remembering she couldn't see without her glasses and the effect would be lost, I said instead, "Marilee, my ensembles are fine. I'm sure you wouldn't approve of anything I own, and I don't have the money to buy anything new."

"It never hurts to look," she said mildly. "We'll do it another time."

"Fine."

"Well, I'm off to collect my car from José. I know it was ready a couple of days ago; one of my friends saw it leaving town the other day. He's probably put a couple of hundred miles on it, showing off in Española with it the last couple of days, but . . . fut the whuck, right?"

Española was the town just north of Santa Fe and was considered by most people to be the home of the lowriders. The main form of excitement for the young men there was said to be driving around, showing off one's car and yelling at the girls. It was past my understanding what they got out of that, but whatever it was, it had enough glamour that driving through Española on the weekends, on the way to or from Taos, was almost impossible.

"You should just tell him, Marilee, that he can't drive your car around. You have to be firm with people like that. Why on earth would he want to, anyway?"

"Oh, who knows how men think, honey. He started doing it when I was married to Harve, the psychiatrist. Harve was really into sharing stuff. And I don't really care if José drives it. He keeps it in tip-top condition and never gives me a bit of trouble over the bill."

"Well, I know I wouldn't want someone driving my car around like that, even if they did keep the tank full. No telling what he does in it—probably takes his girlfriends out for rides. Have you checked the backseat recently?"

She grinned. "All the time, darlin', and all I've ever found is where somebody spilled a little coffee sugar on the floor. I'm telling you, José treats it like it was made of gold."

"It's your car."

"Right."

At any rate, I told myself, if Marilee didn't care that José drove her car around Española and spilled stuff on the floorboard, I certainly didn't either. I had better things to worry about.

I went down to the garage that afternoon after work to pick up my own car and typically for Santa Fe, I had to stand around while José finished chatting with a couple of thugs who looked like they might eat nails for fun. The conversation seemed strained, at least on José's part, and I was surprised that there was something that could override José's good humor and flashing gold teeth like that. He seemed to be explaining something to the others, but they were standing far enough away that I could only catch a word or two. Further, the conversation was in Spanish and I lacked the interest needed to translate it. It was nothing to me what José was up to, I told myself.

While I waited, I occupied myself by checking over my car. José had done a creditable job, at least on the paint and bodywork, but there was a greasy handprint on the driver's door, marring the shiny new paint, offensive, ugly. I went into the maw of the garage, hunting a clean rag, and prowled around for a few seconds in vain amid the debris and effluvia that seemed necessary to car repair. It occurred to me there might be something in the ladies' room that I could use to wipe off the print, and going to the back of the garage, I opened one of the doors. I saw at once that I'd made a mistake. The room was bathroom sized but the similarity ended there. It was windowless and relatively clean and bare, the only furniture being a waist-high bench that ran along one side. I started to close the door again but my eye was caught by a briefcase sitting open on the bench. It was leather, hand sewn—a very, very nice briefcase, and expensive, hardly the thing one might expect to find in a greasy garage owned by a Hispanic ex-lowrider. The briefcase, itself, was an anomaly in the garage, but the thing that caught my eye was that it was half-filled with money, bundled neatly with bill-wraps, and there were more bill-wraps in the briefcase and on the bench. All the exposed bills were hundreds, and I stood in the doorway, stunned by the sight of so much money lying around like that. It seemed that José was very successful with his garage, indeed, but my estimation of his business sense dropped somewhat.

You'd think, I told myself, he'd invest some of that money in a safe.

The other half of the briefcase was filled by what looked to me like scales, a smaller version of the kind chem labs use, lying on its side, partially covered over by loose bill-wraps.

The sight of all that money was irresistible. Before I really knew what I was doing, I'd stepped into the room and picked up a packet of bills.

There's so much here, I told myself. So much that they'd never miss just one. And one packet of hundred dollar bills would make a world of difference in my life. What would it hurt? Who would know?

My mother's face loomed up abruptly in my mind, shocked, appalled, horrified, disgusted. Not Buchanan behavior, it reminded me, sneering. You haven't sunk that low. Remember Buchanan pride; remember Buchanan honor. Common thievery is vulgar—thieves are trash.

Reflexively, I dropped the bills again, stepped back out of the doorway and closed it, heard the automatic door-lock catch. Had the door been completely closed, I would not have been able to open it in the first place.

I was instantly sorry. I grabbed the doorknob again and tugged at it but it was firmly locked and, futilely I beat my closed fist quietly against the door while I tried to twist the doorknob with my other hand. In that small room lay a certain answer to at least some of my troubles, however temporary, and I'd impulsively rejected it. Cursing myself for my idiocy, I leaned against the door, trying not to cry. Resignation quickly replaced the anger, however; by then I'd had a good deal of experience in sublimation.

Well, it's just as well, I told myself. You probably wouldn't have felt good about it. It really wasn't right. Nothing's free.

And with that triteism, I felt somewhat better and firmly put the entire room and its contents out of my mind, not willing to club myself further with yet another bit of evidence that I was incapable of taking care of myself.

The next door was the ladies' room door, and finding a semiclean cloth there, I took it back out to my car and wiped off the handprint. After a few minutes, José joined me, handed me the keys, and I was mildly interested to notice that the flashing gold smile was back again.

I was surprised to realize the depth of feeling I had when I crawled under the steering wheel of the little Bug. It was almost like being reunited with a close relative, and as I drove away from the garage, I patted the dashboard with uncharacteristic glee. I'd gotten a new paint job out of the deal, as well as a new hood and axle, and at no cost to me, except for what little cab fare I'd expended. Further, I'd been without a car for nearly a week and had managed to survive, a realization that cheered me up considerably. My cold had gone without turning into the flu everyone else was having, and I'd been involved with Richard, with all the benefits that entailed. So it was with some aplomb that I drove myself home that evening. For the first time since long before my divorce, I felt that tingle, however slight, that comes with true happiness.

I'm doing all right, I told myself. I'm going to be fine.

The place I'd rented was a two-bedroom adobe that was at least fifty years old and probably older. It sat well back from Garcia Street, down a little lane that ran next to an arroyo. It wasn't cheap but it had charm, an unconventional kind of charm to be sure, but without too much imagination it could be considered cozy and clever. I had not expended too much effort on it, however, lacking the money and more important, the interest to decorate it, so it remained much as it had when I'd moved in, bare walled and with old-fashioned pull-down window shades.

"Lo, how the mighty have fallen," I quoted to myself when I'd first rented it, but now, for the first time, I considered how I might fix it up, personalize it so it reflected something of my essence and might make my coming home to it every evening more than a retreat into a burrow. I'd turned the larger of the two small bedrooms into a closet, having more clothes than the insufficient closet space would even remotely accommodate, and had merely thrown a twin bed and a dressing table into the other. In my haste to get divorced, I'd left rooms and rooms of good furniture behind, and now, as I walked through the place, I looked at everything I had with a judicious eye and wondered at my previous disinterest. I realized I had not been able to think about decorating before, that I had not allowed anyone into my house before that first night with Richard, and that, further, I had not even been aware that the house, which had so much potential, as he had pointed out to me, was barren of anything that might make a statement of any kind about me.

By way of contrast, his house had a great deal to say about him, mostly that he was male, sensitive to fine things, and accustomed to pleasing himself. It, too, was a true adobe built in the pueblo style, but it was three times as large as mine, open and airy, with architectural emphases that mine lacked. One knew immediately a great deal about Richard Sommerfrught just by walking in his front door.

Suddenly, I was excited about fixing up my place. I began to experience a feeling much like a freshman feels at the thought of decorating her first dorm room, a slight sense of justified frivolity. For the first time in my life, I could decorate a place the way I really wanted to, not having to worry about what my mother, my husband, or my friends thought. It was a delicious feeling and intensely liberating.

The phone rang, and when I answered it, Marilee's voice said, "Hi. Come to dinner."

"No."

"Why not? Are you going out with Ricky?"

"No, he's in Albuquerque tonight."

"Then come over. Have you ever eaten meat loaf?"

"No, I don't think so, but—"

"Well, come on. You'll like it. I make a great meat loaf."

"I really—"

"If you don't like it, we can put it in the fridge and make us some omelets or something. We'll eat in front of the fire and get drunk on Mac's wine. Come on. It'll be fun."

"Marilee, I don't think I should tonight. How did Mac take José's bill?"

"That's why I'm calling. He called and said he wouldn't be home. He and the current bimb are gonna party and then stay at her house tonight. So I'm footloose. Come on over. It's safe."

I allowed myself to be talked into going, and as I drove up Hyde Park Road, I found myself thinking about the way my life was finally opening up, and the key had been meeting Marilee Wallace.

It only takes one little thing, I thought. Your life goes on and on, one dreary day after another, and you think nothing will ever change, that life will just be forever dour and gray. And one day, one little thing happens and suddenly everything is different.

I found myself humming as I drove into the driveway.

The meat loaf was surprisingly good. I couldn't ever remember having eaten meat loaf before, but Marilee was right. She did make a great meat loaf, at least as far as I could tell without having had any others to compare it with. I had two servings.

In spite of myself, I was impressed with Mac Carpenter's house. Like a great many wealthy Texans, he'd made some money in oil and gas, but unlike most, had lived off a flat salary, poking the extra money here and there into other things, diversifying and building a financial network that had grown exponentially. From what Marilee told me over supper, it seemed that, no matter what he got into, it prospered without effort, and he, Midas-like, had prospered with it.

I wasn't sure what sort of house to expect, something tacky and ostentatious surely, hideous with bad taste, with a houseful of those appalling wire oil derricks or pumping units or rattlesnake skins or something equally gauche. I was surprised when Marilee took me through it. Mac's apparent abilities in ferreting out good financial deals also manifested itself in choosing competent architects and decorators. If Mac had bad taste himself, he'd at least had the good sense to hire the best and leave them alone.

The house sat halfway up one of the foothills of the Sangre de Cristos, off Hyde Park Road, and commanded an exquisite view of

Santa Fe, the Jemez Mountains to the west, and the Ortiz Mountains and the Galisteo Basin to the south. The south and west elevations of the house were mostly glass, and the landscape architect had had the good sense not to block the views, placing the shrubbery and trees downhill, graded according to their sizes. Because the exterior was in a modified pueblo style, it blended into the side of the small mountain it was built on. I'd caught the rays of the setting sun on the house as I arrived, and it seemed to glow with the same bloodred that had given the Sangre de Cristos their name.

The interior was mostly wood, stone, and glass—an amalgamation of nature in a modern setting. The only carpets in the house were in the bedrooms, and the slate or tile floors in the rest of the house were covered with Indian rugs. My work at the Museum Shop had given me an eye for recognizing genuine Navajo rugs and an appreciation for their cost, and without being too obvious about it, I estimated that Mac had at least fifty thousand dollars in those rugs alone. The rooms were spacious, high ceilinged, done in desert colors, and somehow gave the appearance of being cozy, too. It was quite the most marvelous house I'd been in for some time.

After dinner, Marilee and I sat in front of the fire in the living room, drinking wine. I'd noticed a large Cochiti pot on a stand and was trying to decide if it was a Herrera. If it was, it was worth at least two thousand dollars, my salary for two months.

Why him? I thought. Why him and not me?

Suddenly, I could see why Marilee came back between marriages each time. My cozy little adobe now seemed squalid by comparison to this beautiful house, full of beautiful things. I longed for nice things of my own again, an abrupt yearning that was so strong, it was an actual physical twisting inside my body. It was all I could do suddenly to keep from crying.

I'll never take anything for granted again, I told myself, but even as I did so, I knew that my chances were very slim that I would ever get the chance.

I set my wine down on the glass-topped table, realizing that, in the mood I'd fallen into, drinking it would be the worst thing I could do.

"You okay?" Marilee asked. Even as blind as she was, it was amazing to me she could perceive things that would not have been apparent to another, less sensitive, person.

I started to answer her, to deflect the question, when I heard a door open and a male voice bellow, "Whose piece of shit is that, blockin' the fuckin' driveway and dripping oil all over ever'thang!"

"Uh, oh," Marilee said under her breath. "Mac's home," she added quite needlessly.

Hopping to her feet, she went to meet him. I rose and stood by the sofa, unable to think what to do. As always when confused or frightened, I merely stood, rock still, raised my chin, and froze my face into a mask of haughty disdain. I'd learned that trick from my mother, but with her, it had been no trick. It gave me the appearance, however, of being composed and controlled in the middle of any confusion and had done more than anything else to give me the label of being cold.

Before Marilee could get around the sofa and through the living room, the kitchen door swung open and I got my first look at Mac Carpenter.

He'd been handsome once, a rugged handsomeness that had atrophied from years of hard living to coarseness. The expression on his face, even making allowance for the blustering anger that was there now, was a perpetual craftiness, a shiftiness that made one instantly want to protect one's back. He was of medium height, overweight, flabby, and what hair he had was combed up and over the baldness on the top of his head, accentuating rather than hiding it as he'd meant to do. Whatever skill he'd shown in selecting architects and decorators, he lacked when it came to barbers, haberdashers, and jewelers. He was the epitome of the self-made yokels my family spoke of, those people who, though they might succeed beyond their wildest fantasies, never quite fit in their new shoes and know it without knowing why.

He and Marilee met in the doorway, and before she could remonstrate with him, he peered around her and saw me. Good manners would have made him stop and if not apologize for his rude behavior, at least wait for an introduction. Instead he kept on haranguing Marilee about my car in his driveway, all the while watching me. I realized he was performing for my benefit, and quietly, knowing he would have to shut up to hear me, I said, "I believe you're referring to my car. I apologize for the inconvenience. I was just leaving anyway."

I'd spoken coolly, and combined with the look I knew was on my face, it was almost a sneer. He read it that way instantly, and whatever faults he had, stupidity wasn't one of them. Insecurity, however, was.

The combination of his perceptiveness and that insecurity caused him to say, even more loudly, "Since when do rich bitches drive old Nazi cars?" Since he'd said it ostensibly to Marilee, I ignored it, and picking up my purse and fox jacket, I made my way without haste to the door. Marilee met me there and walked me to my car. I realized then that I was shaking.

"Shit, Karen! I'm sorry as hell about that. He's in a worse mood than usual. The new bimb musta pissed him off. You okay?"

That was the second time she'd asked me that same thing in a few minutes, and without really thinking about what I was saying, I blurted, "Marilee, come home with me tonight. You can't stay here with him."

She laughed and patted my arm.

"Sure, I can. He's just pissed. He'll wind down pretty soon. But thanks anyway. I'll call you tomorrow."

Relieved, I got into my car and eased out of the driveway, aware suddenly I was crying.

Damn you, Jack Travis, I thought fiercely, for putting me into a situation where I would have to associate with such an awful creature.

I managed to make it home, and locking the door behind me, I leaned against it. My dreary little adobe house was a refuge again, and even if it was depressing and miserable by comparison, coming home to it was better than staying in that glass pueblo on the hill would have been.

For no amount of money on earth, I told myself, would I live there and take the abuse Marilee must take every day. There are some things that are worth more than money.

The next morning, Marilee phoned me at work.

"Hi, can you talk?"

"Not really," I said. "The place is full of tourists."

"Well, I just want to say this: You really impressed old Mac."

"Indeed?"

I was hard put not to tell her how Mac Carpenter had impressed me!

"Let's do lunch. Meet me in Pasqual's at noon. I'll get there early and get us a table, okay?"

She hung up before I had a chance to say anything else, and when

I fought my way through the crowd in the tiny foyer of Pasqual's later that morning, I saw she was sitting in the single booth that was large enough for six people.

"Mac wants you to come to dinner tonight," she said without preamble even before I'd seated myself.

"No. No, Marilee. Absolutely not!"

"Why not, Karen? It'd be a free meal."

"Marilee, not for all the free meals in the world would I eat with that . . . with him. There are some things more important than free meals, you know."

"Name one." She grinned.

"How do you know he was impressed with me?" I asked, changing the subject. From what I'd seen of Mac Carpenter, admitting he was interested in me would be the last thing I thought he might do. "I can't imagine his telling you that."

"Oh, he didn't, but I know Mac. When I came back in, he'd calmed down a lot and was really quiet. That's not like Mac so I kept my mouth shut, just to see what was going on. Finally, he asked me again what a rich bitch like you was doing, driving an old, beat-up VW."

"That doesn't mean—"

"I told him you were eccentric and then I changed the subject. After a while, he asked me where you were from."

"Marilee, that doesn't—"

"Don't you see, Karen? That's more interest than he's shown in anyone for a long time. He was quiet all evening. This morning when I got up, he'd left a note telling me to have my 'weird friend' to dinner tonight. It was supposed to be an afterthought, but the first part of the note was stuff I already knew and he knew I knew. I'm telling you, he's *interested* in you."

"Well, I'm not *interested* in him!"

"I've been thinking about this all morning. . . ."

Right then and there, I should have gotten up and left, terminating the conversation and the friendship. I should have seen the signs for what they were and taken the warnings to heart. I should have known better than to listen to anything Marilee Smith Carpenter Finch Sommerfrught Wallace suggested. God knows, by then I'd certainly had enough experience with her crazy reasoning to know better than to sit in that booth and listen to anything she had to say.

"What if he marries you . . . ?" she said.

I stared at her, horrified, unable to think of anything but the fact that she'd lost her mind. No other explanation for her statement occurred to me, but before I could say anything, she rushed on.

"What if he marries you and then dies. Listen, Karen! If he does, you'll inherit *everything*. We can split it. Then I won't have to worry all the time about him marrying one of those little—"

"What!"

I whispered the single word, too stunned to put any more energy into a response than that.

"Working together," she said, her eyes sparkling, "we can get him to marry you, and then, when he beans off, we'll have his money. The only reason he hasn't married any of these little bimbs he's been dating is that he still has me at home to pick at and they're doing everything all wrong. He's sneaky as shit but I know exactly how his mind works. We could do it, Karen!"

"You are the craziest woman I've ever met! You are so crazy that you ought to be locked up! Why they let you run loose, terrorizing this town, is beyond me, and further—"

"It'd work, Karen! I know it would!"

"No," I said, and then, looking at her as fiercely as I could manage, given my state of mind, I added, "Don't say another word about it, Marilee! If you do, I'm leaving!"

"Honey," she called to a waiter, passing by. "We need some wine here. We have some serious business to discuss."

"Not me," I said. "I don't want any wine. I don't want anything to drink. Just coffee, please."

I knew what she was trying to do and I was determined I would be one person, very possibly the first, who Marilee Wallace couldn't manipulate into doing what she wanted.

"Well, bring me two glasses of today's red, honey, please. I feel like drinking a *lot*."

He grinned and brought the wine and two glasses, and set them in front of Marilee.

"Just don't even think it, Marilee," I warned. "If you want me to eat with you, you'll have to change the subject. Right now."

"Just listen, Karen . . . Wait! I won't talk about it anymore, I promise. Sit back down."

* * *

In the end, of course, I did go to dinner at Mac Carpenter's house. In my defense, I can only say it took her four days to talk me into it, four days in which I slunk from my house to work and back again, almost furtively, feeling as if I should peer about me cautiously for the sight of that pink Cadillac and its flame-haired driver before I scurried from the security of either place to hurry to the security of the other.

I was pretty safe from her at work. The Christmas season was approaching and the shop was full of locals as well as the usual population of tourist shoppers, and we were busy enough that her arguments would constantly be interrupted. She had the good sense to realize that, and since I was with Richard most of the time in the evening, her harangues were limited to "doing lunch" together every day.

Refusing Marilee anything, however, was futile. Male or female, no one was immune to her combination of cajolery, flattery, and arguments that were so completely illogical they had no defense—at least, not from a rational person. She was relentless, and the sweet talk with which she peppered her dialogue was sincere, genuinely given, and so artfully tucked here and there into the conversation it was never really blatant enough to remonstrate with. The cumulative effect was devastating, especially since she really believed what she was saying, and as she was fond of saying, she never lied to a girlfriend. I certainly could not fault her there.

"What would it hurt," she asked me, "to just go out and eat with a lonely old man who's anxious for the company of a real lady for a change?"

"Marilee, I could not stand to be in the same room with that man. He has the manners of a warthog."

"He was just chapped at that little twit he was going with or he would never have yelled at you like that. He'll be on his best behavior, I promise."

In spite of myself, I was interested. "How could you possibly promise a thing like that?"

"I know Mac. If he wants something badly enough, he'll do what it takes to get it."

"Well, I don't see why he's so set on having dinner with me. Why me? I thought I made it perfectly clear what I thought of him that night."

"You did, and that's what got him interested in the first place. He's intrigued with your stand-away attitude. It's completely opposite to what he gets all the time. He likes a challenge, and I've said a few things myself to beef it up some for you."

"I can well imagine. What did you say?"

"Nothing much. Just a few words here and there. He acts like he could care less, but I notice he always listens. I didn't live with that man for all these years for nothing, you know."

I sighed, but determined to make her understand my position, I pressed on.

"Marilee, there is absolutely nothing to be gained by my coming to dinner. I am not accustomed to being yelled at. Mac Carpenter and I don't have enough in common to even make polite dinner conversation."

She patted my hand. "Just leave that to me. I'll handle everything. What night would be good for you?"

"Haven't you heard *anything* I've said? I am not going to eat with that man! I can't imagine why he wants me to in the first place. And in the second—"

"I told you, he likes a challenge. Why do you think he lets me live there? I'm the only one in the world who doesn't toady to him. It adds spice to his life."

" 'Spite' would be the better choice of words."

"Well, there! You see, you understand him better than you think you do."

"Marilee . . ."

I paused, trying to think of something else I could pull into play, something that might make some sense to her. Nothing occurred to me immediately, and Marilee, taking advantage of the situation, said, "Listen, Karen, what would it hurt? You're not committing marriage or anything—just four or five hours out of your life to have dinner with a man who finds you intriguing. That should flatter the shit out of you. It would me. Now, listen, how about this? What if we have dinner at some restaurant? Then you'd be on neutral ground."

"No! Absolutely not!"

I could imagine what kind of spectacle Mac Carpenter might make of himself in a public place. Nothing on earth could have made me even pretend to interact with someone like him around other people. I suddenly realized what would be worse than going to dinner at his house. Marilee sensed my horror and pressed her point.

"Look, Karen. Come to dinner. I promise. If he does anything,

anything at all, you don't like, you can leave. No arguments, okay? And I won't bother you about it again. How's that sound?"

It sounded fishy as hell to me, but I was fresh out of rational defenses, and worse, I was becoming confused and as crazy as Marilee.

"All right. All *right*, Marilee, but you listen to me—one hateful thing out of that man's mouth and I'm gone, hear?"

"Of course, and I wouldn't blame you. You'll come?"

"I said I would."

She patted my hand and smiled at me. "Fut the whuck, right?"

"Sure," I said.

Marilee invited herself over to help me dress for the dinner. Walking into the bedroom I'd converted into a closet, she whistled.

"Wow! I thought I had a lot of clothes!"

I had taken straight wooden ladders and wedging them between the floor and ceiling, had suspended metal pipes between them for rods so all four walls were covered with clothes. Additionally, there were two fingers of my makeshift clothes racks stuck out into the middle of the room, and I'd put chests at the end of each finger for those things I couldn't hang. Given the quality of everything, I could conservatively estimate I had at least a couple hundred thousand dollars invested in my clothing, worth practically nothing at the consignment shops. I'd already checked into that.

Why hadn't I bought fewer things, I'd asked myself several times, and filled every pocket with Krugerrands?

The answer—that I wasn't expecting to be divorced—was so obvious I didn't even bother to make it.

"I haven't bought anything new in well over a year," I told her. "Thank God I got good, classic things when I was married."

"Do you believe in organization or what? Little gray suits here, little beige suits next to them, brown suits, black suits. Let's see, where are the blouses? Oh, God, Karen! Pinks, beiges, whites—pretty wimpy stuff! Uh-oh, here's a yellow one. You must have been living dangerously the day you bought that!"

"Cut it out, Marilee. I can't wear the things you can. I would look appallingly . . ."

I stopped, hunting for a word that wouldn't hurt her feelings. I needn't have bothered.

"Where did you buy all this stuff? It looks like it all came from a schoolteacher's warehouse or something." And to herself, "There's gotta be something in here Mac would like."

It was an impossibly clumsy thing for her to say and I was on it instantly.

"It doesn't matter what Mac would or wouldn't like, Marilee. I'm not dressing to please that man. I don't care what he thinks. I don't care if he's happy with what I wear. Understand?"

"Sure. Sure. Where are your scarves? Jesus! I never thought I'd see a bland scarf, but here's a whole rack of 'em. Well, okay. If we can't have color, we'll go for textures. How about this?"

She began pulling things off the racks, seemingly at random—a floor-length, black velvet skirt that, even sans the matching blouse, was much too dressy to wear to an informal dinner; one of Jack's sweaters that had inadvertently gotten into one of my closets before the divorce, a dark-turquoise, cotton heavy knit that still had his scent on it, just enough so it caused me a momentary pang and then was forgotten; a knotted silk scarf that was really a shawl.

"Put this stuff on and let me see what you look like."

Obediently, I stripped and began to dress, feeling a little like a mannequin must feel. It was slightly exciting, this being dressed up, but Marilee squelched that.

"I wish you had more boobs," she said doubtfully, staring at my tiny breasts. "Mac is into tits in a big way."

Defiantly, I grabbed Jack's sweater, and pulling it over my head, I jerked it down, covering my bare breasts.

"It doesn't matter what my breasts are like," I said. "I don't care what Mac likes."

"Well, don't worry about it, honey. That sweater will be fine for tonight, and then we'll get you some push-up bras so you can wear some low-cut stuff."

She stripped a huge Navajo ring off one of her fingers, and looping the scarf around my neck, she slipped the opposite corners of it into the ring and pulled them through, tightening the scarf around my neck.

"Now what kinda boots do you have? Anything that looks even slightly funky?"

*　*　*

True to her word, Mac was on his best behavior—which, as it turned out, was just barely acceptable. As Marilee introduced us, he jabbed his hand out at me, and without thinking, I took a step backward. It was poorly done but I was not comfortable with a man's offering his hand to me before I'd made the first move to shake his. Mac recovered smoothly, however, and putting his outstretched hand on my elbow, he led me into the living room. I permitted it, slightly ashamed of my gracelessness before.

"What're you drinkin'," he asked, and I answered, as pleasantly as possible, "Sherry, please."

"Marilee tells me you're from Austin. I was outta Dallas myself, but I was always runnin' down there to the Railroad Commission for something or other. You knew I was in the awl bidness?" He peered at me and I nodded. Satisfied, he continued, "I liked it a lot. I done pretty good. Not bad for a poor boy. Yeah, I done all right, better than most of them smart boys who went to college."

He'd picked up a bottle of Bristol Cream, but before he could pour it, Marilee traded bottles with him, so smoothly that, intent on what he was saying, he wasn't aware he'd chosen a sherry that was not appropriate for a before-dinner cocktail. I took the glass from him and sipped the dry sherry he'd poured politely, seating myself where he gestured. The crystal glass in my hand was thin and heavy.

"Yes," I agreed, floundering for something to say, "Austin is quite nice."

"Plenty hot in the summer, though."

And Dallas isn't? I wanted to say. Aloud, I agreed again politely, "It can be."

"Though it ain't as hot as Houston. God *damn!* That place is worse than hell! At least, hell ain't humid."

How would you know? I almost asked him, and was surprised at my belligerence. Marilee, sensing the growing strain between us, said, "The only thing I miss here in Santa Fe are the cardinals and the mockingbirds."

Mac and I looked at her in unison. It was so like her to say something that was totally off the wall like that, and neither Mac nor I could think of an answer. She was fine with that, however. Smoothly she asked, "What do you miss, Karen. Anything?"

"Well," I said slowly, forced to think of something besides Mac Carpenter's squatting like a monstrous toad on the Velasquez sofa, "I miss the greenness, I suppose. But then, you can get that here by just driving up into the mountains."

"Yeah, when Marilee moved us out here, I was real upset, but the more I stayed here, the more I got to likin' it, and now it'd be hard for me to move back. That Texas heat is a killer on an old man like me."

We were back on the heat again and I sighed. I knew polite conversation would require that I refute his calling himself old like that, if only out of consideration for Marilee. I resented such an obvious manipulation, but I sipped my sherry and grinding my teeth, made the effort.

"I can't imagine your considering yourself old," I said, hoping the obtuseness of the response would throw him. I shouldn't have bothered.

"Well, this altitude is terrible for my heart. I've had three heart attacks, you know."

I looked quickly over at Marilee, but her face was bland, expressionless.

"The doctor says I ought to have a bypass, but I told him to go fu—to go find somebody else to hassle about it. I ain't building no bedroom onto some doctor's house for him. I'd ruther die happy, without letting him cut on me and then paying him for it. You know, that don't make sense, now does it? They hurt you and you pay them to do it. Now, does that make any sense to you, Marilee?"

"No, honey," she said, leaning over to pat him on the arm.

"Well," he said to me, "that ought to worry me if it don't make sense to her, neither."

He guffawed and I stared at him, my drink halfway to my mouth. Marilee stood, saying, "Why don't we go in and finish putting dinner together? You know, Karen, Mac makes a mean Caesar salad, and I'm going to put you in charge of the bread. I picked up some rolls at Becker's and all you have to do is butter them and heat them up."

She'd accurately estimated my level of culinary competence, and still offended by Mac's remark, I ignored him and followed her into the kitchen. On the way, I drained my glass of sherry, hoping Marilee would pour us some wine in the kitchen. Getting drunk, I suddenly saw, was the only way I would be able to handle the rest of the evening with Mac Carpenter.

I was amazed at the amount of liquor he drank. Over the course of the evening, he had at least three glasses of wine and several cocktails, bourbon cut with a little "branch water," and I diverted myself by wondering just how much he could swill and still remain functional. I'll say this for him, he was a happy drunk, unlike so many people I'd known who came out from behind a bar like Dracula. As the evening wore on, he became more expansive, more and more on stage, and the more he played to me the more I withdrew. I couldn't help it. It was beyond my experience to have someone lead me around his house, pointing out treasures, and telling me to the penny how much each had cost him. I found it unutterably tacky, this relating things to money, but I gamely stuck with him, hating every moment I spent with him and Marilee for talking me into it.

I did find out it was Marilee who'd worked with the architects and decorators, not Mac. It made sense, considering the impressions I'd gotten of his clothing and jewelry and her taste. As if to negate any implied compliment, he said, "That's where she met that little pansy decorator. The next thing I knew, the house was all finished and she'd run off with him. Jesus! First a cop, then an interior decorator—then a shrink. Will wonders never cease?"

At that point, my disgust matching his, I asked him point-blank why, if he had so much money, didn't Marilee have any help. She'd prepared the dinner and with my clumsy help, cleaned up after it, and when I asked her, she told me she did all the housework.

"That's what I pay her for," Mac said, watching me closely.

"Pay her?" I was under the impression that Marilee received no money from him, except what she spent at the market for groceries.

"Yeah, she gets room and board here."

The way he said it, as if defying me to tell him what I thought of it, caused me to pause, and encouraged by my silence, he said, "She had it all but she ran off with that little cop. That was real stoopid."

So, you're punishing her, I wanted to say. Your feelings were hurt and you're making her life miserable because she hurt you. Poor baby!

Instead, I changed the subject, as smoothly as possible, and the evening wound down. Finally, it was over. I knew it was over because, while Marilee and I were talking, Mac had gone to sleep in his chair, his head thrown back, giving us an excellent view of the insides of his nose and mouth. His snoring was amazing, consisting of a constant rumbling punctuated with violent snorts that would have awakened a lesser man.

"Are you okay to drive home?" Marilee asked me as I was leaving. I'd had several glasses of wine and was none too steady, but I assured her I was fine. Nothing on earth could make me spend the night in that house and I knew that suggestion was next.

"Come home with me, Marilee," I said, the wine talking for me. "You can live with me. I know you can find a better job than being Mac's drudge. We'll manage."

She smiled and, patting my arm, she loaded me into my car. On the way home, I was so sleepy I thought I might have to pull over, if only to sleep for a few minutes before I could continue. As it turned out, I didn't have to. I was halfway home when I realized red and blue lights were flashing behind me.

When the policeman walked up to the car, I said breathlessly, before he could comment on anything, "I'm sorry, Officer. I'm really sleepy. This is very late for me. I've been to a friend's house, Marilee Wallace, you might know her. She was married to a policeman here."

I was a little surprised and certainly delighted to see his eyes widen slightly. I hurried on.

"Let's see. It would have been Officer Finch. David Finch? I'll call her to verify what I've said, if you want me to."

This time, I was rewarded by the sight of his eyes, already as wide as possible, contracting to points in the dim light. Encouraged, I continued, "I know she'd be glad to come right down and talk to you. You know how Marilee is."

I smiled at him, my most innocent and endearing smile. It was one I'd copied from Marilee. It was all I could do to keep from patting his arm.

"Yes. No, that won't be necessary."

I had to listen to the regulation lecture about driving recklessly and promised to go right home and go to bed. He carefully avoided any mention of my possible drunkenness and so did I. Marilee's name might be a great incantation for protection against cops, but there was no sense in pushing it.

Fut the whuck, I thought, pulling away from the curb, watching the cop in my rearview mirror as he made a tight U-turn behind me. Will wonders never cease?

*   *   *

"Mac really, really, *really* likes you," Marilee said smugly.

I kicked at the pigeons that swarmed around our feet. They were almost as thick as a carpet, made tame by the constant feeding they got from tourists and locals alike. Walking across the open plaza could be a surrealistic experience in wading through waddling birds, and it was so that day.

Keep Santa Fe clean, I thought; eat a pigeon.

It was an old bumper sticker from another city, but it was still viable, at least for Santa Fe. Other cities might experiment with reviving dying breeds of falcons to deal with their pigeon populations, but Santa Fe's tallest building, by city ordinance, was limited to four stories, and falcons were not apt to nest that close to the ground.

Maybe cats, I thought. We could have plaza cats. I wonder what werewolves eat. Pigeons?

Actually, the pigeons were not all that much of a problem. I was in a lousy mood, hung over from the wine I'd drunk the night before and the aftereffects of the dinner with Mac Carpenter. The bright, high-altitude sunshine made me long for two ice cubes to hold against my eyelids. Wearily, I answered Marilee.

"Look, Marilee. I don't *care* whether Mac likes me or not. I don't like him. I don't see how you can live there with him."

"He's not so bad, I tell you. He was showing off for you. When he's insecure, he does that and I haven't seen him do it in years. He can be a really sweet man, Karen."

"Marilee, you are a virtual slave to that man. There are laws against that now. Remember that nice Yankee, Abe Lincoln? He set all the slaves free over a hundred years ago. If Mac is so sweet, how come he treats you like he does?"

"Well, he does have a few personality traits that could stand some polishing. But you know what they say: Once they're that old, you can't change 'em."

"Good. Let's don't try. Where do you want to eat lunch?"

"I thought the Palace. It's quiet there and we can talk."

"I can't afford it."

Even then and even with Marilee, it was difficult for me to admit how broke I was.

"It's on Mac today."

"What do you mean?"

"He gave me some money to go to the market and then he gave me some extra and said for me to take you to lunch."

"Mac said that?"

"Well, he didn't come right out and say it, but that's what he meant."

"Uh-huh."

"He did. I'm telling you, he *likes* you."

"Uh-huh."

The plaza was filled that day, as on most sunny days, which averaged three hundred days per year in northern New Mexico. The usual mélange of tourists, people who worked downtown, and some apparently rootless young adults, a few with dogs and young children, visited while they ate their lunches. The plaza had its share of weird people, too, and I saw one of them coming toward us. I'd seen him before. Too sane to be locked away in one of New Mexico's overcrowded mental health facilities, he was, nevertheless, decidedly strange. He was a fairly young man, dressed in tatters, and he always wore a football helmet. He seldom noticed the people around him, but he could often be seen talking to people or things who weren't there, sometimes conversationally, sometimes with anger or agitation, complete with gestures and shouting. When he was like this, the plaza policeman would gently herd him away from the tourists so they wouldn't be offended and go off to Albuquerque or Taos to spend their money.

Occasionally, however, he would accost people, plead with them for some kind of assistance with the "others," as he called his own personal demons. The locals were all a little leery of him but true to the Santa Fe spirit, allowed him to coexist along with the other, more normal people. Santa Fe was a great place for alternate life-styles, and some of those were even more strange than that of the young man coming toward us.

As he approached us, I realized that he was in one of his wildly agitated moods and I began to angle away from him. Marilee, however, stopped and waited for him to get within hearing range. I was horrified to hear her call to him.

"Hello, Frank. How are you?"

He stopped in front of her, went through a series of facial gestures, and then, conversationally, said, "Hello, Marilee. I'm doing fine. This new helmet works better than any of the others did. Thanks."

I pretended great interest in the benches in the center of the plaza. It was beyond my understanding why Marilee would make such a public spectacle of us by talking to him. Everyone was watching their conversation, some covertly and some with great interest and amusement. I waited in the strong, glaring sun for her to be finished, my eyes throbbing and my irritation growing.

She smiled at him and said, "Oh, good. Did lining it with tinfoil help?"

"Oh, yes. It's much better. Blocks out most of the rays that way."

She patted him on his arm. "I'm glad. Be seeing you, Frank."

"Yeah. 'Bye, Marilee."

She joined me and we started toward the corner of the plaza again.

"Why did you want to talk to him, for God's sake? He's crazier than a—"

"Well," she said mildly, "I would hate it if I were like that and everyone ignored me. I may wind up on the street myself, you know. And so could you. Who knows what being a bag lady would do to you."

I didn't say anything else. She was right. I had not considered working in the Museum Shop any kind of a long-term commitment. I didn't want to think about my being there long enough to build up any kind of retirement, but the alternative was too gruesome to consider. Chastened, I followed her into the restaurant.

When we'd ordered and scoped out the interesting men in the dining room, she said, "Look at these guys. What a bunch of losers! You know, Karen, you could do a lot worse than Mac."

I laughed, a short laugh that was humorless.

"Let's change the subject, Marilee."

She patted my hand. "Just listen for a few minutes. I've been thinking, what if you *did* marry Mac. No, Karen, just *listen* to me. If you marry Mac, you'd be secure again. You wouldn't have to ask your mother for any money. You wouldn't have to worry about where your next meal is coming from. Do you have any put away for emergencies? What if you get sick? I mean, really sick, so sick you can't work for months and months? What would you do if your car blew a rod or something? If that happens, could you afford another one? You'd probably have to move in with your mother. She's got the beginnings of old-timer's disease, doesn't she? Do you realize what you'll be letting yourself in for? Years and years of it. Mac is a walking time bomb.

You saw how much he ate and drank last night. He's just *asking* for another heart attack. This altitude is perfect for it. Right this minute, he could be on his way to the hospital. If he dies, it's all wasted."

"Surely, he'll leave something to you."

"Well, sort of."

"What do you mean?"

"I'll get a little, but most of it goes to, get this, to fund some kind of petroleum research thing in his name. He never had any education to speak of, and by setting this thing up, it's like he's saying, 'Look at me. I'm just a dumb guy, but I'm the reason smart guys can study.' It's the ultimate power trip for him."

"That doesn't make any sense."

"Not to you or me, but it does to Mac. We're talking about millions and millions of dollars, Karen, all frittered away on some stupid oil and gas research thing that won't do you or me a bit of good."

I didn't say anything. I was thinking about the "millions and millions of dollars" she'd mentioned. It would just about pay off my credit cards.

Marilee hurried on, realizing I was snagged.

"If you marry him, when he dies, we can split it."

"Why don't you marry him, then?"

"He wouldn't remarry me on a bet. Once you've done something to him, he never forgets it. Besides, like he says, why should he buy a cow when he can get the milk for free?"

I stared at her, overwhelmed by the coarseness and the cruelty. It was beyond my understanding what there was between the two of them that bound them together like that. For the first time in my life, I gave some serious thought to the possibility that there might be something to the concept of karma.

"Anyway," she continued, "I'm not sure I want to remarry him. If he's married to me, he might live another hundred years, and I don't think I could take that."

I let the illogic of that go, focusing on what was really bothering me.

"Marilee, I could not be married to that man. I couldn't stand it day after day, and worse, night after night, and," I said, staring at her meaningfully, "I think we *both* know what I mean."

"Oh, you don't have to worry about that. He can't get it up anymore. Why do you think I ran off with Davy Finch in the first place? I think it's the medicine the doctor gave him to keep his blood pressure down, or maybe it's the booze. Anyway, he definitely can't. You'd be safe there."

"And I'm sure you could guarantee that."

She ignored my sarcasm. "Sure. That may not be a problem for you. I personally found it very hard to take myself, being a red-hot little Taurus girl. You know how we are."

"What about all these girlfriends he has?"

"I'll give you a dime against a doughnut he's never slept with any of them. I *know* he hasn't! Why do you think he has so many? He can pick them up without any trouble, if for no other reason than all that gold he wears. He might as well wear a T-shirt that says, 'I'm rich!' But they never last very long and that's why. If he had any kind of a sustained relationship with a woman, he'd have to sleep with her and he can't do that, I'm telling you. He can't get it up. So he blames her, dumps her, and finds another one. Every time he finds a new girl, he thinks maybe she's gonna be the one who can cure his 'problem.' That's why he was so pissed off the night you met him. It was another dud."

"How do you know all this? I got the impression you two never talk."

"I'm telling you, I know him backward and forward, Karen. I've spent thirty years with that man, off and on—mostly on—and I can tell you exactly what's going through his mind at any moment. I've made a career of it, for what *that's* been worth."

For the first time since I'd met her, I sensed a note of self-pity in her voice. It was gone in a flash. She grinned at me.

"That's why you need me. He's too cagey to get married, and marriage is the only thing that will work for us. I can get the two of you married. Trust me."

"I don't *want* to get married, Marilee. At least not to Mac."

"Why not?"

I thought about Richard. Perhaps it wasn't going to be a forever thing, but then again, maybe it was.

"If I were married and Robert Redford came along, what would I do then? I'd be stuck with old Mac and somebody else would get Redford."

"You think Redford's going to be interested in a forty-five-year-old woman without any money?"

"He *might!*"

"Well, you'd certainly have a better chance if you had some money to spend. After Mac dies, you would have."

"Your eyelashes are coming unstuck again," I said, trying to divert her. I needed time to think. What she was proposing was crazy and I was even crazier for listening to it. What bothered me even more than that, however, was the fact that I was beginning to see how it might work.

She got up to go to the women's room to reglue her lashes.

"Just think about it," she urged. "You don't have to commit on anything right now. I just wanted you to think about it some."

The next week was, without a doubt, the worst week of my life, surpassing the week in which I'd been faced with the undeniable evidence of Jack's infidelity, exceeding even the week I'd met Marilee Wallace.

First of all, the credit card people, whom I'd stalled for the better part of a year, all suddenly decided to file suits for the balances I owed them. When I was first divorced, they'd pressed credit on me, not realizing I had come out of the divorce without anything except, literally, the clothes in my closets. I'd spent over a year in limbo, my soul devastated by the ending of the marriage I'd assumed would last forever, unable to initiate anything that would bring on an easier transition into another lifestyle, or to even understand it would be necessary to do so. When I ran out of money, borrowing money on the credit cards had seemed an easy source of revenue until, waking up to the fact I had no chance in hell of paying any of it back, I could only castigate myself for my naïveté. In my defense, I could only say that someone had always paid my bills without question, and I had been given no training in anything but finding a man, marrying him, and living happily ever after, giving little dinner parties and raising funds for charities. And ultimately, I'd even failed at that.

I also spent the better part of the week at the local office of the Internal Revenue. I'd received notice that my returns for the three years I'd been single were being audited, and dutifully, I hauled the grocery sacks that served as my filing system into their office. I was pleased to see the look of dismay on the face of the auditor, a young woman with an incredibly poor complexion and a tendency toward obesity, when she saw them, but it was the last pleasant thing that happened to me in the experience, until the very end. The auditor, finally exasperated almost into apoplexy by my inability to grasp even the most simple (to her) tax laws, finally snapped at me.

"You can't be this stupid," she said.

I knew how to handle that. I leaned back in my chair, rubbed the fingernails of one hand with their thumb, and gave her my mother's stare.

"As it happens," I said coolly, "my IQ is higher than my weight."

She didn't miss the implication. It was a fleeting pleasure, however, and when she was done with me, I owed five hundred and forty-three dollars in additional taxes, penalties, and interest.

"Well," I said, "I'll just have to go to prison. I don't have the money."

At that point, I would have welcomed prison. At least, I would be free of the credit card people, who had become insistent, to the point of sending registered letters and process servers to my house.

"You have assets," she snapped. "You have a car? Well, sell it! This money is owed to the government of the United States of America and I'm empowered to collect it. We're tired of you deadbeats."

"Why didn't you just slap the shit out of her?" Marilee asked me later, over drinks at the Ore House. "What could they have done? Fut the whuck! You could claim temporary insanity. There isn't a jury in this country that would convict you."

"Is that what you would have done? Somehow, I doubt it. Dammit, Marilee! I handled it all wrong. I should have taken an attorney in there with me, or an accountant, or something. I might as well have jumped into a lion's den without any clothes on."

"Can you afford an attorney or an accountant?"

"No. Shit! I can't even declare bankruptcy; you have to have money to do that. I guess I'm going to have to call Mother. This has got to be the worst day of my life, Marilee."

I was wrong. The next day was. When I called Mother in Austin, I was snottily informed that Mother was resting, and when I remonstrated with whichever of her lackeys I was talking to, I was referred to the firm that handled her legal work. Calling them to find out what was going on, I learned I'd been summarily disinherited. One of the registered letters I hadn't bothered to pick up from the post office was from their firm, informing me of the action. It was so silly, so Victorian, that I actually laughed, thinking it was a joke. It was not. Mother, tired of my "feckless irresponsibility and stubborn absence from the protection of hearth and home," had decided I was no longer a daughter of hers, had changed her will, and instructed my sisters, on pain of also being disinherited, to have nothing more to do with me. I knew them well enough to know where I stood, or rather didn't stand, with them. Both of them would sell their children for a bigger slice of the pie.

When Richard picked me up that night, I said, "Let's go somewhere and have a drink before dinner. I could use one."

"That's probably a good idea. There's something I want to talk to you about."

What he wanted to tell me was that he didn't want to see me anymore. It wasn't what he said, but it was what he meant.

"I think we both need to date other people right now," he said. "I'm feeling a little claustrophobic with you."

"Oh?"

I realized it was inadequate, but I literally couldn't think of any other response. He took it as a good sign and continued, "Of course, I'll want to see you again, now and then. We make a good-looking couple, the two of us."

Suddenly, it all seemed so very funny. I tried vainly to keep my lips from smiling, pursing them severely, while I watched his earnest, handsome face. Finally, I was able to control myself enough to say, "In other words, I'm a great arm-decoration but not suitable for anything else."

"That's not what I said, Karen. You're doing it again."

"Doing it?"

"Pulling away, sneering like you do."

I suddenly had an image of Mother in my mind, nose lifted in haughty disdain. Richard thought I was sneering? He should have seen Mother's sneers. She was a master at it and in her prime, could reduce a grown man to a whimpering, bloody pulp. Richard wouldn't have lasted a second under her quiet scorn. I saw him, suddenly, groveling on the floor in front of her, his shirt in ribbons and his back lacerated with whip marks. She could do that to someone and never raise her voice.

Now I realized I was actually laughing and told myself it was no laughing matter, that I should calmly reason with Richard, open up dialogue in order to work out whatever was bothering him. For some reason, however, I couldn't stop laughing, and seeing that I was making a public spectacle of myself and unwilling to sit there and have everyone stare at me, I rose and walked out of the place with as much dignity as possible.

The sharp, piñon-smoke-scented air did a lot to slap the laughter out of me, but irrationally, I realized that now I wanted to cry, that I wanted to sit down on the dirty curb and bury my face in my hands, or better yet, throw myself in front of the first car that drove past.

I walked down the street for a little way toward a pay phone and called Marilee. When she answered, I asked her to come and get me. I had the money for cab fare, but suddenly, I wanted to talk to her, to have her sit and listen to all that had happened to me that week, to put it into perspective as only she could do. I wanted her to tell me I was overreacting, that everything would be all right, though even the frybrain on the plaza could see that it wouldn't be. Most important, I wanted her to point out any reason I hadn't seen why I shouldn't just kill myself and get it all over with.

"Where are you?" she asked, and when I told her, she said, "Stay right there. I'll be there in a second."

When the pink Cadillac veered to a stop next to the curb, nearly clipping the pay phone as it did so, I opened the door and crawled in.

"Well, you look like shit," she said cheerfully, and overwhelmed by all that had happened to me, I started crying again.

"A friend would tell you," she said. "I'm taking you home. You look like you need a strong cup of coffee and a good bawl."

"First of all," she said when I'd cried myself out, "first of all, this isn't the end of the world, you know. These things can all be handled."

"Oh, sure. Tell me how."

I felt logy and stupid, the tears having loaded my sinuses with cement, as well as having destroyed my makeup. I was lethargically argumentative, unable to respond positively to any reasonable assessment of the situation.

She put a cup of coffee in front of me and I sipped it dutifully. She was right, it was very strong and it helped a little.

"I've made such a mess of my life," I continued, wallowing in misery and self-hate. "How anyone could do some of the stupid things I've done is beyond me. And now, the IRS is making me sell my little car."

I started crying again.

"All you need is some money. If you had money, you could pay the IRS off, or hire some attorneys and accountants and fight 'em. If you had money—"

"But I don't! I don't have *any money*," I said, enunciating the last two words carefully. "And I *never will*. I have no chance of *ever* earning any. This is what the rest of my life will be like, Marilee."

It was something I'd just realized, and the awful enormity of that understanding was staggering. I stared at her, panic-stricken.

"Mac had his nitro pills refilled," she said, patting my arm.

"What?"

I did not want to hear about Mac's nitro pills. The end of my world was looming and I couldn't spare any energy to think about someone else, much less Mac Carpenter or his nitro pills, whatever they were.

"Don't you see? That means he's having chest pains again. We're running out of time, Karen."

I sat there, looking at her. From somewhere, deep inside me, a voice cried, No, you're not *that* desperate! Don't listen to her! You're just weak right now. Things will be better in the morning.

But I knew they wouldn't be.

"Karen, if you marry him, he'll not only pay everyone off, but he'll take care of it personally, too. You won't have to deal with the IRS or anyone yourself. He'll do that. And he can do it better than you; he's had lots more experience at it, at dealing with assholes like that."

"Marilee, I couldn't. I just couldn't . . ."

"Why not?"

"It seems dishonest."

"Oh, bullshit, Karen. Grow up, honey. If you can't take care of yourself, you have to find somebody who will. And Mac will. You and I *need* to be married, honey. We were born too soon to learn we might have to take care of ourselves. Marriage is the only answer for us, now isn't it?

I switched tactics.

"Doesn't it bother you to talk about Mac dying like that? Surely, there must be something left, some spark of love somewhere for him. It's like he was some stranger. Really, you'd show more sympathy for a stranger than you do him. You talk about his dying like you would talk about a new dress or something. Don't you have any feeling for him?"

"Karen, I started coming to grips with this sixteen years ago when he had his first heart attack. I could see he wasn't about to stop what he was doing just so he could live longer. That's the way he is, the selfish ass-hole. Anyway, he's made his choices and I've made mine. And, God *damn* it! I'm *not* going to let the University of Texas have all that money if I can help it! I'd put it to a lot better use, believe me."

"But, Marilee..."

"What, Karen? Tell me what we'd be doing wrong. You'd marry him, he'd be happy, and then, when he dies, you and I split the proceeds. That's a lot better than winding up broke and hungry, isn't it? I don't know about you, but I don't want to be a bag lady somewhere down the line. Neither one of us are chickens anymore, Karen. It's not as if we have the time or the energy to start over, and I'm tired of marrying cookie bandits just to have some spending money."

I sat there, staring at her. Suddenly, there was a pounding on the door.

"Don't answer it," I whispered.

"Why?"

"It's probably a process server."

We sat there and looked at each other while the pounding continued and finally, stopped. In that time, I'd made up my mind, but to give me credit, I tried one more time.

"Are you sure," I asked her, staring fiercely at her so she would know I meant business, "are you sure Mac is impotent? Are you *positive?*"

"Sure, I'm telling you it's been so long since he used his dingle for anything more than standing in front of a urinal that he might as well not have it."

"Because if he isn't, Marilee Wallace, if he isn't, you'll be the one who dies. Get me?"

"Sure." She grinned. "I wouldn't lie to a girlfriend."

She patted my arm again. "Now here's what we'll do," she said.

2

The next morning, Marilee picked a fight with Mac and using that as an excuse, moved out of his house.

"If I'm there, he won't ever remarry," she explained. "No man will change his environment unless he's unhappy. And if he's not happy, you can count on him doing something about it. Women will sit around for years, miserable, just tolerating things and waiting for them to get better. But if a man's unhappy, then he'll do something about it, real quick. Now, in a few days, Mac'll call you, looking for me. You act surprised. You imply you and I are not in contact. He has to think you're more his friend than mine. You imply you don't approve of my actions, but don't tear my ass off to him because he'll feel like he has to defend me. Whatever you say, just imply things. Tell the truth as much as possible. He can sniff out a lie better than Sherlock Holmes. Be polite and nice but a little cool, and this is important, you're too busy to talk to him at the shop. Pretend there are several interruptions and you can't quite concentrate on what he's telling you. Apologize without groveling. Let him know that, if you had the time, you'd be interested in what he's trying to tell you. Okay?"

"All right."

"Now, he won't do anything right away so don't feel upset if he just hangs up on you. He might do that. What we have to do is replace me with you, but very, very slowly. Let him think it's all his idea."

"How do you know so much about men?" I asked, impressed in spite of myself.

"Not men—Mac. A lifelong study, darlin'." She grinned. "We'll put a little stress on old Mac to get the ball rolling."

"What if this puts so much stress on him it triggers another heart attack?"

"Don't worry, this'll just piss him off." She laughed.

"Well, all right," I said with some degree of doubt.

"Trust me. I wouldn't lie to a girlfriend."

What she did do was move in with me.

We put another twin bed in my bedroom and I cleared out the closet in there for the things she didn't put in storage.

"Now you understand," she warned me, "I won't have any money for a while until my alimony check from Harve, the psychiatrist, comes in. It's not much but it will pay the rent, if you can spring for the groceries in the meantime."

"Sure. I can do that. How long is this going to take, do you think?"

In spite of myself, I was caught up in the excitement of the thing. Marilee could do that to you, take something you would probably never have dreamed up, not in your wildest fantasies, and turn it around and around so it became not only a considerable thing but something fun and exciting, as well. Every morning I would have coffee with her before I went to work, listening to the plans she outlined, speculating on their possible consequences, arguing, conspiring, laughing with glee or grinding our teeth, depending on how things were going. Every evening, after work, I came home to a clean house, to the smell of dinner in the kitchen, a table set before the little kiva fireplace in the sitting room. There was usually some new thing in the house, something Marilee had picked up at the Goodwill or the Salvation Army Thrift Shop, the "Sally" she called it, a sofa pillow, a tablecloth, a lamp, something to decorate the house I'd lived in for two years, turning it finally into a home with a personality.

Her skill at taking someone else's discards and using them in unique ways was phenomenal. She had an unerring eye for quality, and she often showed me some small treasure she'd picked up for nothing because the unsophisticated girls who worked in the thrift shops didn't recognize what they'd been given and had priced it routinely, without thought.

She could do that with people, too.

I began to realize how really alone I had been, and not just since my divorce, either—all my life, really. By the very contrast, Marilee's moving into my house had highlighted the low-grade misery that I'd always merely taken for granted. I'd certainly never shared a bedroom with anyone before, except, of course, with Jack, and somehow, the presence of someone else in the warm darkness, someone to whom I could tell things I couldn't talk about in the light, was immensely comforting. Somehow, in the anonymity of the darkness, I could whisper aloud all the things that frightened me, things that I wouldn't be able to admit to during the day, things that, before Marilee's coming, could roll up higher and higher in the night, growing like some giant wave, until they threatened to overwhelm me. Marilee's answering whisper—"I know, honey. It'll be all right. It'll look better in the morning"—reassured me, allowing me to fall asleep, to sleep peacefully until daylight came.

"Is this Karen Travis?"

"Yes, it is."

"Well, this is Mac Carpenter. Have you seen Marilee in the last few days?"

I paused, took a deep breath, and then said into the phone in my hand, exactly as if I'd just connected names with faces, "Oh. Hello, Mac. Is Marilee missing?"

"Have you seen her?"

Keeping Marilee's instructions in mind, I said, "Excuse me just a moment, Mac." I laid the phone on the counter, counted to fifty, picked it up again, and said, "I'm sorry, Mac, this place is a madhouse. Now what were you...Oh, yes, I saw her the other day. She was driving down Palace in that pink Cadillac of hers. Has something happened to her?"

"She got pissed off and moved out. I'm trying to find out if she got married again or what. What day did you see her?"

"Well, it was...I'm sorry, Mac. Excuse me again."

I put him on hold and walking to the other end of the shop, had a short conversation with one of the volunteers concerning the symphony concert the Sunday before. When I picked up the phone again, it was humming. I put it back on the cradle.

When I told Marilee about it that night, she said, "Great. You did perfectly, perfectly super. Now, he'll call you again tomorrow morning. Do the same thing, except be just a scooch irritated with him for calling you when you're so busy. When he asks you to go to lunch, you say, 'I can't today, Mac, thanks anyway. What about tomorrow?' "

"How do you know he'll call tomorrow and ask me to lunch?"

"He will."

"Why can't I go to lunch when he calls?"

"Because your social calendar is *not* something that's open for drop-in lunch dates, that's why. God damn, girl! Didn't you ever date before you got married?"

"This is a lot of game-playing, Marilee. More than I'm used to."

"That's all life is, Karen. Games. You take everything too seriously. Now don't get upset if he tells you he can't have lunch with you the next day. Just blow it off and make sure he knows you're just blowing it off. Don't be hateful; it's just not that big of a thing to you, okay?"

I'd had a couple of lunches with Mac, and as Marilee had instructed, I'd made them hurried affairs, tantalizing him. When I was with him, also per her instructions, I was totally with him, hanging on every word, ignoring anyone and everyone who came and went through the dining room. I found this pretending to be interested in him hard at first, very energy- and emotion-consuming, but the more I was with him, the more I could see what Marilee had meant when she said he could be sweet—when he wanted something. I'd had no experience with someone like Mac, however. His manners and treatment of the serving people were horrifying, and often, I felt like throwing my napkin over my face and rushing out of the dining room—not that I worried so much about the waitperson's feelings particularly, but that he was so very loud with his offensivenesses.

When his drinks began to tell on him, I was more than glad to leave, pleading some official reason I had to cut the meal short—I had to go to the post office; I had a staff meeting. Each time, as I fled to the sanctuary of the Museum Shop, I swore I'd gotten in over my head and that, no matter what, I could not ever see myself actually married to Mac Carpenter.

Every time it happened, I would begin to have doubts about what we were trying to do. What if, I asked myself, we couldn't get him to marry me? What if he married someone else first? What if he moved away? What if—God forbid!—what if I should manage to marry him and he didn't *die?*

"Don't worry about it," Marilee counseled. "Let's just take one thing at a time. Now here's what we'll do . . ."

Trained from childhood to be obedient to any kind of an authority figure, I swallowed my doubts and allowed Marilee's assurances to soothe me.

"After all," she said, "anything's better than what you've got now, isn't it?"

And when confronted with that kind of logic, I had to admit that, yes, anything, *everything,* was better than what I was experiencing as a single woman, on my own, and that nothing could be as bad as the mess I'd made of my life.

Finally, as if obeying some cue from Marilee, Mac asked me out to dinner. She was beside herself with glee. She'd accurately predicted his doing so, had even told me, almost word for word, what he would say.

"Now," she said. "We have to get you ready."

"Get me ready?"

"Figure out something for you to wear."

"I thought I'd wear my taupe raw silk—"

"No, no, no! You cannot wear anything in your closet for a dinner date with Mac Carpenter. He would be so *intimidated* by your little power dresses."

"Power dresses?"

"Well, you don't mean them to be, but they are, just the same. Your clothes would say to a man like Mac, 'I have lots of class and you don't and what's more, you can't buy what I've got, no matter how much money you have.'"

"What?"

"Don't worry about it. You can wear something of mine."

I pointed out to her, with some asperity, I wasn't worried about it. What Mac liked or didn't like, whether I intimidated him or didn't, was absolutely nothing to me and I certainly wasn't dressing to please him.

"Besides," I said, "he's seen me at lunch in my little 'power outfits' and they didn't intimidate him in the least."

"Well, I'm telling you they did. You just didn't notice it. He's like a magician about hiding what he's thinking, but he could excuse them over lunch, since you were working. He could tell himself those were your work clothes. You have to look professional at work, but when you go out to dinner with him, you want to put forth a completely different image. He's got to think you can be fun, too. Besides, I'd kill you before I'd let you wear that gorgeous silk to Ernesto's. No telling what would happen to it there."

"Ernesto's!" I was aghast. She'd named one of the toughest, rawest clubs on Cerillos Road.

"It's Mac's favorite watering hole."

"I am not going to Ernesto's!" I said with a great deal of certainty. "Not for anything would I go into that place!"

"There you go, getting all excited again, Karen. You should watch that. You'll be the one having the heart attack if you're not careful."

"I'm not going to Ernesto's!"

"Mac'll take care of you. Nothing will happen to you there."

"Marilee, I am not worried about something happening to me there. It's just that . . ."

"Well, what?"

I couldn't think how I could tell her that just being there, amid the rough element of Santa Fe, would be impossible for me. I could not imagine what kind of people I would have to deal with, and furthermore, I was positive I not only wouldn't have a good time but might catch something horrible there, as well.

"Oh, piffle," Marilee said. "You won't see anyone there you know. My mother always said, 'Never pass up new experiences because they can be very enriching.'"

"Like marrying Mac Carpenter," I muttered.

"What?"

"Nothing."

"Karen, you miss out on so much of life because you're such a stick. Unbend a little. Have some fun. I give you permission to have fun now and then."

"I am not a stick."

"Well, a friend would tell you. Now, have you ever even been in Ernesto's? I thought not. How do you know you won't like it? It can be a lot of fun there."

I couldn't think of anything to say to that, and taking my silence for agreement, she started digging through her closet. I poured us both a glass of wine while she hauled things out, looking at them judiciously and then throwing them indiscriminately on her bed. She handed me a pair of orange spandex pants and I obediently began pulling them on, but I'd only gotten them halfway up when Marilee stopped me.

"Take those panties off, Karen! You can't wear spandex tights with underpants on. Major panty line! It's a giant fashion no-no!"

I was aghast. "Not wear underwear!"

"It won't kill you one time," she said. "What did you do for fun before I came along?"

I ignored the question and its implication, but I took the offending panties off. The orange pants were exceedingly tight and pulling them on took some effort.

"I haven't worn a girdle since 1965," I grumbled, working the stretchy fabric back up my legs.

Finally, I got them up. Since I was taller than she was, they went down only to midcalf and fitted me like skin. I stared at them in the mirror.

"I hope this stuff is stronger than it looks."

"Sure," Marilee said. "I wear it all the time. Spandex is your friend. It'll never let you down. Here, put this on."

She handed me a padded, push-up bra. Dutifully, I put it on and fastened it behind me. Without any embarrassment on her part, she dug her hand into each of the cups, pulling my breasts up and wiggling the bra to seat it firmly on my rib cage. I permitted it, knowing there would be no use in resisting. When she stepped back, there was a satisfactory, and very foreign, bulge over each of the low-cut cups. In spite of myself, I was a little pleased.

"There! That looks great! You've just increased your bust size by at least three inches."

I arched my back a little, twisting, to observe the effect in the mirror.

"Where did this bra come from?" I asked. "It's not one of mine. Is it yours?"

"No, God, darlin'. I haven't owned a padded bra since I was ten. I got it at the Sally."

"What!"

I had a sudden image of a flat-chested, scrubby-looking woman wearing my bra. I'd never shared underclothes with anyone and certainly not a stranger. I stared at Marilee in horror.

"Stop worrying," she said defensively. "I washed it."

"Did you disinfect it?"

"Sure."

I knew she was lying. "What with?"

"Lysol, for God's sake, Karen."

"I didn't think you ever lied to a girlfriend."

She grinned at me in the mirror. "Well, fut the whuck," she said, shrugging. "Once in a while, it's good for you. Keeps you on your toes."

Then she'd bullied me into a tight fuchsia tank top. When I pulled it down, the bulges over the neckline appeased me somewhat. For the first time in my life, I knew what it was like to have obvious breasts. It was a heady feeling.

"This is pretty bright," I said doubtfully, surveying the effect of the orange and fuchsia together in the mirror.

"Yeah, isn't it great? Here. Wrap this scarf around your waist for a belt."

The scarf was kelly green.

"Are you color-blind?" I asked. It was a serious question.

She ignored me, handing me a blouse that could only be called wild, having great fuchsia, orange, and green flowers that looked like nothing I'd ever seen growing in real life printed frenetically on the fabric. It was more of a shirt than a blouse, and putting it on me and tying a knot in each of the bottom corners, she stepped back to get the effect.

"Not bad," she said. "Not bad at all. Now for some jewelry."

"Marilee, you surely aren't going to suggest jewelry with this garb, are you? Because if you are . . ."

We argued with some heat over a necklace that suggested it might double as an Argentinian hunting bolo, and finally compromised with earrings that looked like they had probably been part of a child's jacks set in a prior life. I put them in the holes in my ears and observed the result. They dangled almost to my shoulders, a wild froth of geometric shapes on tiny chains.

"Great, just great," Marilee said. "Men just love dangly earrings. Catches their eye and makes you seem vivacious to them. Now what we need is something to call attention to your boobs. Do you have a long chain or something that will tuck into your bra?"

She pawed through my hanging chains and finally selected one, fastening it behind my neck. She poked the bottom of it between my new cleavage into the bra, clawing me slightly with her Dragon Lady nails as she did so.

"Leave that tucked in like that. Makes 'em wonder what's on the end of it. Now for some makeup. Come over here and sit on this stool."

She poured us both another glass of wine and hauled out her makeup basket.

"I have makeup," I said firmly. Sharing underclothes was one thing, but makeup couldn't be disinfected.

"Not like mine, you don't. Drink some wine and trust me."

I sat, as still as possible, for the better part of thirty minutes while she worked on me, muttering to herself. Finally, she stepped back.

"Okay. That's perfect. See what you think."

I walked back to the mirror and stared in horror at the clownlike stranger who stared back at me. She'd used color freely, much more than I would have thought possible on a single face. My eyelids alone were four different colors, and the weight of the coats of mascara she'd used made my eyelashes seem heavy, foreign. My cheeks screamed at me, and the shiny lipstick on my mouth was a very definite scarlet, outlined with brown. I looked like something out of a John Travolta flick, but when I told her that, she merely laughed.

"You don't even know what a John Travolta movie is like. Have you ever been to one?"

"Marilee, I cannot go out of this house looking like this."

"Why?"

"Because . . ."

I stared at the tarted-up stranger in the full-length mirror. Marilee had brushed my hair and pulling it up to one side of my crown, had fastened it into a ponytail with an orange elastic band. I looked like a horrified woman who, under the influence of some virulent psychedelic drug, had lost her mind and gone into some kind of frenzy and then awakened to the result of her being out of control staring her in the face. I started to take the earrings out of my ears.

"What are you doing? Karen, stop that!"

"Marilee, the deal is off! I would die, absolutely die, before I let someone see me like this. This isn't me! This is . . ." With the earring I'd managed to get out of my earhole in my hand, I waved it helplessly at the wild woman in the mirror, who gestured back at me.

Marilee grabbed my hand.

"That's perfect! With just one earring in, opposite your ponytail, it balances off your head perfectly. We'll just put a little one in the other ear."

I grabbed her upper arms, made her look at me.

"No! I am not leaving this house looking like this, Marilee. If this is what it takes to rope in Mac, count me out!"

"Have some more wine." She smiled, managing somehow to pat my underarms with her hands. "What do you care who sees you like this in Ernesto's? There's nobody there you want to impress, right? Besides, if someone you did know saw you dressed like that, they wouldn't recognize you, would they? Now, would they?"

"Who would I meet that I know?" I asked suspiciously. Too late, I realized I'd fallen into her trap and tried to drag the conversation back to the pertinent subject. "Marilee, I absolutely cannot carry this off. I look like . . ."

Pausing while I tried to think of an apt analogy for the spaced-out look she'd given me, I hesitated too long.

"Look at yourself, Karen, no, really look."

She turned me to face the mirror. Embarrassed, I forced myself to look.

"You look ten years younger than you really are, and in that dark bar, you'll look even younger than that. You've got great legs that come all the way up to my armpits and a body that's terrific, especially with that bra. Why not show it off?"

"Marilee, this is tacky!"

"If you show up at Ernesto's wearing your little evening suit and pumps, you think you won't stand out? You'll look like shit there; people will laugh at you and Mac will be embarrassed."

The idiocy of that statement was so obvious I just stared at her, having no defense for it. She hurried on.

"Now, when you walk in there, everybody's gonna look at you. 'Wow!' they're gonna think. 'Look at that absolute fox! That old geezer is sure lucky, having a woman like that!' Mac'll be in heaven."

"Marilee—"

"It's a game, Karen. It's just a role you're playing. Didn't you ever do any acting? Didn't you ever want to step out of that prissy little knees-together, ankles-crossed life of yours and do something really wild? You know you have and here's your chance."

Put that way, I could almost see some excitement in what she was telling me. In spite of myself, I was intrigued with the idea of playing a part, stepping out of myself completely like that.

"Now, when you walk in there, you walk in with your shoulders back and your knockers up and a big smile on your face. Strut a little. You aren't Karen Travis, the Texas princess; you're someone who doesn't have any worries and likes to have a good time and who nobody there knows. Jesus Christ, Karen! Don't you think Di and Fergy don't sneak off once in a while and let their hair down, too? Why can't you? Hell, I'll give you permission if you need it!"

She talked on and on, and the more she talked, the more sense she made to me. Finally, I said doubtfully, "But won't Mac be just horrified when he sees me. After all, Marilee, he's seen me in my regular clothes and without all this makeup. Won't he be embarrassed to haul someone like this around his drinking buddies?"

"Are you serious! I'm telling you, he'll absolutely love this look. To him, you'll look like just another one of the bimbs he dates all the time, at least at first. He'll be able to relax with you for the first time. You intimidate the shit out of him, you know, and it took quite a bit of talk from me for him to gut up enough to ask you out."

"You talked to him? When?"

"Yesterday. I had a drink with him and told him I was moving out for good. I let him think I was getting married again."

"What did he say?"

"Well, he was furious, but before he could really get wound up about it, I sort of hinted he should consider you as a replacement."

"You did that? How?"

"Well, I used a little reverse psychology on him. I made him think I didn't think you would be a good replacement for me. I suggested you were too into having a good time to settle down, but if you ever did, you would be a rock. I told him that you weren't what he wanted or needed, but of course, he immediately got it in his mind he did."

"Won't Mac recognize these clothes?"

"Are you serious! He won't see anything but those boobs. Besides, if you lined me up with three other women and covered our heads, he wouldn't be able to pick me out. He hasn't looked at me in years, Karen, much less at what I wear. And anyway, I never wore all that stuff together at one time like that."

To do myself justice, I tried one more time.

"But Marilee, I couldn't carry this off. I really couldn't. I wouldn't even begin to know how to act. The clothes would say 'bimbo' but I would still be Karen Travis inside. What would I do?"

"Do whatever you want. Do all the things Karen Travis has always wanted to do but didn't dare."

"I can't imagine what that would be. I've always done what I wanted to do."

"That's wrong, and if you really think that, you're lying to yourself."

"Perhaps."

"Well, a friend would tell you. Now, first of all, you don't walk like you have a stick up your ass. You bounce. Like this, see?"

She pranced across the room and I tried it, feeling like a complete idiot. She made me walk for several more minutes, saying, "When your boobs bounce, you know you're doing it right. Now you keep walking. I'm going to go hide my car."

Mac stood inside my front door, filling it up with his gross toad's body, looking around my shabby little living room, his disdain plain on his face. Belatedly, I realized I should have met him somewhere, that he could tell by one look at my house I was poor. That knowledge would give him an advantage and worse yet, put me at a disadvantage, at least to my way of thinking.

"Cozy little place you got here," he said, and I wanted to slap him for the condescension in his voice, but knowing Marilee was hiding in my closet-room, listening, I gritted my teeth and ignored it.

"It suits me," I answered, walking to the table where my Houser sat, drawing his attention to it. I might have saved my energy. I'd guessed correctly; he was completely impervious to good art and therefore wouldn't have recognized it had it reared up and bitten him, much less been impressed by it. I had been correct in my guess that Marilee had chosen the pieces in his house.

I stared at him, thinking the best thing I could do for myself was to tell him I'd changed my mind, thank him for the invitation, and send him on his way. The tax auditor's sneering face in my memory reminded me, however, that I didn't really have a choice, and realizing also that, at any minute, a process server might begin banging on the door, I grabbed up a coat against the cold New Mexican winter night and hustled him out the door. What he thought of our precipitous leaving without my so much as having offered him a drink, he didn't say. Gallantly, he opened my car door for me, and getting behind the wheel, he adjusted his stomach under it and started the engine.

"If you don't care, little gal, I wanna run by my office first."

"Fine," I said, implying by my attitude I couldn't care less. I realized his question for what it was, a territorial display, a see-how-important-I-am kind of thing, but part of me was surprised he would bother preening before me. I wondered if he did that with all his women, decided he probably did, and then, just as quickly, dismissed the whole thing as being unimportant.

It was a quietly elegant office, and there again, I recognized Marilee's influence. I waited in the receptionist's foyer and watched through the door he'd conveniently left open while he went into his private office, rummaged around the things on his desk, and pretended to read something. I wasn't fooled; nor was I impressed. It was merely something that was part of the evening, something to be endured. When he came out, I had my back to him, examining a Gorman on the wall, and so I missed the expression on his face as he said, "This is just a little office compared to the one I had in Dallas before Marilee got that wild hair up her ass to move out here."

At that crudity, I turned and stared at him, realizing that, IRS auditor and irate creditors or not, I could not stomach an entire evening of Mac Carpenter, much less marry him.

"Would you mind taking me home?" I asked as pleasantly as possible.

"What?"

"I'd like to go home, please."

"Why? We just got started, little gal. What's the matter?"

"This isn't going to work. It would save us both some time if you just took me home."

"Why won't it work?" he asked with some belligerence.

"Look, Mac, you and I have nothing in common. I don't know why you wanted to ask me out in the first place, and I certainly don't know why I accepted. I don't want to go to Ernesto's with you and—"

"Well, where do you want to go?"

"Home. I want to go home."

"Well, sure. We don't have to go out. I don't mind a little home-cooked meal once in a while." He leered at me.

"You don't understand, Mac. I don't want to cook for you. I can't cook, anyway. I want you to take me home and then I want you to go to your home. This was a mistake."

He stared at me, but when he started to say something else, I turned and walked out the door, leaving him to follow if and when he wanted to.

"Is this a joke?"

I stopped and turned to look at him. "What do you mean?"

"Is this something you and Marilee cooked up between you? Because if it is, little gal..."

Marilee was right; he was very perceptive—and certainly no dummy.

"It should be obvious to you Marilee and I have very little in common, Mac."

That certainly was no lie, and I was able to say it to him without flinching my eyes away.

"Then what's all this bullshit—"

"Mac, there's no need for us both to waste a good evening. I could be home, reading a good book, and you could be..."—I paused, trying to think of something he might be interested in, and finding it without much effort, continued—"at a dogfight or something."

The sarcasm was wasted.

"Well, we don't have to go to Ernesto's. You're all dolled up to go out and I thought Ernesto's would be a fun place. Marilee said you don't get to let your hair down much, a woman your age and all."

Now I was furious, with Marilee as well as with Mac, but before I could think of an answer, he took my elbow in a firm grip and using it as a steering lever, pushed me out the door.

Ernesto's was all I'd dreaded—and more. I could hear the beat, beat, beat of the music even before we were fully out of the car, and the sound hit me like a wall when Mac pushed open the door in front of me. The place was dimly lit and so smoky I had the eerie feeling I was underwater, and without thinking about it, I held my breath exactly as I would have done in any hostile environment. The smoke eddied and wafted in the beam of green spotlights that were focused on a live band, but before I could really assimilate anything, Mac had pushed me into the room and bulldozed our way to a table, calling boisterous greetings to several people along the way.

He pulled out a chair for me with showy gallantry and waved down a harried-looking waitress.

"What do you want, darlin'?" he asked me, shouting it above the roar of the band.

"White wine," I screamed back, resisting an urge to dust the chair off before I sat in it. The waitress stared at me, her eyes narrowed slightly.

"Naw, dammit, you don't want a sissy drink like that," he informed me. "Bring her a real drink," he yelled at the waitress. "Bring her a— a pink lady."

The girl said something to him, smiling, and moved off to be obliterated almost immediately by the darkness and smoke, leaving me to ponder the reason why white wine was a "sissy" drink and a pink lady wasn't.

"Smoke?" Mac yelled at me.

"Yes, it is, rather," I screamed back. I realized suddenly he was offering me a cigarette. "Oh, no, thanks. I don't smoke."

Just as I was shouting it, the band stopped playing with a final crashing chord, and I finished the sentence, yelling it into comparative silence. The houselights went up a little and people finished applauding and turned back to their drinks, ignoring the lead guitarist, who informed us cheerfully the band was taking a short break and we'd be treated to canned music for a few minutes. The canned music was only just a little quieter than the other, and the country and western singer moaned and sobbed her way through it with clear agony. A young woman came up to our table, staring at me hard, and Mac reared back in his chair to look up at her, grinning. I had the quick impression of a tiny, skinny body, top-heavy in too-tight clothes, capped with an incredible mass of hair that might have been red or blond. She finished her hard look at me and turned to Mac, smiling sweetly.

"Hello, Mac. How're you?"

"Well, just fine, little darlin'. This is my friend, Karen Travis. Patsy Brown, darlin'."

I acknowledged the introduction, but Patsy wasn't looking at me, pointedly. I took a healthy swig of my drink, raised my eyebrows, and stared off into the crowded room, implying a crashing disinterest in Patsy Brown and her poor manners.

"You haven't called me, Mac," she said, and I could have slapped her for her whining pridelessness.

"Now, darlin', I been busy, and that's a fact for sure. I'll git around to it. One of these days."

"Well, you and me had so much fun together and I was wondering what had happened to you."

I was concentrating so hard on the conversation at the table, I hadn't realized I was staring at a cowboy who sat with three others on the periphery of the gloom. Now he rose and waded through the tables between us, purposefully. I looked away, but I did it too late.

"May I dance with the lady?"

He pronounced it "daince" and Mac nodded, grinning, but the grin evaporated when the cowboy turned to me. It was suddenly obvious he'd thought the cowboy had indicated Patsy.

"Care to dance, ma'am?"

Without waiting for my answer, he pulled me to my feet and led me toward the tiny dance floor. He tucked my left arm against his shoulder, my body tightly against his, and holding my right hand hard against his chest, he imprisoned my head under his chin. Before I could resist this offensive manipulation, however, we were off, gliding around the floor in a swooping parody of a waltz. I found it hard to dance with him, at first, but as the drink began to take effect, I looked over his shoulder and saw Mac watching us. Patsy had pulled my chair next to his and was sitting close to him, whispering urgently into his ear.

Screw you, I thought, and relaxed a little, allowing the sweating hand at the small of my back to guide me through the steps. I was suddenly aware of the scent of my partner, a spicy after-shave kind of fragrance, mixed with a clean soap-smell and a tantalizing male scent, slightly smoky. I breathed it in, sniffing discreetly, realized it was definitely turning me on, and suddenly did not care. After all, as Marilee had pointed out, no one knew me here, no one knew I was Karen Buchanan Travis of the Texas Buchanans, and no one would care, anyway.

I relaxed a little more against the hard body and began to enjoy myself, even forgetting Mac Carpenter and Patsy Brown.

"That's right, honey. Don't fight me," he whispered in my ear.

It was all I could do to keep from shivering at the whispery roughness of his voice.

When the music was over, he led me back to my empty chair, thanked Mac, and went to join the others at his table. I took a deep drink of the pink lady and then another one, careful to keep from looking his way again.

"You know him?"

I looked at Mac, slightly surprised, refocusing on his presence at the table, and answered, "No, of course not," and then, with malicious innocence, added, "Do you?"

"Let's dance."

He lumbered to his feet and I obediently followed him to the dance floor and allowed him to pump-handle me around it until the dance was over. As we were walking back to our table, Patsy Brown stood in front of me, however, barring my way. I stepped aside to go around her, but she moved, blocking me again. I stared at her, surprised.

"I was going with him first," she said belligerently.

I raised an eyebrow. "All right," I said.

"Well, you just better not git any ideas about you and him."

I stared at her, using my mother's witheringly icy stare. It was wasted. Patsy was drunk and, worse yet, she was obviously a mean drunk.

"Nobody ast you to push your way in here," she said. "Mac is mine."

"Fine."

I turned to look at Mac, expecting him to do something about the disgustingly unladylike behavior of his ex–"little darlin'," but he just stood there, grinning down at the two of us, and I suddenly understood he was enjoying it, this being the cause and center of an impending catfight. Looking around, I saw people were watching us, and helplessly, I stood there, allowing Patsy to berate me, not knowing what I should do about it, other than stare at her as witheringly as possible.

Apparently, that was the wrong thing to do because my lack of reaction seemed to enrage her further, and suddenly she hauled off and hit me with her doubled fist, a manlike slug—right to my left breast.

Marilee's padded, push-up bra saved me. What breasts I had were lifted up, out of the way, and Patsy's blow landed on my rib cage, padded somewhat by the bra. It would have been devastating had it landed as Patsy had intended, and as it was, it hurt like hell. Without thinking, employing a primitive tit-for-tit reasoning, I doubled up my fist and punched her back, right in the center of one of the points of her tight sweater. I had the advantage of size on her, and without any padding or pushing up, she was much more fragile than I. I had the satisfaction of seeing her crash backward into the tables and chairs behind her, eyes wide with pain and shock, already grabbing her chest as she fell. She rolled over onto her knees and one elbow, clutching the offended part of her body with her other hand, and cried—loudly. I realized everyone was staring at us, and getting that strange, savage joy my punch had given me under control, and suddenly embarrassed by the obvious spectacle I was making of myself, I turned to Mac and asked him to take me home.

It was foolishly done. I should never have turned my back on her.

I heard a rattling of chairs over the music, but before I could turn around, I felt my head jerked backward, and pulled off balance by my hair, I fell. She'd landed under me, but without hesitating, she scrambled out from under me, and grabbing the side ponytail Marilee had been so proud of, she used it like a handle to bang my head repeatedly against the floor. Several things went through my mind almost simultaneously: The floor was indescribably filthy and I was wallowing on it; I was getting Marilee's clothing dirty; Patsy was causing me a great deal of pain; everyone in the place was staring; Mac was laughing like a hyena above us. The thoughts were just as quickly dismissed, however, pushed away by fear—not the relentless, dully constant fear I'd experienced since my divorce and fall from moneyed grace. This fear was sharp, searing terror, freezing me from any overt action. It became obvious to me Patsy was crazy and that she meant to kill me or worse, disfigure me, and further, she could do it, too. I felt her nails scrape against my almost bare chest, pulling my top away from the bra underneath. Reflexively, I put my hands up to protect my face and tried to roll away from her. She scrambled around, however, straddling me, yelling all the time, pinned me down, and began beating wildly at my forearms, which covered my face, and succeeded in landing one blow on my cheek. The pain made me angry and that unfroze me. Reaching up, I tangled my hands in her wild hair and pulled as hard as I could in opposite directions, jerking furiously. It was all I could think of to do and it worked, for she stopped hitting at me and grabbed at my hands, trying to lessen the effect of the tugs. It occurred to me that hitting her in the chest had worked very well for me so far, but when I tried to do it again, I found I couldn't get my fingers free from her wiry hair long enough to do it. Jerking frantically at her hair, I heaved my body and rolled it over, throwing her to the floor, and pinning her with one of my legs, I pounded her head fiercely on the filthy floor. From somewhere, I could hear an atavistic screaming over the roaring in my ears, even over the beating music, a banshee's chilling screech, and as hands began pulling me off Patsy, I realized the demented screaming was coming from my own mouth. Frenziedly, I fought the men who were trying to separate us, driven by a rage so wild I was momentarily crazy with it. I was running on pure impulse, pure emotion, and without the restraining hands, I might have killed her.

Suddenly, I stopped dead still, horrified. I realized that, for the first time since I'd met her, Marilee had been proven wrong about something.

"Spandex is your friend," she'd counseled me. "It'll never let you down."

I realized suddenly, however, it was no friend to *me*, it *had* let me down, that in the rolling around on the dirty floor, the seam in the back had split and I was, in effect, mooning everyone. Quickly, I scrambled to my feet, took off my blouse, and tied it around my waist, hiding the offending rip, and with as much dignity as possible, I turned to the laughing Mac, who'd collapsed weakly into a chair, wiping at the tears on his face.

"If you don't take me home immediately," I said with quiet menace into the laughing room, "I intend to hit you with a chair."

It was then I realized that Marilee had been right about one thing: Mac Carpenter needed to be dead. Someone as hideous as he was deserved to be dead, would be better off dead, and the entire world would be better off for it as well.

Mac continued his gasping, sobbing laughter almost all the way to my house, and peripherally, I considered that it would be just my luck he would laugh himself to death before I could get him married. I stared out my window at the lights as we drove, aware I had become what my mother considered the lowest form of organism, human scum, and that, without a doubt, I could not top the experiences of the last couple of hours no matter how far I fell into depravity. I could feel the rip in the pants underneath me, and carefully I focused my attention away from the scene that threatened to loom up in my mind, that of my bare fanny waving around in the breeze as I tried to beat Patsy Brown to death on the dirty floor of Ernesto's. Instead, I focused on Mac, or rather my hatred of him, present from the first time I'd seen him and grown now until it was something that I could have used to knock down a concrete-block wall with very little effort on my part. Added to his other sins, which were many, was the fact he had not behaved like a gentleman, had not protected me as a true gentleman should have done, and further, had actually enjoyed my discomfiture so much he was now in danger of laughing himself to death in the seat next to me. I considered what I would do if he suddenly collapsed with his expected heart attack, how I would steer the car and bring it to a stop. I focused on anything and everything but the fact that I now was no better than he was, that all my breeding and prideful heritage was lost when I agreed to consort with such a lowlife. The only good thing I could see about the situation was that, as Marilee had pointed out, no one knew me at Ernesto's, and therefore, no one could tell my mother how tackily I had behaved. That, at least, was something.

Mac had the temerity to ask if he could come in for a drink when we got to my house, but I gave him my mother's stare, and even as insensitive as he was, he caught on right away. When I got into the house, I closed the door behind me and leaned against it, closing my eyes.

"Are you alone?" I heard Marilee's whisper, and then, in her normal tone, "My God, Karen! What happened to you?"

"I had a date with Mac Carpenter," I said, enunciating every word clearly and staring at her malevolently as I did so.

"He did this to you? That's not like Mac. What—"

"No. He did not do this to me! A cretinous little she-warrior named Patsy Brown did this to me, and you know those damn tights you said were my friend? Well, look . . ."

I untied the blouse from my waist and turned so she could see the rip that parenthesized my bare fanny. I was mollified a little by her gasp, and retying the blouse around my waist, I went past her into the kitchen.

"I need a strong drink, Marilee. Do we have anything that's more than a hundred proof?"

"All we have is some wine. Here, I'll get it. You just sit down and tell me all about what happened."

Briefly, I went through the horrid events of the evening, but as I was telling them, I realized they had lost something of their horror, and by the time I'd finished, I could sip the wine and know I wasn't going to cry—or kill someone.

"That was the best thing you could have done, Karen."

I stared at her, disbelieving my ears.

"Look, Marilee. I did not go through this evening rationally, I can tell you that. What happened was pure chance, and by the way, while we're on the subject, what was all that bullshit that you fed me about Ernesto's not being such a bad place? I found it utterly reprehensible."

"No, what I was saying is, now that you've had this little fracas with Patsy, Mac won't be so intimidated by you and he'll—"

"Marilee! For just a few minutes, let's us just not talk about Mac, all right? I've had a gutful of him for one evening."

We drank a bottle of the wine and were well into the second one when I suddenly, inexplicably giggled.

"What?" Marilee asked, peering owlishly at me.

"I wish you could have seen her face when I punched her."

"Yeah?"

"She looked like Bozo the Clown with all that hair sticking out and her face like this."

I made a surprised face at her and Marilee laughed.

"You ever punch anyone before?"

"No, of course not. My mother wouldn't have approved."

I'd made my voice as sarcastic as possible, and Marilee, catching the change in my mood, stood up, shakily.

"Come on. We have to do something with that eye. Too bad we don't have a steak to put on it, but it'll have to be an ice bag."

I allowed her to minister to my eye, and by Monday morning, when I had to go to work, the swelling was down enough so Marilee could disguise the discoloration pretty effectively with makeup. No one would know, after all, that Karen Buchanan Travis had been wrestling with one of Mac Carpenter's "ex-bimbs" on the floor of Ernesto's the previous Friday night.

Over the next few weeks, I led Mac through a dance choreographed by Marilee, an intricate series of steps that kept him interested in me far longer than he'd been with any of the other women in his life since Marilee. She'd been right about one thing: He was an extremely complex man, and without her help, I wouldn't have stood a chance with him. Of course, without her, I would never have even considered such a thing as binding Mac to me, but that was another story. As it was, I was alternately cool and sweet to him, at times interested in his work, and other times, obviously bored with his conversation. Between us, we kept him on the edge, praying his overdue heart attack would hold off long enough for us to get him married to me. Marilee had been right when she'd told me he was taking his nitro pills again, and several times while dating him, I'd seen him suddenly break into a sweat, his eyes gone glassy and his lips blue, and then, when the attack was over, boisterously cheerful again as if he'd put yet another one over on Father Death.

As Marilee had instructed me, I ignored his attacks when they happened.

"He wouldn't want you to know he wasn't young and healthy, Karen."

"But for Christ's sake, I do know that. It's as obvious as mud on a fence. How could he be young and healthy when he's sixty-six years old and—"

"This way, Karen, he can delude himself into thinking he's all right. If you acknowledge his attacks, then he can't pretend anymore, see?"

"Oh."

She patted my arm, squinting up at me through her fake lashes. "Trust me, okay?"

"Sure," I said.

I had to admire her, however. She certainly knew Mac Carpenter inside and out. I reflected briefly that if he'd taken the time to know her as well as she knew him, there would have been no divorce, but like Marilee would say, fut the whuck, that's the way men are.

* * *

Finally, true to Marilee's word, and much to my relief, he proposed. Obeying Marilee implicitly, I'd danced around Mac, leading, enticing, goading sweetly, and keeping out of his bed religiously. No nun would have been more prissy about sleeping with him than I was.

"What do you mean, stay out of his bed?" I wanted to know when she'd first told me to do so. "I thought he was impotent. You told me he was—"

Arm patting. "Well, he is, honey, but you don't want to be the one who reminds him of that, do you? To him, you're a lady, not one of the 'bimbs' he's been taking out. If he can get you into bed, two things will happen: You will no longer be a lady, you will be a bimb, and therefore not marriageable, and you will know he's impotent. And then, it's good-bye, Karen, see?"

"Well, yes. I guess so."

"So whenever he insinuates that you two should hit the hay, you merely act like you don't understand what he's suggesting, and when he gets real overt about it, then you look at him like he's suddenly lost his mind."

"Well, all right. That, at least, I have no problem with."

In spite of myself, I was impressed. Marilee had all the tactical acumen of a general and a chess master's ability to think several steps ahead. There was a lot more behind those unstuck eyelashes than people would ever have assumed was there, and as I got to know her more, I found myself wondering what she might have done, had she been born male, or been born a few years later, at a place and time when femaleness was not automatically linked to dependency and helplessness.

Marilee was far from helpless. I often wondered if she even knew that.

"Tonight's the night," she pronounced one evening as I was getting ready for another one of my dates with Mac.

I paused with the mascara wand hovering in front of my eye and looked at her in the mirror. She lay across our two beds we'd pushed together to give us a little more floor space in the tiny room.

"Really?"

"Yep," she said, sipping from her glass of wine. "He's probably real frustrated by now, probably about to pull his hair out, but he's also tintillated, too."

"Titillated," I corrected automatically. "Why do you think tonight's the night?"

I had pretty much stopped asking her weeks before how she knew something was going to happen. The answer was always the same: "I just know," and she was always right.

"He can't take frustration very well and he's had about all he will take without exploding. Probably what will happen is he will make one last hairy stand to get you in bed, and then, if you refuse, he'll just suddenly blurt it out. 'Well, all right, then. Let's get married.' Something like that."

"And then I accept," I said smugly.

"No! You definitely do not!"

"What! The whole point of this thing, Marilee, is—"

"The minute he says it, he'll want to take it back unless you just look at him and maybe kind of laugh and say something like, 'Don't be silly, Mac.' That'll set the hook. After that, he'll get marriage in his mind and nothing you can do will change it. He'll marry you if he has to kidnap you."

"But—"

"If you agree to marry him right away, he'll find some way to get out of it. Trust me."

"All right."

It went exactly as she said. I felt as if I were an actress in a play and it was as if Marilee had written the script. On cue, I smiled, frowned, shrugged my shoulder daintily, gave him Mother's stare, peered, obviously awed or sometimes amused, into his eyes, and finally, when he became impatient and blurted, 'Well, let's us just get married!' it was all I could do to keep from laughing, it had been so close to what Marilee had predicted. Instead, I looked at him as if he'd just made a little joke, smiled a little, and said, "Don't be silly, Mac." I changed the subject abruptly as Marilee had instructed me to do, and just as she'd predicted, he swung the subject back to matrimony.

"Why not?" he asked with some degree of belligerence.

"Why not what, Mac?" I said with fake patience.

"Why shouldn't we get married?"

"Oh, I don't know," I said, toying with the wineglass on the table, rotating it back and forth. "I don't think I want to remarry. I've been married, you know."

"Well, I know Jack Travis, and you'll excuse me for sayin' it, but he's an asshole."

And you're not? I wanted to say. I was surprised at the sudden urge I had to defend Jack, and I wondered how much of that smoothing of troubled waters I'd done for him in the past, all without realizing it.

Instead, I said, "Well, you're probably right."

"When in doubt, agree with him," Marilee had told me.

"But," I continued, sighing a little, "I really got hurt over that and I don't want it to happen again." I looked him straight in the eyes, saying, "I don't have anyone to look after me now. I have to do it myself."

It was straight out of a melodrama, a poor-me kind of statement that would cause any man not born in the South before the Second World War to hoot with derision. I saw a slight softening of the lines around Mac's eyes, however, and he reached across the table and took my hand, pulling it away from the wineglass, pinning it down on the pristine white cloth.

"I wouldn't do nothin' like that to you, darlin'."

"I know you wouldn't, Mac, but I . . ."

I let the sentence trail off. Marilee had also instructed me to let him take the lead in any conversation I was unsure of.

"Don't you love me?" he asked, plaintively for him. It was right on cue. Carefully, I looked up in the corner of the room, to the right, as Marilee had instructed me to do. When she'd pressed him once, Mac had told Marilee he could always tell when someone was lying if they looked up and to the right when they talked. Incredibly, she'd remembered it and it stood us in good stead now.

"I don't think so, Mac," I said softly, gazing up at the corner of the room. "I don't think I can love anyone, ever again."

"It'll be a new challenge for him," she'd said, and she was right. He almost jumped to meet the hook.

"I think you don't know what you want. I just bet you do love me and just don't know it yet. I can make you happy again, darlin'. You'll see."

"Well, I don't know," I whimpered. "Let me think about it a little. This is just so sudden."

We were married at The Little Chapel of the Mountains outside Tahoe. I had willingly signed a prenuptial agreement stating that, if we divorced, I would receive only what I'd brought into the marriage—in my case, the clothes in my closet. Mac was touched at my ready willingness to sign the agreement, but as Marilee pointed out, divorce wasn't in our game plan and the agreement wouldn't make any difference one way or the other.

He had wanted to be married in Reno, but Reno and Vegas had always been the epitome of tacky to my mind, and when I sweetly insisted on marrying somewhere else, he'd compromised by driving up the mountain from Reno to the chapel. We were married using another couple as witnesses, who were married right after us, and to whom we returned the favor.

Mac was ecstatic. All through the ceremony, he kept my hand in a tight grip as if he were anxious I would break and run, and when it came time for me to repeat my vows, I faltered on the "till death do us part" bit. Idiotically, I suddenly realized, for the first time, the enormity of what I was committing myself to, and it was frightening to me, frightening and overwhelming. It was as if I had just suddenly understood that what I had considered to be a game all along was now an actuality, was something that would be real, was not just late-night girl-talk anymore, but was real, a definite surety. I stood there, paralyzed, staring at Mac, wide-eyed, while I tried to make my mouth work to end the travesty.

"Come on, honey," he whispered, shaking my hand a little, urging me. "Don't give out on me now."

The minister, if that's what he was, intoned the offending phrase, repeating it for my benefit, and I realized there was a very real possibility I might throw up. Frantically, I worked my throat, swallowing down bile, and as I did so, I heard my voice repeating the last of the vow.

"I now pronounce you man and wife," the minister said, bored. "You may kiss the bride."

I steeled myself. Mac had kissed me before, of course, and I readied myself for what I knew would be unpleasant. It was quickly done, however, and then Mac, his bum ticker notwithstanding, stooped, hugged my hips, and whooping, hoisted me over his head in a childish display of exuberance. Weakly, I smiled down at him, looking hopefully for any signs that his impulsive gesture might have triggered a fatal coronary.

His face remained unclouded, pink cheeked, and dry, so I smiled shakily at him and suggested that he put me down. He did so, and after we'd witnessed the other couple's marriage, one in which the bride and groom were obviously very much in love and made a travesty of mine, we drove back down to Reno, my second least-favorite place in the world, Vegas being the first.

Mac insisted on going straight up to our suite and going to bed. Nothing I could think of would convince him to postpone it, and so with great resignation, I followed him into the elevator and rode up to the floor on which our suite was located, girding myself for what was coming.

"Just submit and pretend you like what he does," Marilee had counseled me, much as a Victorian mother might have counseled her virgin daughter, the difference being, of course, that I was no virgin sacrifice to the god of matrimony but one who had willingly gone into the fire, knowing exactly what was coming up. "He'll roll around and grunt a lot, and then, when he can't get it up, he'll stop," she'd said. "You be understanding and kind. Say something like you didn't marry him for the sex anyway, which will certainly be no lie, and then change the subject. Get it onto something he feels powerful about."

"Do I have to look at him while he's naked?" I asked. It was not a joke; I couldn't think of much else that would disgust me like the sight of Mac Carpenter's corpulent, flabby body, unclothed.

Arm patting. "Married women do it all the time, honey. You'll get used to it."

Mac led me into the suite and closed the door behind us.

"C'mere, Miz Carpenter," he leered, and obediently I walked into his arms, a smile pasted on my face.

Mrs. Carpenter, I thought wildly, trying to focus on something besides the sudden onset of the persistent stomach churning. Mrs. Karen Carpenter. It was true. I was now firmly and finally wedded to Mac Carpenter, something for which Marilee and I had worked so hard, and now it was time to pay the piper. I had visions of eighteenth-century French nobles being led to the guillotine, jeered by the rabble. It was not the thing to think about, and I thrashed about mentally for another image to distract myself while Mac tore at the buttons to my new suit.

I'll say one thing for Mac: He was an energetic, enthusiastic lover. But being mauled by a large, friendly dog is no more enjoyable for the amount of energy that's put into it and in fact, is worse for it. I really thought he would break the bed down. I focused on that, I focused on paying off the IRS and my many creditors, I focused on what I would wear to his funeral, how I would act, dabbing my eyes while people offered their condolences, anything except what I was having forced on me by my own choice. I had never before had the experience of having to have sex with someone whom I despised, and now that it was happening, I wondered just how bad the IRS and my creditors could be.

"He's impotent," Marilee had said, but she hadn't said he wouldn't try. And try he did, with a single-mindedness that was just short of hysterical obsession. Suddenly, I realized there were things worse than ejaculation and consummation, and one of them was trying and trying and trying . . .

Finally, when I thought I would have to stop it if only to relieve my aching body of the pain, he suddenly stiffened and relaxed on top of me, and I prayed that he'd died, that his heart had exploded inside him, spattering itself all over the inside of his rib cage, and he would finally leave me in peace. Just as I was about to roll him off me, he suddenly jumped up and whooped, the second time he'd shouted that day. The suddenness of it startled me, and I grabbed the sheets and pulled them to my chin, hiding my bruised and battered body. I peered over them at the incredible sight of a naked, fat old man capering around the bedroom, laughing and giving short, excited yells, punctuating them with sharp thrusts of his fist in the air, much as men do on the tennis court when they've done something wonderfully impossible. He ran to the side of the bed, and kneeling, he grabbed my aching shoulders and dragging me toward him, kissed me soundly on the mouth.

"Thank you, baby, thank you! You're a jewel, yeah, you are. I love you, darlin', I love you! You're more woman than a man has a right to expect! You won't be sorry! I'll treat you like a queen, you'll see! Queen Karen, that'll be you!"

Cowering under the sheets, which I had pulled up over my nose, a weak protection against an obviously crazy man, I stared at him. He leaped up again, belying his age and physical ailments, and still whooping, went into the bathroom to shower. Suddenly, it dawned on me that the impotent Mac Carpenter, for some reason unknown to me, was no longer impotent and he thought I was the cause of his cure. I scrambled to the edge of the bed and grabbing the telephone, started punching numbers.

"Hell-looo," Marilee crooned into the phone. It was her usual way of answering it; it made you think she'd been waiting all day for you and you alone to call, and that she was as excited as hell you'd done so and that she wanted to talk to you and only you and no one else, ever.

I ignored it this time, however, and whispered, "Marilee!"

"Is it done? Are you married?"

"Yes! Yes, we sure as hell are, and Marilee, when I get back there, I am going to *kill* you. Do you understand? It'll be *you* that'll be dead— by my own hand! Why I let you talk me into this—"

3

My honeymoon should have been the high point of a good many dreary months, and in retrospect, there were some good things about it. Instantly, I no longer had to worry about how much something cost anymore, mentally adding and subtracting numbers in my head before I decided whether or not I could buy it. The wonderful thing about having money, I realized, was you never had to think about it.

Mac had given me a packet of credit cards in my new name on our wedding day, and I was genuinely touched by the significance of that gesture. I sat looking at the cards in my hand, tears running down my face, while Mac anxiously asked me why I was crying.

How could I tell him of the hell I'd been through for the past few years, which he had just relieved with a single, casual gesture? How could I explain so he, who had money and the security of knowing he would always have money, would understand how constant that fear was, always with you, going to bed with you at night and there, waiting for you, in the morning? How could I tell him what it was like to realize you wouldn't have the rent money on time and you would have to call your landlady and put her off again, a woman so slatternly my mother wouldn't have hired her to do her floors? How could I explain that suddenly I no longer had to worry about getting sick, my car's breaking down, having my teeth cleaned, losing my job, having my eyes checked, a car's hitting me as I crossed the street? How could I make him understand what it was like to have to choose between eating and buying gasoline for the car, knowing you couldn't afford health insurance because the state made you buy automotive liability, scraping and scraping, just to be able to go and have a drink with the girls after work, hoping, by some miracle, you might meet someone who would lift you out of that dreariness, emotionally if not financially, and knowing you wouldn't?

The relief as those burdens were suddenly lifted off me was so great, at that moment, I almost loved Mac Carpenter.

Suddenly, I could go into any of the shops in the hotel, buy anything that caught my eye as I had done before my divorce, but savoring it this time, exulting in the ability to indulge myself, allowing the obsequious attentions of the shop clerks, knowing that a few days before, I had done the same things that they were doing for me for the moneyed women who were my customers at the Museum Shop in Santa Fe.

To my great credit, I had learned humility, at least a little, and took nothing for granted. When we went home, I already had several gold Krugerrands hidden in my purse, just in case.

It became obvious to me early in the honeymoon, however, that the only way I could keep my sanity, not to mention my self-respect, was to never appear in public with Mac. Alone with me, he was smugly attentive and sometimes even kind. If I could get enough booze in him, he'd go to sleep and I'd be free of him until the next morning, when he would suddenly jerk awake, bound out of bed as if he'd never taken a drink in his life, and pull the covers off me, insisting I get up and see the sunrise with him, or worse, start fumbling with my body. I, however, always felt, at those impossible hours, that I was suffering from the aftereffects of a three-day drunk, no matter how little I'd had to drink the night before. Before my marriage, when I was working, I'd had to confront mornings out of necessity, but I saw no reason to do so now. Finally we compromised. He got up in the mornings without waking me, went down to the casinos, and did his gambling, which I had no interest in. I met him for lunch and we either shopped or gambled, and then I would start on my trying to lure him up to the rooms and out of the public's eye. It sometimes took several hours— he could be amazingly stubborn—but all the while I was pouring drinks into him so that, when we did get upstairs, he would collapse on one of the couches in the living room and suddenly deprived of any of the external stimulation that he fed on, would fall instantly to sleep.

If he decided to see a show, I worked doubly hard afterward. The bare-breasted show girls turned him on, and he could be indescribably vulgar in public. It was nothing for him to take my hand and pat his crotch with it, baby-talking with "Mr. Whoopee," his name for his penis, no matter who was present, or put his hand on the back of my head and playfully push it downward in the same general direction. I found it incredibly demeaning and told him so repeatedly, but he didn't mean it maliciously—it was his idea of a joke—and he saw no reason to stop it. There were times when I had to sit, my face burning with mortification, while he gave a blow-by-blow description of our sex the night before to a waiter or someone else equally unsuitable, or fumbled inside my blouse in the elevator. I learned early that to protest would only fuel him, and a better course of action was to pretend to ignore his lapses as best I could.

His grotesque manners were tolerated in the casinos and hotels because he spent a lot of money while he was there and never really did anything that would get us thrown out. He made friends easily with all sorts of people, and I often found myself sitting at a table with a gangster or a senator, or both, that he'd known from previous trips.

Marilee had been right when she said he was into breasts; he was constantly mauling mine when we were alone and would insist that I wear only my peignoir or a gown in the suite so he would have ready access to them whenever he felt like grabbing for them. I often shuddered when I allowed myself to think about how low I'd fallen, but it kept him happy even though I never really got accustomed to parading around the suite in high heels and practically nothing else.

Quite by accident, I discovered a sure way to get him to sleep was to get a couple of six-packs into him and allow him to nuzzle one of my breasts while I cuddled him against me. It was a sure soporific for him, and although I found it revolting, it was less disgusting than the alternative, sex, and worked better than any sleeping pill might have done. Mac, indeed, had a breast fetish if anyone ever did and had absolutely no shame about expressing it.

Once, he actually got it into his head that he should get a hooker to come up to the suite.

"I'll get one with real *big* tits since you don't have much."

That's fine with me, I thought. Let her suffer Mac's crudities. Better her than me.

"All right," I said pleasantly. "Let me know when and I'll go shopping or something."

Mac was appalled.

"No, baby! I wouldn't do that to you. I wouldn't never fuck around on you. You're my Queen Karen. It'll be you and her and me. We could take pitchers and ever'thin'. Have somethin' to remember our honeymoon by."

It was with great effort I talked him out of the idea, but that was something I would not do, not for money nor for anything that Marilee could think up to say to me, and when he realized that I was seriously walking out the door and out of his life, he finally backed down.

"Well," he said regretfully, "I guess that's not really the thing to do on your honeymoon, is it? Maybe next time."

"Yeah, maybe," I said sourly, praying to God his black heart would stop its beating before another chance like that ever came up again.

I found his grossness extremely disgusting and my part in his antics distressful, but nothing I could say would convince him I actually was serious when I implied I wasn't having the time of my life.

The low point came when he flushed my birth control pills down the toilet.

"What are you *doing?*" I asked, aghast.

He grinned at me, a wolf's grin.

"We're married now. I wouldn't mind having a boy to leave all my stuff to."

I stared at him, horrified beyond speech. Not only was I unwilling to become a mother at forty-five, and more important, unwilling to be the mother of his child, but even I knew that, should he actually produce an heir, Marilee and I could kiss all our work and his fortune good-bye.

"Honey," I said, making my frozen mouth smile, "let's talk about this, shall we?"

But nothing could change his mind on that point, and having been thwarted once, he was not about to allow it to happen again. When I threatened to leave him again, he called my bluff, saying, "A man without a kid might as well not have a wife, either."

All I could do after that was to pray fervently I would not become pregnant until I could get back to Santa Fe and surreptitiously get my prescription refilled.

* * * *

In the matter of half a day and some phone calls that, in their aggressiveness, exceeded what I would have considered the limit of good taste, Mac had all my financial troubles cleared up. I was profoundly and truly grateful.

"I can't tell you how much I appreciate this, Mac," I said. It was no lie, I *couldn't* tell him. It was beyond the scope of my vocabulary to thank him enough. Just to wake up in the morning and know I would not have to worry about creditors and the IRS made almost anything that Mac did forgivable.

"How did you git into that kinda mess?" Mac wanted to know. His awe was not something he would particularly want me to see, but it was obvious, nevertheless.

"I don't know, Mac." I sighed. "I've always had money to spend and it didn't occur to me I wouldn't always. What with the divorce and then my mother's doing what she did, I just didn't pay attention to what was happening, until it was too late."

"Well, you're my Queen Karen. I wouldn't do anythin' to you like Jack Travis did."

"Thank you, darling," I said, and meant it.

Mac's impotence continued to be a thing of the past. He considered me his good-luck charm, felt I'd given him back his lost youth and manhood, and was exuberant enough to be telling me so constantly. Whatever it was that triggered overt sex in his mind kept him in a state of randiness that caused me to dread his coming home more and more every day. It didn't seem to matter that I was cool to him, in fact, that seemed to whet his appetite. His lovemaking was extremely physical, and nothing I did seemed to chill him out. What he lacked in technique and finesse, he made up for with energy and staying power, however, and after a particularly gruesome encounter, I would push his unconscious body off mine and going into the den, pour myself a strong drink to take with me while I took a hot bath to relax my aching and stiffening muscles.

"I can't take much more of this," I told Marilee one day over lunch. "I'm losing weight and getting these dark circles under my eyes. Look."

"I know, honey, but try to hang in there. His heart can't hold out much longer."

A dark suspicion flitted through my mind, slowed, and stuck there.

"Are you *sure* he's had three heart attacks, Marilee? This isn't just something you told me to talk me into this, is it?"

"I told you I wouldn't lie to a girlfriend. I'll show you the medical records if you like."

"No," I sighed. "I believe you. It's just that he seems perfectly healthy to me. He hasn't shown any signs at all of feeling bad since we were married."

"He seems to have gotten a new lease on life at that," she mused. "I don't understand it. What is it you do to him?"

"I'm not doing anything! Literally. I just lie there as inertly as possible, and he bounces around and mauls me like some bird-dog puppy, and just when I think I can't take any more, he yells in my ear and falls asleep on me."

"That's our Mac, all right. At least, it's the old Mac. He hasn't been like that for fifteen years that I know about. He sure wasn't like that the last five years we were married. He was always oversexed, but after that first heart attack, he got it in his head he was impotent and cut me off. That's why I divorced him and married Davy, the cop. A girl's gotta have some fun."

"Well, I can't take much more of this. It's *every night*, Marilee. Every night! For God's sake, he's an old man!"

Arm patting. "You have to, honey. Sooner or later, it's gonna catch up to him. Wiggle a little. Show some enthusiasm. Keep after him, morning, noon, and night. Make him really sweat. Screw him to death."

"Did it ever occur to you it might kill me? I can only take so much and I'm not a young woman, either. I'm not sure it's worth it."

"Sure it is, honey. Just keep your mind on all that money. It doesn't matter how old you are if you have money."

I tried, I really did. Rather than being the Ice Lady, I began to be aggressive, to take the initiative more and more in our lovemaking. Mac would no sooner lumber through the door every evening than I'd be on him, clinging, sweet-talking, nuzzling his fat neck, hating myself and him for my degradation. At night I forced myself to show some reaction to his body-mauling. I thrashed around and moaned heartily, trying to match his level of excitement and to spur him on his way toward a fatal climax.

At the end of a week of that, two things happened: I realized I was severely depleting myself physically, and Mac became impotent again.

"I don't understand it, Marilee. That's twice in two nights that he's been dysfunctional. He's beginning to act wary now, and the more I chase him, the more he acts like I'm diseased or something."

Marilee chewed on a swizzle stick. The Pink Adobe was full of single cookie bandits, but neither of us was aware of them, concentrating as we were on the new problem at hand, this new glitch in our progress to kill Mac Carpenter.

"You know what I think it is?" she finally said. "I think that's been his problem all along. Most of the women who hit on him were always the aggressors, high-powered little twits who scared the stiffness out of his dingle. That's gotta be it! Back off, Karen. Be the Ice Lady again. If he says anything about this past week, tell him you were ovulating or something."

"You think so?"

"Sure! It *has* to be that. I'll be damned, who would have thought there was something to old Mac I would miss like that."

I could see she was intrigued with this lack of understanding, no matter how small it was, of the psyche of Mac Carpenter, but I let it go, relishing the sudden relief I felt, knowing I could ease up on chasing Mac around the sofa every night.

"Thank God," I said fervently.

Marilee peered at me, squinting fiercely. "I know this hasn't been easy on you, Karen."

"It's just that I rattle around in that house all day with nothing to do and then have Mac to contend with all night. I never realized how much I would miss my work and the people I met there. I guess I'm just bored. Consuela does a great job with all the housework and I don't have anything to do with my time. I used to do a lot of volunteer work, but Mac won't let me do that. He wants me to be there, in case he comes home during the day to 'tear off a piece,' as he so endearingly puts it."

"Would it help if I were there, too?"

"Sure, but you know he won't want you there now we're married."

"Just leave it to me."

* * * *

Dutifully, I backed off my aggression, and just as Marilee had predicted, Mac became robustly potent again. It seemed, indeed, there was an inverse relationship to my participation and Mac's enjoyment; the less I moved, the more he enjoyed himself, and during the nights following my return to nonreaction, Mac became more and more energetic until I thought I would have to kill him overtly, if only to have a little peace.

"Don't you feel good?"

I looked at Mac across the breakfast table. He'd paused in his food-shoveling and was sitting very still for him, staring at me.

"I guess I'm just tired," I told him, smiling weakly. It was the understatement of a lifetime. It was all I could do to sit in my chair and lift food to my mouth, food that was tasteless and seemed to take a great deal of effort to chew and swallow.

"Are you gonna have a baby?"

I wanted to slap the hopefulness off his face. Trying to hide my irritation, I said, "No, I don't think so. I'm just a little run-down. You know"—I shrugged feebly—"I'm a little out of practice with this marriage business."

"Jack didn't hump you enough, is that it? Well, I been noticing you draggin' your tail around these last few days and I'm gonna do something about it."

A flicker of hope began to grow but aborted itself abruptly as he continued, "You need somebody to help you around the house here. That Meskin gal ain't doin' enough and you're too sweet to make her hustle. So I fired her and hired Marilee to take her place."

He beamed at me.

"Marilee?" I stared at him, willing my brain to function fast enough to keep up with what was going on.

"You know, my ex-wife. You don't mind, do you?" he asked. "That marriage of hers fell through and she don't have no place to live. She don't have the sense God gave a screwdriver, and we got plenty of room here. You need some help, baby. You look wrung out like a dishrag. An' I need a good meal once in a while. You ain't no cook, that's for sure, darlin', but I didn't marry you for your cookin', now did I?" He leered at me and I smiled wanly. "This'll work fine. Marilee kin do the cookin' and cleanin' agin and you kin be my Queen Karen. That okay for my baby-girl?"

I smiled at him. I knew it wouldn't have mattered what I thought, but pathetically, I was glad Marilee was moving in. That meant there would be two of us to divide Mac's limitless energy and constant attention needs. If nothing else, she could talk to him, occupy him, while I took a nap on the weekends.

It was so very like him that he didn't even think to wonder how Marilee and I might feel about the arrangement.

"Oh, Mac," I simpered. "You're so sweet to me. Thank you."

He got up and walking around the table, planted a hearty, slurping kiss on the side of my face.

"Well, nothin's too good for my little Queen Karen. I gotta get to the office, darlin'. Marilee'll be movin' back in sometime today. You go to bed and rest up. I can't have my little wifey gettin' all tired, now can I? There's more important things to do than cookin' an' housework, now ain't there?"

He leered at me, fumbled inside the front of my peignoir, and left, whistling. I snatched my napkin and scrubbed his drool off my face, trying to decide if it was too early for a quick drink, and deciding that it was, I went to the phone to call and rehire Consuela, the "Meskin gal" who did for me.

Things settled down into a pattern after that. With Marilee there to take some of the pressure of the rambunctious Mac off me, I began to relax. I started playing tennis again, something that I'd done a lot of while I was married to Jack. While not tournament material, except in the smallest way, I was good enough that I enjoyed it, and as I'd done while married to Jack, I took my frustrations with my husband out on the ball. After a couple hours on the courts every afternoon, I felt that I could even handle Mac that evening.

With Marilee there to diffuse his tantrums if he came home and found me gone, I began to do volunteer work again, mostly docent work for the museum. Marilee and I had lunch together often and occasionally ran down to Albuquerque to shop. Marilee had a great many acquaintances whom she "did lunch with," and at least a couple of dates a week, but as time went on, we spent more and more time together, from choice, falling into a sisterly relationship that was closer than any pair of sisters whom I'd ever observed. It seemed that our oppositeness balanced each other neatly so that, as the spring went into summer, I couldn't even remember what it was like not to have her around me.

Consuela came in twice a week, did the heavy stuff, told Marilee in great detail the latest mean thing her husband had done to her, and departed well before Mac was due to come home. What she thought of the first and second Mrs. Carpenter living under the same roof together with Mr. Carpenter, who she thought was meaner than her husband had ever dared to be, she never said, but Marilee and I both realized she had a great deal of pity for us both.

I began to gain back some of the weight I'd lost after my marriage. Marilee was cooking all the things Mac loved, every single thing that was on the doctor's list of no-no foods. I could understand Mac's attitude about her cooking, however; it was excellent and occasionally, when we had nothing better to do, she began teaching me the rudiments of cooking. Under her easy tutelage, I began to see it as an art form, a creative effort, rather than the drudgery I had always assumed it to be. Our lunches were totally different from the breakfast and dinner fare she prepared for Mac's nonbenefit, and the day I could prepare and serve our lunch with no help from Marilee, I felt a smug satisfaction that I had not felt for a long, long time.

There were other perks, too. I found myself talking and talking, emoting endlessly about things I would never have spoken of to anyone else, things I had pushed back and locked down even from myself. Marilee listened, patted my arm when I cried or got angry, and said, "Fut the whuck," in all the right places. After a few weeks of that, however, I began to be bored with the miseries of my life, and except for the nightly mangling by Mac, I began to feel more comfortable with myself than I had for a long time.

We were coming back from Albuquerque one afternoon, and because it was such a pretty day, we eschewed the interstate and drove back on the old highway that went through Madrid and Cerrillos. After we'd passed the two towns, Marilee suddenly directed me to turn off onto a dirt road. It was a measure of our relationship by then that I did so without arguing. After we'd driven a few miles, she pointed to one of the hills, the *cerrillos*, that stood isolated on the floor of the Galisteo Basin.

"See that house on top?"

I looked up, maybe two hundred feet, and saw that the top of the hill had been cut off and a large, sprawling house and smaller buildings crowned it. It was built in the pueblo style, apparently true adobe, stuccoed over, and the entire complex of house, trees, and outbuildings was surrounded by a high wall of the same material. Only the top half of the buildings could be seen from the road below. The entire hill, as far as I could see, was enclosed by a high Cyclone fence, one that appeared to be gateless.

"Somebody spent a bundle on that," I said, awed in spite of myself.

"Yeah. Harve."

"Harve?"

"My last husband."

"You lived here?"

"Well, not exactly. He has a condo in town and we stayed there."

"You never *lived* here?"

"I've only been out here a couple of times. It's really nice. It even has a landing strip and everything. Harve flies himself to all those conferences and meetings in California and places."

"This place isn't even thirty minutes out of town. Why would he have a condo in town when he could live out here? That doesn't make sense to me."

"Well, Harve uses it for some workshops and seminars and stuff, I think. I wasn't married to him long enough to talk him around to letting us move out here."

I grinned at her. "Weren't you married longer than ten minutes? I can't imagine your not being able to talk somebody into doing what you wanted them to do."

"Harve is a weird duck, Karen. Every time I thought I had him, he'd go off with the Space Brothers or his Spirit Guides or something. I couldn't get him to pay attention to what I was saying, and when I finally did, he'd leave town on one of his trips. I really got pretty frustrated."

"I can imagine."

"Anyway, that's Harve's place."

I turned the car around, carefully.

"Why did you show it to me?" I asked.

"I don't know. We were passing by and I just thought it might be interesting. I'd take you on up to the gate, but there's always a guard there and I'm pretty sure he wouldn't let us in."

I drove back to the highway and said, "Well, I'm not sure I would want to live there. It looks like a fortress to me."

"They have to have all that security stuff, Harve said, because they're so close to the state pen."

"Are you guys still friends?"

"Sure. We still do lunch all the time. He's a nice guy, just strange. I'll take you next time I go and introduce you."

"Thanks, but I have enough strange guys in my life right now."

"Well, fut the whuck, darlin'. It could be a lot worse."

"How, Marilee? Just *how* could it be any worse than life with Mac is?"

"Well, he could eat seaweed like Harve does and make you eat it, too. At least Mac eats real food."

She grinned at me, and in spite of myself, I grinned back.

"Yeah, right," I said.

Occasionally, triggered by some change in my emotions, Mac would ask me hopefully if there was a baby on the way, and each time, I felt the anxiety of Mac's continuing good health.

"You've given me a new lease on life, baby," he said to me once, and it was so. He seemed to be healthier than he'd ever been, and with horror, I realized one day that I was becoming accustomed to his mauling of my body, his wet, slurping kisses, his pawing at me in front of other people, his prurient suggestions, which had absolutely no place in the neat, clean, refined way of life I'd been taught was the only one that was acceptable.

"We have to do something else, Marilee," I told her. "There has to be something we could do that we're not doing. He's as healthy as a horse now."

"I don't know what it could be, Karen. His arteries have to be completely clogged now. He's not drinking as much but he's staying up later every night and smoking more. I don't know what else we can do."

"You know he told the pharmacist not to refill my prescription for my pills, don't you? I've had to sneak over to Planned Parenthood to get them, and I live in terror he's going to find them one day."

"Maybe we should let him."

"What! Are you crazy? He'd have an absolutely killing fit . . . Oh, I see. . . . I don't know, Marilee. I'm not sure I can handle anger like that anymore. Especially not directed at me."

"Maybe not that, exactly, but maybe we should make sure he gets really, really mad at someone."

"Who?"

"Well, not us. For one thing, he would just get pissed and then blow off anything we did. We're just women, you know. He wouldn't expect us to do anything smart anyway, and he wouldn't stay mad long enough to have a heart attack. No, it has to be some man."

"Who?" I asked again, pushing it. "Who would make him the maddest?"

She looked at me with that slightly unfocused gaze of hers and smiled, slowly, smugly.

"One of my ex-husbands."

I thought about it. There was a good deal of ingenuity behind her thinking. Mac was the kind of man who would be constantly on guard around another man, aggressive enough to be suspicious of any kind of interaction with another, equally aggressive person. His acceptance of Marilee and me was based on the fact that we never showed him any kind of overt resistance and that we were sweet, mindless little women with whom he could relax. Therefore, it made sense that the opposite would trigger the most stress in Mac—some man who was aggressive, unafraid of Mac's blustering defensiveness, and some kind of a power figure.

"The cop," I said.

"Exactly. We'll call Davy and talk to him. I'll just bet he'd help us out."

"Marilee, I don't think a cop is going to help us kill Mac. Somehow, I just can't see that happening."

"Trust me. Get your clothes on and we'll go talk to Davy. Right now."

David Finch, like all of Marilee's ex-husbands except Mac, was young, good-looking, handsome in the way that cigarette-commercial actors are handsome. As before, I marveled at her ability to interest and snare men who were the very apex of Santa Fe's tiny population of eligible men. He was at least ten years younger than I, and his eyes were something that would strike even the most hard-hearted, cynical female dumb with wonder.

As we made our way toward the desk he was sitting on, he looked up and saw me, dismissed me as being harmless, and then, looking behind me, he saw Marilee and a look of extreme wariness crossed his face. He half-rose from his seat on the desk as we approached, a reflex that was just short of flight.

"Hello, darlin'." Marilee smiled at him, a delighted smile that told him she'd missed him very, very much and couldn't wait to talk to him again. From the side of her mouth, she whispered to me, "Let me do all the talking."

"Marilee, I'm married now," he said, warning her with his eyes as well as his voice.

"I know, darlin'. I've met your wife and she's gorgeous. She seems really nice, too, and it's no more than you deserve. You two should have babies together; the population of this country could stand some upgrading."

"Well, we did have a baby, last October—"

Somehow, I had the feeling Marilee already knew about the baby, but her face showed nothing but delighted surprise at this information.

"Did you? Oh, how nice. Do you have any pictures?"

Before he quite knew what was happening to him, David Finch had photographs out and was showing them to us. I made the required sounds over them, and handing them back to David, Marilee introduced me to him as the second Mrs. Carpenter. He looked me over carefully, much as he would have done a suspect who might possibly be armed. I smiled at him, one of Marilee's smiles.

"We're stepwives, you might say," she told him.

"How is old Mac?" David wanted to know, still watching me. I started to answer but Marilee cut in, so smoothly that, had I not known what was going on, I wouldn't have noticed the interruption. David missed it and I couldn't help thinking, regretfully, that all those months he was married to Marilee hadn't taught him a thing about her.

"He's doing just fine, Davy."

David Finch winced at this use of his baby-name in public, and I noticed the uniformed Hispanic officer at the next desk was watching the proceedings, grinning broadly. David got up and walked around his desk, and taking our elbows in each of his hands, he began to walk us toward the door. I followed willingly enough, but Marilee, catching on immediately to his manipulation, stumbled, fell against him, and swore, prettily.

"Damn these high heels! I just *knew* I was going to turn my ankle in them, but you know me, I *had* to have them."

She sat down in a chair near an empty desk, rubbing her ankle, and gave every appearance of taking root there. The look in David's eye was now that of an animal that's just beginning to realize he's fallen into a trap through no fault of his own. I was beginning to feel a little sorry for him.

The Hispanic cop got up and approaching Marilee, said, a little more heartily than necessary, grinning at David, "Miz Finch, how you doin', man?"

"Why . . . Tony Garcia. You sweet thing! But it's not Mrs. Finch anymore, darlin'. It's Mrs. Wallace now. What have you been up to?"

He perched himself on the corner of the desk and beamed at her. David looked around at the tiny crowd that was beginning to gather. His lips were white and there was a faint sheen of perspiration on his upper lip and brow.

"Marilee," he said urgently. "I'm real busy now, so if you could—"

"Oh, that's okay, darlin'. You go ahead with what you're doing and I'll just chat with Tony and the boys here until you're through."

She was merciless. David grabbed her arm and using it as a lever, propelled her out of the chair and toward an empty office. "Detective Finch," it said on the door. I followed meekly. He shut the door behind us and said sternly, "What's all this about, Marilee?"

"Well, I hate to bother you with this, Davy, but . . . I need some advice and I don't know who else to turn to."

"What kind of advice?"

"Well, we think that . . . a friend has gotten into something he doesn't need to be doing."

Instantly, David Finch was all cop. "What do you mean?"

"Karen felt bad about coming down here, but I thought maybe, since you were an old friend, you could help us out. Sort of under the table, you know."

"Now, Marilee . . ."

"We just need some advice, Davy, that's all. What would you do if you thought a . . . a friend of yours was, might be selling . . . stuff he shouldn't be selling?"

I stared at her, aghast, but before I could say anything, David asked, "What kind of stuff? Who?"

"We're not sure what kind of stuff. Karen and I, well . . . We wouldn't want him to get into any trouble, but there's some stuff in his car we've seen off and on that . . ."

"What kind of stuff?"

"Karen didn't want to come down here, being so close to the problem and all, but I told her we could get some advice from you as to what we should do about it."

"What kind of stuff?"

"Now, Davy, I don't think I know what it is and I don't want to know. What should we do? Confront him with it? Try to talk him out of . . . what he's doing?"

I tried not to gape at her. Fortunately, David's attention was focused on her and he couldn't see my face. In his own way, he was merciless.

"What kind of stuff?"

Marilee suddenly stood up.

"I think we ought to go and let you get back to work, Davy. Come on, Karen."

I followed her out the door and David followed me, saying, "Marilee, if you know anything you need to—"

"Well, I don't! I was just asking you for advice, Davy, that's all."

He grabbed her arms and forced her to look at him. "Marilee, don't screw with me. I want to know what you know, right now!"

"Why, Davy! This isn't like you. What's the matter, honey?"

"I want to know what stuff you're talking about."

"We don't know anything. It's just suspicions, Davy."

"Well, what did it look like?"

"I don't know, honey. You know how crafty . . . Look, we don't know anything, Davy. When we do, we'll call you. It was nice talking to you again, honey, but we have to go now."

Firmly, she walked us out of the station, and getting into my new car—another German model, but this one a Mercedes—she blew out her breath.

"There! That ought to do it."

"Marilee, I don't think you should have lied to the police like that. David might be one of your exes, but he's still a cop and—"

"That's right," she said with a healthy degree of satisfaction. "I know how they are. Now they'll be on him like a chicken on a grasshopper. At least for a while, anyway, and it will drive him absolutely wild."

I waited with some trepidation for Mac to come home that evening. When he finally did, he was an hour and a half later than usual. He burst into the house through the garage door, and with only a short look at his face, I knew David Finch and his fellow officers of the law had been at Mac.

He was almost inarticulate with rage, and I watched his face hopefully for the signs he was overloading his heart. Eventually, they were all there.

While he ranted and raved, more or less in my direction, I distracted myself by planning what I would wear to his funeral. Marilee had told me not to offer any kind of solace or in any way commiserate with him, and I sat there on the couch, a mannequin for all the help I offered, while he described in endless detail his treatment that afternoon at the hands of Santa Fe's finest. Finally, after nearly an hour of pacing around, drinking one whiskey after another and blustering, he suddenly got very quiet and, putting his glass down on the bar shakily, he went into the bedroom we shared.

"Are you all right, honey," I called after him.

He mumbled something and I waited, suddenly unwilling to follow him and confront a man having a heart attack. Finally, however, he came back into the living room, subdued, and quietly asked about supper as if nothing had happened.

The three of us sat at the dining room table, toying with the high-cholesterol, high-calorie food on our plates. As we usually did, Marilee and I had eaten a veggie plate before Mac came in to take the edge off our hunger so we wouldn't pork out on the fattening stuff, and Mac, having had his first brush with angina since before our marriage three months before, was uncharacteristically picky. That night, for one of the few times since our marriage, Mac didn't leap upon me in bed and roll us around enthusiastically. Sometime in the middle of the night, I woke up to find his place empty, and in spite of myself and Marilee's counsel, I got out of bed and went to find him. He was in the living room, staring out of the glass walls at the lights of Santa Fe that jeweled below, a drink in his hand.

"Mac?"

"It was that little cop of Marilee's," he said without turning around. I realized he was actually drunk, the first time I'd ever seen him more than just a little high, even though he could drink as much as a fifth in an evening. In his state, he was unaware of me as anything more than a voice coming out of the dark room behind him.

"He stole my wife and now he's after my balls," he added, apparently forgetting I was now his wife of record. "Marilee never woulda run off with him on her own. She ain't smart enough. He done it to me. I'll get that little fucker if it's the last thing I ever do."

There was something about the way he stood there and his words that was very menacing, and not knowing what I should do, I turned and went back to bed, to lie there for several hours, staring up at the *vigas* of the ceiling, trying to get some control over the shivering that had taken over my body, shivering that had nothing to do with the chill of the night.

"Hello, Karen, how are you?"

I knew whose voice it was before I turned around. I was surprised at the quick jump of my heart and the sudden joy that hit me in the stomach. Carefully, I tried to arrange my face in a mask of carefree unconcern so I could turn and answer Richard Sommerfrught with some degree of aplomb. Marilee squinted at me and then turned her brilliant smile on him.

"Ricky, darlin'," she said, obviously beside herself with delight at seeing him. "Imagine running into you here!"

She held out her hand and he took it, smiling down at her.

"You know I eat here often. It's convenient to my office."

"Of course, I knew that! I must be getting old-timer's disease or something, forgetting a thing like that. Sit down, darlin', and join us."

By this time, I had myself under some measure of control, and I was able to offer him my hand and say, quite coolly, "Well, hello, Richard. How've you been?"

He took my hand and I felt the tingling current run up my arm from his hand, making the tips of my breasts sting. Confused at the suddenness and the intensity of the feeling, I returned his stare, suddenly unable to think of anything else to say. Marilee, to her great credit, interrupted, breaking the contact between us, and said, "Sit down here and talk to us, darlin'. We're dying of boredom and you're just the person we want to talk to. Karen's thinking about redoing the breakfast room and . . . Oh, you knew she'd married Mac, didn't you? We're stepwives now, in a manner of speaking."

Richard released my hand and sat down.

"Yes, I'd heard," he said, his eyes still on me and suddenly hard.

Santa Fe, for all its cosmopolitan sophistication, was still a small town, and very little went on without everyone's knowing it shortly after it happened.

"Congratulations," he added after a short pause.

"Thank you."

"I hope you'll be very happy," he added sardonically, watching me intently.

"Thank you," I repeated, hating myself for my lack of inventiveness. I nudged Marilee's leg under the table with my foot, and thus cued, she said, "We were thinking of doing it in a teal blue. That's a good color for Karen and—"

"Did you get your Houser repaired?" Richard asked me.

"Yes. Yes, it's just fine now. You can hardly tell it was chipped. Thank you," I added, kicking myself for the repetition.

"Well, anyway," Marilee doggedly continued, "we might put in a tiled table with a server to match and—"

"I suppose you let the cottage go," he interrupted, ignoring Marilee.

"Yes."

"It's too bad. I liked it. It had a good feeling to it. I enjoyed being there."

Incredibly, I felt myself blushing. Helplessly, I stared at him, just managing by a great force of will not to thank him.

"It *was* fun, wasn't it," Marilee said. Part of my mind realized she was sweating, and I remember being surprised that there was a situation that could have that effect on her. Richard reached across the table and took my hand again.

"Karen . . ."

I seemed to be unable to look away from him. His holding my hand had made me suddenly will-less, completely powerless to make my muscles work enough even to withdraw it from his.

"Karen has just done *wonders* with Mac's art," Marilee babbled. "You know she has *such* a flair for groupings and . . ."

"Karen, you didn't have to do that. It wasn't necessary. Marrying him, I mean. I was an asshole, sure, but I didn't mean for you . . . I thought . . ."

"She's put the Santo Domingo pots together with the . . ."

"Is he good to you?"

"He treats me like a queen, Richard."

That, at least, was true. The waiter approached the table and the contact was broken between us. Richard focused on the menu and then, abruptly, stood up. Marilee looked up at him, surprised.

"If you'll excuse me," he said, "I think I'll skip lunch today. I've just remembered something I need to take care of."

"Well . . . Of course, darlin', you . . ."

He walked away, leaving her to stare after him.

"Shit," she said.

"Yeah," I said miserably, staring down at my plate.

The harassment by David Finch and his fellow officers, either real or in Mac's imagination, continued, off and on, for the better part of two weeks, and during that time, Mac became increasingly withdrawn and irritable, sleeping very little and drinking a great deal. I enjoyed the respite from his sexual mauling and began to sleep better than I had in months. It was heaven, knowing that, when I went to bed, I could go to sleep immediately without having to endure Mac's only form of physical exercise, that of tandem aerobics.

Then the harassment stopped, and in another week, Mac was his old, virile self again.

"How can he need so much sex?" I moaned to Marilee one morning. "He's nearly seventy, for Christ's sake. When is he going to slow down?"

"You should have known him when he was younger. He's always been oversexed, except when he thought he was impotent."

"There's got to be something else we can do."

"Well, maybe we ought to do some research on giving somebody a heart attack. Maybe we're going about it the wrong way."

"Oh, sure. Let's just go down to the public library and check out a book on how to cause a fatal heart attack in your husband."

Even then, I still considered Mac as much Marilee's husband as mine, perhaps even more.

"No," she said, patting my hand that lay beside my coffee cup, "let's get some real advice."

"What do you mean, 'real advice'?"

"I mean, let's go right to the source. Get some medical advice."

"Where are we going to . . . Oh, I see. Marilee, I don't think I can take any more of your ex-husbands."

She knew exactly what I was thinking about. She patted my hand, squeezed it gently.

"I'm sorry about that thing with Ricky, Karen. I didn't realize you two were so taken with each other. I thought it was just a little whiz-bang affair."

"Even you can be wrong," I pointed out to her.

"Yeah, I guess so. It just never occurred to me you two still had that much between you. I thought he was going to set the tablecloth on fire, the way he was looking at you."

"Let's change the subject."

"Yeah, okay."

In spite of my words, however, I was secretly pleased to think about Richard's obvious interest in me and then, just as suddenly, depressed—because it was all so futile.

As Marilee had told me, Harvey Wallace, M.D., was a New Age holistic psychiatrist with a good-size reputation for success around Santa Fe, one that was beginning to spread to both coasts. Being in his presence, she said, was like being in the presence of an irreverent Jesus; he was calm, kind, sweet, benevolent, and fatherly without being patronizing. His greatest professional attribute, I came to realize, was his ability to confer permission on his patients. It was a knack he had, an ability to ferret out each one's secret desire and then imply it was perfectly all right to give rein to it, to exercise that right as a Child of the Universe, that everything was karma anyway, either past or future, that everything was just merely a stick floating down the river of Taoist experience. In a hundred years, what would it matter what you did, except that you didn't deny your soul growth, and if running away with your secretary and living in a hogan in the desert contributed to your soul growth, then wouldn't it be a greater sin to refuse that experience?

His second-greatest attribute, according to Marilee, was that he could and did sleep with most of his patients, making them feel they were special since he had karma to work out with them.

"You think Mac is oversexed," Marilee told me, grinning, as we walked into the courtyard of the building where he had his office.

"Isn't that unethical for a psychiatrist, porking all his patients?"

"Well, sure, probably. His deal is he won't take on any patients that are really sick, just those with a few hang-ups that permission-giving would alleviate. He's pretty picky and everyone thinks he's just wonderful when it's over."

"Is he?"

"Sure! I'm a former patient and I tell you, he does wonders for a girl's self-esteem. I'd recommend him in a minute."

"What about his male patients? Does he sleep with them, too?"

"No, God, Karen! He runs support groups for them. He says women always have a built-in support system in their women friends and their mothers and their daughters, but men never, but never, talk about stuff that bothers them, except maybe to their wives. He gives them permission to let their hair down and get feedback from the other guys in the group in a protected environment. It's kinda like AA or something. Anyway, there's a waiting list for his men's groups. I'm telling you, this guy is dynamite. Wait'll you meet him."

"Why did you divorce him then?"

"He eats weird stuff."

"Weird stuff?"

"Yeah, I didn't have any trouble with the veggies, though I had to sneak around to eat a steak, but I did have trouble with the psyllium husks and spirulina and shit. He actually encouraged me to screw around on him, but if I ate part of a cow, you would have thought I'd betrayed him in the worst way. I hadda draw the line somewhere, and the seaweed got to me. I never could figure out how to cook it so it didn't taste like seaweed. Besides, it was like he said, our karma together was resolved."

"Resolved?"

"Yeah, we'd finished what we came here to share with each other this lifetime. It was time to move on."

She grinned at me as she opened the door to his office. A soft chime sounded as we stepped over the threshold and mixed melodically with the New Age music that whispered into the room from speakers hidden somewhere that I couldn't see. The scent of incense, patchouli, wafted out to greet us and pull us into the monochromatic-blue waiting room. Walking over the thick carpets toward the heavily pillowed couch, I felt myself relaxing in spite of myself. By the time I reached the wide couch, I was soothed almost into slumber. It was like being in a cloud.

"Ricky did a great job in here, didn't he?" Marilee said with obvious satisfaction as she seated herself on the couch.

"Richard decorated this?"

"Sure. Harve was going to do everything in rainbow colors and crystals, but I got him and Ricky together and he's just happy as a pig in fresh mud now."

The inner door opened and a man walked out. He was tall, thin, tanned, and completely bald, probably artificially so, but those impressions were all that I noticed at first. I was instantly mesmerized by his eyes, which were blue, a sharp blue, steady, penetrating, all-knowing. He stopped and held out his arms, smiling at Marilee.

"Darling!" he said, obviously delighted to see her.

Marilee stood and held out her arms, smiling. "Darlin'!"

They commingled and their kiss was of such intensity and duration that I became nonplussed. Just as I thought I might have to examine the monochromes on the wall, which consisted mostly of planets and solar systems in unlikely configurations, they broke, and Dr. Wallace said to her, "Let me schedule some time for you, sweetheart. I've forgotten what a wonderful essence you have."

"Maybe later, darlin', but right now, I want you to meet my stepwife, Karen Carpenter."

He looked at me and raised his eyebrows.

"Mac?"

"Yes," I said, holding out my hand, adding, "I'm the second Mrs. Carpenter."

He ignored my hand, and taking me in his arms, he hugged me tightly, rocking us side to side for a long time. I endured it, but when he tried to kiss my mouth, I pushed him firmly away. He was philosophical about the rebuff, however, and smiled down at me.

"When you've had all you can take, my dear, come in and we'll talk. Mac is pretty heavy karma and you are such a delightful person."

I couldn't resist it. "How do you know?" I asked suspiciously.

"It's your aura. All pink and gold, but with a little touch of brown here and there that we need to work out. You're very sexually oriented, aren't you?"

I snorted, thinking of my inert body under Mac's heaving one, and suddenly, unbidden, I remembered my fierce responsiveness to Richard's lovemaking. I gave him Mother's stare, feeling my face growing hot and doing my best to ignore it.

Before I could say anything, however, Marilee smoothly interjected, "Darlin', this is really sweet of you to see us like this. I know how busy you are, but we're in a world of hurt and we need some information from you."

"Come on in and let's talk."

He put his arm around her and with the other, pulled me against him firmly. I allowed him to lead me into his inner office with his arm around me as well and to seat me in a hedonistically soft chair in front of his desk. He put Marilee in another just like it and when he was seated himself, said, "Okay, what's up now?"

"Well, darlin', we need to talk to you as a medical doctor."

"It's been a while, Marilee, but I'll do what I can."

He smiled benevolently at her.

"Well, we're worried about Mac's heart. You know he's had those three heart attacks and he absolutely *won't* take care of himself. Karen is worried that the rigors of married life might trigger another one. What do you think?"

"In other words, he might fuck himself into another one."

"Well, yes, something like that."

"You needn't worry about sex. It's good for him. If anything, it'll keep his chances for another coronary way down. The infarcted area is probably healed by now. How long has it been since the last one, three years?"

"It was when you and I got married."

"Don't worry about it, ladies. Enjoy yourself, Karen. You can't give a man a heart attack. Now, what else can I do for you?"

"But the stress he's under," I said, beginning to be very nervous. "What about that? Won't that cause him to . . ."

"What kind of stress is he under?"

We were on dangerous ground now, and cautiously, I turned to Marilee. She picked up the ball and ran with it.

"Well, the police have been hassling him and we're worried they'll cause him to have another one."

"It's almost impossible to give someone a heart attack, Marilee. It's not the flu, you know. Reinfarction of postcoronary patients is a completely internal thing."

"What?" I was startled out of my caution. "What do you mean?"

"I mean that no matter what you or the police, or even Marilee, did, you could not give Mac, or anyone else for that matter, a heart attack. A stroke, maybe, but not a heart attack. That's something that's controlled by our Inner Selves, our own self-regulatory mechanisms."

I was speechless. Marilee, however, had no such trouble.

"So you're saying that, no matter what happens to him, he won't get another heart attack? What about those he's already had? Something caused them?"

He gave us his Jesus smile. "I'm telling you he allowed himself to have them, and when he's ready for another, he'll allow himself to have another. It's our body's way of getting rid of unmanageable stress. It's really beautifully simple when you stop to think about it."

"Well, that was worthless," I said as we crossed the parking lot and climbed into my car. "What an idiot!"

"I don't know, Karen. It had the ring of truth to it."

"I can't believe that, Marilee. I just can't allow myself to believe that. I have to have hope that, any day, Mac will have another attack. If I didn't think that, I'd . . ."

I realized that I was getting shrill and made myself breathe deeply, calmed myself down.

"What if it's true?" Marilee asked.

"What do you mean, what if it's true? You're the one with all the ideas. You tell me. I'm the one who's going to be stuck with Mad Mac for the rest of my life. Or at least, until I have a heart attack myself."

"We'll just have to think of something else."

"Yes, I guess we do! And I have another question, while we're on the subject."

"What's that?"

"Have you read his will lately? Has he changed it since we were married? What if he dies and the will hasn't been changed?"

From the look on her face I knew the thought hadn't even occurred to her. Relentlessly, I pressed on.

"Yeah. And how do we go about finding out without tipping him off?"

"Oh, *shit!*"

"And while you're at it, will you please stop introducing me to everyone as your stepwife."

The next afternoon I went shopping, anxious to get out of the house, to try to mitigate some of the effects of this new miasma that hovered over it, but when I pulled back into the curving driveway, I saw that there was a police car sitting there, waiting. Instantly, I tensed, guilt making me nervous and wary. As I got out of my car, the officer got out as well and approached me.

"Detective Finch sent me. I need to speak to Mrs. Carpenter."

"I'm Mrs. Carpenter," I informed him.

"No, I mean the other Mrs. Carpenter."

As if cued, the Cadillac roared up the driveway, around a stand of piñons, nearly clipped the police car, and swerving wildly, came to a stop inches from mine, skidding sideways in the gravel. The officer, trained to react quickly, leaped to safety, putting his car between him and the Cadillac. I stood there beside mine, however, frozen with confusion, staring, unable to move until Marilee got out, dragging her huge bag with her.

"Hello, darlin'," she greeted me, grinning. "Sorry about that. Are you okay?"

Before I could answer, the cop came around from where he'd been crouching behind the front of his car and said, "You Marilee Carpenter?"

"Well, I was. I'm Marilee Wallace now."

"Well, Detective Finch sent me to tell you your husband is in the hospital."

"Mac!"

"Yeah. Mac Carpenter."

"What happened?"

"Somebody took a shot at him."

We stared at each other. Her surprise appeared to be equally as genuine as mine, and even as upset as I was, I had to admire her acting ability. But then, I reminded myself, I'd seen it before, many times, and I shouldn't have been surprised at all.

"Is he all right?" she asked breathlessly.

"Well, he got winged pretty good and lost a lot of blood, but it really didn't look too bad to me. Detective Finch says for you to come on down to St. Vincent's."

"I'll drive," I said, scrambling for the Mercedes.

As I drove back down the winding driveway with Marilee in the passenger's seat, I said, "Are you *crazy*! What were you thinking of, shooting at him like that? You know as well as I do that—"

"Me? I thought *you'd* done it! You didn't?"

"No, of course not! I don't even know the first thing about shooting a gun, much less hitting someone. Marilee, please, tell me if you did it. I won't—"

"Karen, I wouldn't lie to a girlfriend. I did not shoot at Mac. Someone else did it."

I stared at her. "You mean, someone else is trying to kill him, too?"

"Looks like it. And guess what? I've been on the plaza all afternoon, sweet-talking Mac's lawyer, trying to find out the status of his will. You were right. He hasn't changed it yet. Karl told me everything still goes to the University of Texas. This is a community-property state so you'll get half, but you'll probably have to sue for it or something, and the lawyer said it will take forever. I, of course, won't get anything."

"Marilee, we can't let him die until that will is changed!"

"Yeah. God, please, don't let his heart give out on him now! I can't imagine anything more aggravating to his heart than being shot at."

I stared out the windshield, driving automatically, thinking.

"Marilee, who could be trying to kill Mac? Who else would want him dead?"

"There's no telling. But we can't let it happen. Not until that will is changed. We have to keep him alive, no matter what happens— at least until then."

4

The policeman had been right; Mac had been clipped pretty good. When Marilee and I got to the hospital and were directed to his room, we found him lying in a bed, his eyes closed, his face gray against the white of the sheets. His hair had been shaved on one side and bandages applied, and his blood-soaked clothing lay heaped in a chair.

I stopped in the doorway, hesitating, but Marilee pushed around me and hurried to his side.

"Darlin'," she whispered, "are you all right?"

His eyelids flickered. "Get me outta here, Marilee. I'm gonna kill me a fuckin' nurse if you don't."

"What happened?"

"Just get me outta here and stop asting stupid questions, willya?"

"I'll do it," I volunteered. The sight of the usually robust and vibrant Mac supine on a bed, wounded, had unnerved me more than I could have guessed it would have done. I left the room, hunting someone in charge. I met David Finch at the elevator. He greeted me, a tight look around his mouth.

"Karen," I told him. "You might as well call me Karen. What happened?"

"He was apparently stopped at a light, a car pulled up next to him, and the passenger shot him. It wasn't an accident or a random shooting. It was an execution-style thing. Somebody wants him dead. What's going on here?"

"Sorry?"

"I want to know what you and Marilee found in his car. I want to know everything you can think of that might pertain to this shooting."

I stared at him, trying to decide what to do. How could I tell him Marilee and I were trying to kill Mac ourselves, and to that end, she had concocted some crazy story about finding stuff in Mac's car to sic the police on him?

"Well," I said, trying to remember exactly what Marilee had told him. "I don't know too much..."

"What was in his car?"

"I'm not sure...It was a sack of something," I lied desperately, hoping what I was saying was plausible. "You'll have to ask Marilee. She was the one who found it."

I had no compunctions about tossing the lie back to Marilee. After all, it was her lie and not mine. Let her handle it, I thought, and excusing myself, I went to find someone to authorize Mac's release.

I tried Marilee's smile and Mother's stare but both let me down. Mac was doomed to spend at least one night in the hospital, for observation, no matter what I did or said, and finally giving up, I made my way back to his room, just in time to hear him bellowing and see a nurse firmly escorting David Finch out of the room. Marilee followed them, soothing, placating, but ignoring them all, I went in and sat on the edge of Mac's bed, picking up his hand and curving mine to fit it.

"Honey," I said, "they won't release you. They want to keep you in here tonight because of your heart."

He looked up at me and said pitifully, "I want to go home."

Incredulous, I heard myself saying, "I'll stay with you, okay? I won't leave. I'll be right here all night."

"Queen Karen—"

He was interrupted by a nurse who bustled in and perfunctorily gave him a shot of something, but before he could remonstrate with her, I said, "Hush now. I'm not going anywhere. I'll be right here."

As I had hoped, his anger at her was diverted, diffused, and he smiled at me as his eyes glazed over.

"My Queen Karen. Don't leave me, okay? Don't go away and..."

His voice trailed off as he went to sleep, his mouth wide open and his breathing vibrating his nasal passages until the snore was almost of jackhammer quality. I disengaged his hand from mine and sat down in the chair next to his bed.

Well, what else could you do? I asked myself, disgusted. You can't take a chance on his having another heart attack. At least, not yet. Anything to keep Mac happy, and if it means sitting by his hospital bedside all night . . .

Marilee came back into the room, interrupting my train of thought.

"Whew," she said, giving me a look of wide-eyed intensity. "I just learned something—don't ever, ever, *ever* lie to a cop, even if he is an ex."

"You didn't tell him you made it all up?"

"No, of course not. I'm not *that* crazy. It's just that the problem with lying is that you have to remember what you said. I did find out one thing, though. Mac was set up."

"I know. David told me. What's Mac into, I wonder, that someone wants him dead? And who is it?"

She closed the door to the room and whispered, "Davy thinks it's the Mexican Mafia."

"The what?"

"Mexican Mafia. It's kind of an underground Hispanic thing. They do a lot of dope from South America and they're real mean. You don't want to mess with them. Poor Davy. He says somebody's running tons of dope in and nobody can figure out who's doing it or how. He's got the DA and the feds breathing down his neck and he—"

"Dope? Do you think we got Mac into trouble by telling David that story?"

"How?"

"I don't know. It's just that . . ."

"I don't think it has anything to do with us, Karen. It's something Mac has gotten himself involved in."

"Marilee," I whispered frantically, "we can't let anything *happen* to him until that will is changed. We have to keep him alive until we can get him to change it."

"I know. Got any ideas?"

I didn't. I was fresh out. Not for the first time, I cursed the day I'd met Marilee Smith Carpenter Finch Sommerfrught Wallace.

We brought Mac home the next day, installed him in his bed, fluffed his pillows, and sighed when he lay there for a few minutes and then bounded out again and began dressing.

"Where are you going?" Marilee asked him. "The doctor said that—"

"Fuck the doctor! I got to get down to the office."

"But honey," I said, "I'm afraid you're getting up too soon." I gritted my teeth. "I'd hate for you to have a relapse or something. I'm worried about you. Please, darling, stay in bed—just for me?"

He kissed me, a kiss such as a big, friendly bird dog might give, patted my fanny, and said, "You don't worry about me. Here's some money. You girls go shoppin' today and buy you something purty. Ole Mac can take care of hisself."

"But Mac, I really think that—"

"By the way," he said casually, so casually that Marilee and I were instantly alerted, "I might be late for supper tonight. I got to see a man about a dog."

As he left the room, Marilee and I looked at each other.

"We have to follow him," she whispered.

"Right!"

We sat in the parking lot across the street from Mac's office building all afternoon in a rented car, waiting for him to leave. Finally, exactly at five, he lumbered out to his car, climbed in, and drove away. We followed Mac's Lincoln stealthily through the Cerrillos Road traffic and parked behind some lilac bushes when he stopped at a building on Piñon. He sat in his car for a few minutes, and just as Marilee and I were almost crazy with boredom, he got out and accosted a well-muscled, tattooed young man who'd come out of the building and was walking down the sidewalk.

"That's an ex-con," Marilee said, putting her glasses on and squinting fiercely.

"How do you know?"

"Look at all those muscles and those jailhouse tattoos. They don't have anything to do in the pen but work out in the gym and tattoo themselves with pencils. They're a dead giveaway."

In spite of myself, I was impressed.

"Don't look so surprised," she said, laughing. "I was married to a cop, you know. Besides, that's the parole office he came out of. Now, what I want to know is *why* is Mac meeting an ex-con?"

We watched as they talked for a few minutes, and then the young man got in the car with Mac and they drove off. I followed, trying to be as unobtrusive in the traffic as possible. They stopped at a restaurant on St. Michael's and went in. Marilee and I watched from the parking lot as they sat down at a table away from everyone else and ordered. They talked for some minutes, drinking coffee, and then, getting up, Mac left some money on the table and walked out. The young man picked it up, put it in his jeans pocket, and continued to sit there, drinking his coffee.

"Well," Marilee said. "Do we leave and follow Mac or do we wait and see what the ex-con does?"

I gnawed my lip.

"Maybe we'd better get home. Mac will be there by the time we turn this car in, and I don't think we ought to upset him more than he has been already."

Mac was in a terrific mood all evening, whistling over his before-dinner cocktails and even teasing Marilee about the cold supper she served us. That night in bed, in spite of his head wound, he groped between my legs and whispered, "You know what I feel like doin'?"

I begged off, citing the fact I'd spent the previous night sitting upright in a chair beside his hospital bed, and he thankfully backed away, a rare gesture for him. I went to sleep with his hand inside the front of my gown, kneading my already sore breast.

The next morning, Mac was gone when I woke up, and staggering into the kitchen, I accepted a cup of coffee from Marilee and sat at the table, cradling it in both hands while I came back to life. Marilee was accustomed to my early-morning antagonism and was quiet, waiting for me to signal that I could think again, talk coherently, function. While I drank the coffee, I glanced over *The New Mexican*, reading the headlines without comprehension, staring at the pictures. One of them caught my eye, and focusing on it, I concentrated, trying to remember where I'd seen the face before. It was a full head shot of a Hispanic male, devoid of expression, a flat, hooded look that was somehow a little intimidating. It was several minutes before I linked it up. The story accompanying the picture was about someone who'd been found dead the night before, dumped on the highway to Clines Corner.

"Get your glasses," I told Marilee abruptly.

"What?"

"Look at this picture. Recognize him?"

She put the newspaper against her nose and squinted at the picture and then at the caption underneath it.

"Oh, damn," she said finally.

"Yeah, right."

She sat down at the table and looked at me.

"What's Mac into, Karen? This guy was the guy he was talking to yesterday and now he's dead."

"I think it's safe to say Mac hired him to do something—"

"Probably to handle what happened to him."

"—and this guy got himself killed in the process."

We stared at each other for a few seconds. Finally, Marilee said, "Maybe not. Maybe it was totally unrelated."

"Come on, Marilee."

She made a face and then said, "So that means that Mac knows who tried to get him the other day."

"Do you think we ought to tell David?"

"No. If we tell him, he's gonna want to talk to Mac about it and Mac'll just croak for sure. We can't risk it."

"Well, what are we going to do then?"

The phone rang and Marilee answered it, paused, and then said, "Oh, hi, José. . . . Already? It seems like it was just yesterday I had it in. . . . Well, okay. I'll haul it down there today. This afternoon be all right?"

She hung up the phone and said, "I have to take the Caddy in for an oil change this afternoon. I'm almost sure José changed it last month. I'll bet he's got a new girlfriend he wants to impress. Could you follow me down there and—"

"Will you just shut up about that damn car for a minute and concentrate on what's important? What are we going to do about somebody who's trying to kill Mac?"

"I don't know. Maybe we ought to focus on getting him to change his will."

She sounded as uncertain as I felt about the subject.

"How are we going to do that? You, of all people, know what he's like when he thinks he's being railroaded into something."

"Maybe if you're pregnant—"

"What!"

"Sure. I know Mac. Then he'll want to provide for the baby and—"

"Oh, no! Oh, no, Marilee! Just forget that! Don't even *think* about it!"

"Well, you won't have to actually be *pregnant*. We can just pretend you are and—"

"Absolutely not! That has to be the craziest idea you've ever had, even surpassing the one where you lied to David—a cop, for heaven's sake!"

"It was just an idea."

"Well, find another one!"

She sat down at the table with a fresh cup of coffee and I watched her think with a good deal of outraged determination. I had nothing against motherhood per se, had even mourned the fact that Jack and I had never had children, but anything that smacked of having Mac's baby, real or imagined, was too much. Enough was enough.

"Okay," she said finally. "Here's what we'll do. You ask him if he has any life insurance on you. Tell him you've been thinking about his being shot. No, don't tell him that—he'll think you're fishing to find out if he has any. Just find a good time and ask him about you. No matter what he says, drop the subject. Let him stew about it for a couple of days, and then, if he doesn't bring it up again, you do it."

"In other words, we're getting him to think about the will, right?"

"Atta girl. Now you're catching on." She patted my hand and grinned at me. "Pretty soon you'll be thinking just like me."

"God forbid!" I said, shuddering.

Mac was in a foul mood that night at dinner, in direct contrast to what his mood had been the night before. Both Marilee and I knew why: Nothing would chap Mac worse than paying for something and then not getting his full value. It wouldn't matter to him that the guy had died trying to do it; he would consider it the breaks of the game. His anger was directed at what he considered worse—being cheated.

Marilee and I worked frantically to diffuse his temper, praying his heart would hold out through it, and finally, after several drinks and Marilee's coddling, he was mellow enough to go to bed.

I tensed for the inevitable wrestling match, but we were hardly into it before I realized his heart wasn't in it. I decided to take us both off the hook.

"Mac, why don't we lie here for a minute or two and let me get my breath? I'm just not as young as I used to be."

"Well, okay. Anythin' for my Queen Karen."

He rolled off my inert body and lay there beside me, huffing in the thin atmosphere. When the silence began to stretch out, I decided it would be now or never.

"Honey, I was just thinking..."

He groped for my hand and finding it, squeezed it. "Now, you don't go worrying your pretty head about things. That's my job, hear?"

"But I was just thinking. What if something happens to me?" I blundered on, mentally cursing myself because I had none of Marilee's tact. "Am I insured?"

"Why would you want to know somethin' like that? That's crazy talk! Nothin's gonna happen to you while I'm around to take care of you."

"But I will die someday, Mac. I would hate for you to have to bury me with—"

"I told you not to think about that! I don't wanna hear no more about it."

"Okay, honey. I'm sorry. I was just wondering."

"Well, don't."

I turned toward him and gathered him in my arms, much as I would have done a child, and thus comforted, he fell into his usual noisy sleep.

It happened again the next day. As Mac was driving down the winding Hyde Park Road, going into the office the next morning, a flatbed pulled out onto the road behind him and on the downhill run, caught up and pulled out to pass. Instead of passing, however, it nudged into the side of the Lincoln, pushing it firmly toward the edge of the road and the drop-off into the canyon. Mac had the presence of mind to hit his brakes and then, when the truck passed, make an abrupt left-hand turn into the entrance of a housing addition. While the truck was turning around, he managed to slip past it and careen on down to the foot of the hill. The driver of the truck, trying to catch up, lost control on the steep hill and ran into a pole.

Marilee and I didn't know about it until almost noon when David Finch himself came out and told us.

"Goddammit, Marilee! I want to know what's happening here!"

"Davy..." She shrugged. "I just don't know what to tell you, darlin'. Mac is so secretive it's like pulling hen's teeth, getting anything out of him."

He ignored the mixed metaphor and said, "If you know anything, if you find out anything, I want to know about it immediately. Okay?"

"Why is he so upset about this?" I asked as he was driving away. "I would have thought he wouldn't care that much what happened to Mac."

"I don't know. Nothing about this makes any sense."

She closed the door and leaning against it, squinted up at me.

"I do know one thing, though. We have to do something. Sooner or later, if they keep trying, they're going to get him. We've got to get him on that will and keep him safe until it's done. Dammit, dammit! Why is everything so slow with him? Just once I'd like to be able to say, 'Do this, Mac,' and have him do it. This working all around Robin Hood's barn all the time is beginning to get to me."

"I know how to keep him safe," I said slowly, thinking it out as I went along. "We could get him out of town, get him away from here for a few days. Maybe he could run down to Dallas for something, take care of some business. Does he have anything left there that he might have to check on?"

"I have no idea. You know what he's like. I wasn't lying to Davy when I told him Mac is secretive. It's a thought, though. If we could just get him out of town for a few days..."

She looked at me, a look full of speculation and purpose and I was suddenly *very* nervous.

"You could get him out of town, Karen. You could ask him to take you back to Reno. Or maybe Vegas."

My nervousness exploded into horror. "No, Marilee! You can't imagine what it was like with him on our honeymoon! If you had any idea, you wouldn't ask me to do it."

"I know, honey," she said, patting my arm soothingly, "but I can't think of any other way to get him out of town. We need some time. At least, until we can figure just what's going on."

I was almost in tears.

"Marilee, *please* don't ask me to go to Reno with Mac again. It's the most degrading thing I can think of. At least here I don't have to be seen with him in public. There, there's absolutely no privacy and you *know* what he's like."

"We've got to keep him safe. I don't know anything else to do. You work on getting him out of town and I'm going to talk to Karl, his lawyer, and see if I can't figure out a way to get him to mention the will to Mac. Mac would listen to him."

"How are you going to do that?"

"I don't know. I'll think of something. Will you do it?"

"You're sure there's no other way?"

"None that I can think of."

"I wish I had never let you talk me into this, Marilee."

"I know, honey."

Mac called at the end of the day, requesting a ride home. Since the Cadillac was also ready, it made sense to me that Mac could bring it up, saving me a trip down, but Marilee told me he would walk before he would be seen in it, much less drive it somewhere.

"It's the color," she explained. "Pink is for sissies, you know."

"Then why doesn't he get you another one?"

"I'm being punished for running away from him."

"Still?"

"Sure."

"Doesn't that bother you?"

"No, but what does bother me is that it always takes José so long to change the oil and filter in it. How busy can he be, for God's sake, that it takes him two days?"

"Maybe he has a contract with the citizens of Santa Fe to keep you off the streets as much as possible."

I was only half kidding her. She grinned at me.

"Maybe. But it's more likely he joyrides around Española in it."

"Don't you check your mileage after you get it back?"

"Oh, god, honey. That odometer has been broken for years. I have no idea how many miles are on it."

I pulled into the parking lot of Mac's building. He plodded out to the car, sweating like an overworked mule in the high-altitude sun.

Marilee dutifully got out and wadded herself into the small space behind the front seats of the Mercedes, sitting sideways on the hard bench, leaving the passenger's seat for him.

"What happened to your car?" she asked him.

"It's in the shop."

"Was it the alternator again?"

"Naw. It needed some bodywork."

"It looked fine this morning."

"Drop it! I don't wanna talk about it right now."

I glanced up into the rearview mirror and caught the small, secret smile on her face. It was something I knew, but realizing it again was still something of a shock. Mac wasn't the only one into power.

While Marilee was working on Mac's attorney that evening at dinner downtown, I gritted my teeth and began trying to talk Mac into taking me back to Reno. He argued with me, but I could see it was done for the sake of form and not from any real antagonism to the idea. I played on his pruriency, and curled up next to him on the couch, I shamelessly whispered reasons we should go, things so suggestive that I was forced to contemplate again the fact that I had probably become what Mother had always indicated was the lowest sort of trash. Mac, of course, loved it.

The next morning, after Mac had left for work in my car, Marilee and I met in the breakfast room and compared notes.

"Well," I said morosely, "we're going. Tomorrow morning. Thanks to you, I have to get up early and fly to Vegas with Mac. I hope you're happy."

"I know, darlin'. It's really too awful to think about. You know I'd do it for you if I could."

"I doubt it. How did you make out with the lawyer?"

"For a supposedly intelligent man, Karl's got a head full of cement. I thought I'd never get the old fool on the right track, but I think he's going to call Mac today and suggest it. If you softened him up some last night, Mac should be open for it."

"You know, Marilee, I never worked this hard at the Museum Shop."

"Yeah, and you were starving to death, too. Keep your eye on the big picture, as our Mac is so fond of saying. If Mac agrees and the lawyer works on it while you're gone, it'll be ready for Mac's signature when you get back, and once it's signed, then they can do whatever they want to him."

"Well, there's that," I agreed, somewhat cheered. "If everything goes okay, it could be all over in a few days."

"Sure," she said, patting my hand. "Fut the whuck! Nothing's forever, now is it?"

"No, I guess not. I just wish the next few days were over."

"We're too old to wish days away." She grinned at me. "We don't have any to spare."

As I had feared, it was the honeymoon all over again. Mac instantly resumed his childlike delight with the casinos and shows and his exuberance in sex, and that comparison to the morose and tense man who'd boarded the plane, more than anything else, pointed out to me the strain he'd been under in Santa Fe. His energy knew no limits, and if he wasn't tormenting my body in the hotel suite, then he was down on the casino floors until all hours, gambling and drinking with all sorts of unsavory characters, none of whom I cared to meet, much less be seen with.

I kept to the suite as much as possible, hiding from everyone and the gross public displays of affection he was so constantly demonstrating. When he suggested I meet him downstairs, I sweetly implied I would rather wait for him upstairs, suggesting with a smile I wasn't interested in seeing anyone else but him. It was only partially a lie, however; most of the people he knew, I certainly did not want around me.

One evening, as I was reading in the living room of the suite, I heard his voice coming down the hall. I looked up, my face arranging itself into a smile of welcome for him, but when he came in, he was leading a young, aggressively gum-chewing woman by the hand. He had the look on his face that I had learned by then meant he was planning something, was anticipating trouble over it, and relishing the thought of it.

The young woman had the face of a twelve-year-old and the body of a woman many years older. Her tight blouse was tied beneath her breasts, showing some remarkable cleavage, and the skirt was nothing more than a small strip of fabric, leaving a great expanse of legs and skinny stomach showing. She smiled at me, happily. From the vacant look in her eyes, I was surprised she could manage to smile and chew her gum at the same time.

"This is my wife, Sheila. Darlin', this little girl has come up to party with us."

I was momentarily confused. "Party? I didn't know we..."

I stopped as the realization of his meaning hit me.

"Mac, no! Absolutely not! I—"

"Hi," Sheila said, catching up in the conversation.

"Now, darlin'," Mac said, "I promised you and you promised me. Remember? When we was in Reno? Remember?"

"Mac—"

"I promised you I'd get us a gal with big tits, remember?"

I remembered all right, and this was apparently to be the continuation of the nightmare. I thought frantically. Short of walking out of the suite and Mac's life, never more to return, I was unable to formulate anything that would deter him. I knew him well enough by then to know that a flat refusal would only goad him worse, and then I would have to choose between walking out of the suite into penury or giving in.

"Mac, darling—"

"Just look at them tits, darlin'. Show her your tits, honey."

Sheila dutifully began working at the knot in her blouse, looking down and concentrating carefully on it, her gum resting at last in her mouth.

"Mac, that's not necess—"

"Now, hush, darlin'. You know how I feel about you. Nothin's too good for my Queen Karen, an' Sheila's the best, aincha, honey? Lookee *there!*"

Sheila had managed to get the knot undone and shook her breasts free of the restraining cloth. She grinned at me as if she'd just learned a new trick, arched her spine, and rolled her shoulders back, giving us the full effect. Mac was almost overcome on the spot.

Sheila was truly gifted. I stared at her, amazed that one woman could have so much and the rest of us so little. Mac, obviously delighted beyond restraint, filled both his hands, smiling with an expression akin to religious fervor on his face. As before, I wondered why on earth Mac had insisted on marrying me when his fetish for large breasts was so well developed. It passed my ability to understand.

"Just lookit them knockers, darlin'!" he said. "Come over here and grab you a feel. Sheila don't mind, do you, darlin'?"

"No," said the simple Sheila, giggling. "No, I don't mind. I *like* it."

For several reasons, I wanted to slap her.

"Mac, sweetheart. I wonder if I could just speak to you a second in the bedroom. It's really, really important, darling," I added at the look growing on his face.

"Now, darlin', Sheila's gonna get her feelin's hurt if you don't be nice. Aincha, darlin'?"

Sheila screwed up her face into a pretty pout. "Yeah," she said. "I want to party."

She shook her shoulders again and her breasts danced merrily out of Mac's hands. Delighted, he grabbed for them again. Sheila smiled again, this time at Mac.

My God, I thought. What am I going to *do?*

I knew the look on Mac's face; by then I was very familiar with it. Nothing short of death would stop him now. Frantically, I inspected and discarded everything that came to mind.

"Mac, darling, I want to talk to you. I wondered, sweetheart, could we just—"

"What's the matter with you? You promised, remember, and I said nothing was too good for you."

"Mac . . . Mac, I just can't."

"Why not?"

"Well, I . . . I just can't, that's why."

"You mean, you don't want to."

"Yes. No, I don't want to."

"Why not?"

"I . . . just don't."

"This ain't like you. You always liked to have fun before. Unless . . ."

He stared at me, hard, Sheila's talents momentarily forgotten.

"Are you gonna have a baby?"

He held the straw out to me and I grabbed it.

"Yes," I said, "I can't because I'm pregnant. Maybe," I added, hedging my bet. "I think maybe . . . I just don't . . ."

It made no sense, but Mac, whooping, grabbed me in a bear hug and then, still holding me with one arm, used the other to scoop

Sheila against us. Her cologne was aggressive, sweet and cloying—
and very cheap.

"I'm gonna be a daddy!" he yelled in my ear.

"Oh, that's nice," Sheila said, wriggling fiercely, rubbing her breasts
all over us. "I like babies."

"I think I'm going to be sick," I said, and it was true. My stomach
lurched and rolled.

"Now, darlin', you come over here and sit down. I don't want you
upset. Not for a minute."

Sheila's cologne clung to my clothing, filled the room, making it
implode on me. I tried to calm myself by breathing deeply, but the
cologne-laden air gagged me.

"I have to leave," I gasped. "I have to go . . ."

"Here, darlin'. Here's some money. If you wanna go shoppin' you
can. Me and Sheila don't mind." He paused, frowning. "That is, if
you don't."

"No," I gasped. "No, of course not."

And grabbing my purse, I fled the suite to the sanctuary of the
shops downstairs.

Mac found me several hours later, sitting in one of the lounges,
drinking my fourth salty dog. He was somewhat subdued, and warily,
I watched him approach my table. He'd showered, I was glad to
see, and Sheila's bad-tempered scent was missing. So was she.

"Hello, darlin'," he said.

"Where's Sheila?" I asked cattily.

He refused to look at me.

"I sent her off. She just had all them tits and nothin' else. It was
lousy and I gave her some money and got rid of her."

In other words, I thought, she was too much for you and you couldn't
rise to the occasion.

I sipped my drink and said coolly, "You know, there are times when
I wish I'd never met you."

I would never have overtly antagonized him before, but the gin had
gotten to me and I was unable to contain my anger. I was determined
that, no matter what the result, I was going to make sure he never
again treated me in such an outrageous manner. There were some

things that were more important than money and security, I told myself, and pride was one of them.

Mac, however, was uncharacteristically remorseful.

"Baby," he whined. "I'm sorry, baby. I just didn't think. I never shudda . . . Well, you know what I always said about you, you're my queen and I don't want to do anythin' that'll upset you."

"I'm very angry."

"Now, don't get all snooty on me, baby. You haven't been that way for a long time. You and me get along so good, no woman ever was so nice to me, not even Marilee. I don't want you to get upset, 'specially not now."

"And that's another thing."

I started to tell him I was not pregnant and further, tell him I would never be, at least not with his child. The gin, however, had made my mouth clumsy, along with the rest of my body, and I paused to get it in hand, concentrating fiercely. Mac reached out and touched my arm.

"Darlin', you shouldn't be getting drunk now. I'm sorry, I shudda thought before I . . . It was just them tits, I never saw nuthin' like them before. Jesus! But she just wasn't you, baby. You're all I want. Now come on back up to the room with me."

"I don't think so, Mac."

"What?"

I enunciated very carefully, trying to make him understand. Suddenly, it was very, very important for me to tell Mac everything, to kiss him off and get out of the craziness I'd let Marilee talk me into.

"I don't think that we—"

Abruptly, the cavernous room spun around me and I swayed. Mac caught me as I was falling out of the chair, lifted me up, and started for the elevators.

"Mac, your heart . . ." I said weakly, shutting my eyes against the gyrating room.

"Get outta the way," he roared. "My wife's pregnant and she's sick."

Mother's admonitions against making a public spectacle of myself made me cringe with mortification and I shut my eyes, alleviating somewhat the effects of the spinning room.

There were people suddenly all around us. Someone took me out of Mac's arms and then there was a gurney under me, solid and reassuring. I clutched the sides of it, keeping my eyes closed from the embarrassment, ashamed I'd made such a scene, and finally, we were back in the suite. Mac got rid of the hotel people and came back into the bedroom. Tenderly, he undressed me and tucked me in. I opened my eyes and looked at him.

"I'm sorry, Mac," I said weakly. "I shouldn't have had so much to drink."

"Well, you don't worry about that, baby. You just can't hold your liquor and that's one of the things I like about you. You're a real lady, darlin', and my queen. Now you just lay there and go to sleep. I'll stay right here with you."

Suddenly, I was exquisitely drowsy and felt myself slipping into the welcome tunnel of sleep, feeling safe and secure. As I drifted off, I heard Mac say, "Now if you just had them tits of Sheila's, you'd be plumb perfect."

But whether I actually heard it or merely dreamed it, I couldn't say for sure.

Our relationship changed after that. It was a subtle thing, nothing overt, nothing specific I could put my finger on, except Mac had changed his attitude toward me, and I, relishing the power of having made a stand and winning—even if by lying—felt more secure and even more cool toward him than before. He chalked it up to my supposed pregnancy, and the cooler I became, the more tenderly and warmly he treated me.

We'd arrived back at the Albuquerque airport the next evening, and when he saw Marilee, who'd driven down to pick us up in Mac's Lincoln, he informed her smugly I was pregnant. Marilee looked at me, surprised, but at my expression, she only made some polite comment and changed the subject. Mac hovered over me constantly, and therefore, it was the next morning before we could talk.

"I thought you didn't want to tell him you were pregnant. What happened?"

"Marilee, I didn't know what else to do."

I told her about Sheila and Mac's determination that the three of us would "party," and when I finished, she blew out her breath and patted my arm, which was lying on the table beside my coffee cup.

"That's our Mac."

"Was he like that when you were married to him?"

"Not as bad. I could usually divert him, and when I couldn't, I would just leave for a few days. It would piss him off something terrible, but then, I had quite a bit of power in the marriage and he wouldn't push it. It was always a favorite dream of his, though."

"And it probably helped that you aren't flat chested."

"Well, darlin', I wouldn't go so far as to say you're flat chested."

At that bald lie, I looked at her with a good measure of scorn on my face and changed the subject.

"Do you think Karl has the will changed yet?"

"I hope so. I'm tired of having to put up with the old fool. He's worse about legs than Mac is about boobs. I've got bruises all up and down my thighs from having dinner and lunch with him."

"Why do we put up with things like that?"

"Because, darlin', we got to do what we can, however we can."

"Well, I, for one, am sick and tired of all the game-playing."

She looked at me with some surprise. "How else are we going to get anything done?"

I had no answer for that. We'd both been raised in the South, and even though we were from different sides of the railroad tracks, we'd been taught exactly the same rules to the game of life.

I was crossing the plaza the next day, wading through tourists and the kids playing hackysack, and had just made it to the other side when a cream-colored Porsche swooped to a stop at the curb next to me, blocking traffic. There was no way I could escape, and so I made myself smile when Richard's face was revealed by the lowering window.

"Hello, Richard."

"I understand congratulations are in order."

"What?"

"The word is that you're expecting. Congratulations."

I was astonished. Even given the small-town grapevine system that existed in Santa Fe, overnight spreading of such news was phenomenal. Mac must have rented a mobile public address system, I told myself.

"Where did you hear that?" I asked.

The natives waited patiently behind him, accustomed to people's stopping in the middle of a street or highway to chat, the rest of the traffic notwithstanding, but the tourists were beginning to honk.

"Get in," he said.

"What?"

"Get in the car. I can't sit here all day and I want to talk to you."

"I don't think—"

"Get in this car!"

He was obviously furious with me and I couldn't think of anything I wanted to do less than get in a car with a man who was mad at me. The tourists were beginning the long horn-blowing that signals breeding arguments. The foot patrolman on the plaza began to saunter in our direction. People were beginning to stare. I got in the Porsche, ever mindful of not making a public scene.

He slammed the car in gear and drove away from the plaza, past the Pepto-Bismol building, called that because of its color, and skidded into a turn onto Artist's Road. I thought he was taking me home, but at the entrance to Ft. Marcy Park, he turned in and parked the car, killing the engine. He sat behind the wheel staring out the windshield at the city spread below us. I was suddenly very aware of the scent of his after-shave, and the memories it evoked made my breasts begin to tingle and then to sting.

Finally, unable to tolerate the charged silence any longer, I said, "I don't know what you have to be angry about. Weren't you the one who wanted us to date other people?"

He turned to me, and at the anger in his eyes, I involuntarily leaned back against the window, putting as much distance between us as possible.

"Sure. I said that but I didn't mean you should go out and *marry* somebody. Or get pregnant with his kid."

"Richard—"

"It sure as hell didn't take you very long, did it?"

Suddenly, I remembered the power of standing up to Mac in the hotel suite. I felt my face grow hot and I stared at Richard with a good deal of my own righteous anger.

"Listen, Richard, you were the one who wanted out. If the results of your commitment-phobia weren't what you ordered, then blame yourself, not me!"

I was prepared for hot words from him in retaliation, or maybe even physical violence, but what he did was to grab my shoulders and pull me against him, kissing my mouth with the kind of kiss that only he could do. The charged atmosphere in the car suddenly exploded, going through my body like a huge lightning bolt. Frightened at the intensity of it, and at my response to him, I jerked backward, out of his hands, and sat in the seat, staring at him.

"Stop it," I whispered.

"You liar," he said. "You craven little liar."

"Stop it."

"You're lying to me and to your husband, and if you think you're not, you're lying to yourself."

"Stop it."

"The problem is, Karen, we don't get anything for free in this world and that's what you're trying to do."

I thought of all the misery I'd been through since my marriage to Mac, the conniving, the manipulations, the sweating Marilee and I had done, the energy we'd expended to make things work the way we wanted them to. Instead of making me angry, however, his misunderstanding only made me sad and I stared out the window, not seeing the beautiful city below us nor the wide sweep of the desert plains that extended almost to Albuquerque, sixty miles away.

"You don't know what you're talking about," I said. "You have no idea what's going on."

"Then tell me," he said urgently, taking my hand. "I want to understand. I want to know why you're doing this. You didn't have to. If you wanted to get married, I . . ."

"You what?" I asked when he hesitated, looking at him again. "You didn't want to date me anymore, much less get married. You wanted to screw me and then, when I got boring, find someone else, another one to add to the list of your disposable lovers. I feel sorry for you, Richard. You sit there and sneer at me but it's you who's flawed. I'm just a liar. You're a cheat. You cheated me, and worse, you've cheated yourself. What we had was something better than . . . Well, what the hell. What does it matter anyway? It's over. I just feel sorry for you. Now take me back to the plaza."

"Karen, come home with me."

I was tempted. God knows, the memories alone were enough to tempt me, not to speak of the multitude of miseries that being Mrs. Mac Carpenter entailed. But I'd signed the prenuptial agreement and I knew, if Mac caught us, I'd be out faster than lightning, back to what I'd been before, broke, poor, unable to make my life work in any kind of decent fashion, and I knew that I couldn't count on Richard to back me up. He'd already demonstrated that.

"I may be a liar but I'm not a cheat, Richard. I made a bargain and I'll stick with it."

"Karen, I . . ."

Suddenly, I'd had all I could take of the argument, his after-shave, the bittersweet sadness being near him caused me. I got out of the car, flagged down the Chile Line, and rode it back down to the plaza, trying not to cry in front of the trolleyful of tourists.

I collected my car from the parking lot, and forgetting completely that I was to drop in on the girls in the Shop, I drove up into the mountains toward the Ski Basin, weaving in and out of the forested curves easily in the powerful car, my mind fixed on the misery that followed me like a swarm of deerflies, stinging, hurting, making my eyes tear up and my throat ache.

Finally, unable to see at all, I pulled over, stopping at a wide spot in the road, and leaning my forehead against my hands on the steering wheel, I cried. I wasn't sure whether I was crying because of despair at my situation or whether it was because I was angry at Richard's accusations and attempts to blame me for any unhappiness of his. He'd loaded me up with guilt over our aborted relationship and the one that I now shared with Mac, making them my fiasco, my doing entirely.

How dare he blame all this on me? I asked myself why I should allow his guilt to rest on my shoulders, but still, it was there, as if it had been made for me, fitting me like a well-worn harness would a plowhorse.

When I finished crying, I got out of the car and looked at the large expanse of land sweeping away from the foot of the mountains below me. Clouds were beginning to form far away to the south, moving toward me. It was the beginning of the "monsoon," that couple of months beginning around July Fourth in which every afternoon was cooled by a ten- or fifteen-minute rain shower, making Santa Fe a haven from air conditioners, even in the summertime.

I knew that, down on the plain far below, there were cars going to and fro with people in them who had problems, but from the height where I stood and looked down, I couldn't even see the cars, much less the people in them. The feeling of isolation grew until I felt I was alone in the world, alone with all the miseries that I'd hatched myself, doomed to carry them forever, until I died.

Richard was right about one thing, I thought. I felt dirty, unclean, and the lies I'd told Mac leaped up to confront me with their uglinesses. I'm certainly not acting like a lady, that's for sure, I told myself.

"'Oh, what a tangled web we weave,'" my mind taunted me, and angrily, I got back into my car and drove home.

When I drove into the driveway that circled the front of the house, Marilee opened the front door and met me on the walk.

"Where have you been all afternoon?" she asked me, displaying a good deal of excitement. "I've been hunting everywhere for you."

"What's the matter?" I asked listlessly. "Did Mac sign the new will?"

"It's all legally executed and filed. Mac took care of it this morning first thing, and I had what I fervently hope is the last lunch of his life with Karl today."

"So now we get the money?"

"You get most of it and there's even some for me. If there's any left over after you die, it goes to any children you might have, or failing that, to the University of Texas."

"Fat chance."

"Right." She grinned myopically up at me. "They'd just waste it, wouldn't they, darlin'?"

"So it's okay for Mac to die now?"

"Yep. He can blow his heart up or get run off the road or . . . What's the matter with you?"

"Nothing."

I didn't want to go into my little confrontation with Richard that afternoon. It was something I didn't even want to share with Marilee. I focused instead on the small, niggling feeling of guilt at our hopeful profiting at Mac's expense.

"I'm beginning to feel kind of sorry for Mac," I said.

"Mac? The same guy you just spent five days in Vegas with?"

When she put it that way, the guilt evaporated instantly, leaving not even a puff of remorse behind. Marilee could do that for me.

"Well," I said, brightening a little. "Let's go and celebrate. I could use a drink anyway."

"I got a roast in the oven. Let me put it on time-bake and then I'm ready. Let's take my car and leave it with José again."

I followed her into the kitchen, where she began to adjust the dials of the oven, peering intently at the tiny letters and numbers, her face inches away from them.

"Didn't you just get it back from him?" I asked her.

"Yeah, but he left something off or something. He said it won't take but a minute to fix and we can have a drink while he's doing it."

"Why doesn't he just ask you if he can drive your car? He must know you'd let him without any trouble."

"Ask a woman for something? You don't know José."

"You ought to sell that thing, Marilee. It's getting to the point where José drives it more than you do."

"What? And make Mac happy? No way! Neither of us could stand it. Come and look at this oven, darlin'. Is it on time-bake or what? I don't want to cremate another good roast again."

I obediently inspected the oven dials and said, "It's fine. I don't know why you don't wear your glasses."

"I lost them again. They're somewhere in the house. The problem with glasses is that, when you lose them, you can't see to find them. I'll run across them sooner or later."

"Well, in that case, I'm driving the Cadillac. Come on."

With a good deal of growing anticipation on my part, we grabbed our bags and went out to the Cadillac, parked in front of the garage. Finally, things were beginning to go right for us, I told myself. All the planning and waiting were finally beginning to pay off. There was a God in heaven, after all.

In the distance, thunder rumbled.

Getting in behind the wheel, I started the motor. It purred to life with the hungry sound that only a huge engine, well-tended, can make.

"Where's the thingy that makes the top go up?" I asked Marilee, who was settling herself in the passenger seat.

"José said that, whatever we did, we were definitely not to put the top up until he's had a chance to work on it. It might get stuck halfway up and then we couldn't drive it."

"God forbid we should not be able to drive this car on the streets of Santa Fe!" I grinned at her. "I don't care. I'm not tearing around with the top down and drying out my hair worse than it already is. Besides, it's going to rain—look at those clouds. Where's the switch?"

She showed me, and sure enough, when the top was halfway up, it shuddered, hesitated, and then stopped abruptly. The motor that winched it growled ominously. I took my finger off and turned to look at her.

"Oops," I said.

"Damn!" Marilee said, getting out of the car. "When I pull on it, you try it again. Rev the engine a little—see if that helps any."

I leaned on the toggle and gunned the engine.

"Wait! Wait!" she called. "It's hung up on something. Here's the problem."

I turned in the seat and looked back as Marilee tugged with both hands in the well where the top lay when it was down.

"What is it?"

"I don't know. It's . . . Shit!"

"What is it?" I asked again. I could see her face, but the half-raised top hid what she had in her hands. Her face showed shock.

"Karen, come and look at this."

I got out of the car, walked around it. She was holding a quart-size Baggie in her hands, filled about two-thirds of the way with a white powder. It looked like sugar.

"What is it?" I asked for the third time. Marilee looked at me, her eyes wide. I noticed almost absently that the skin around her mouth was white, making her orange lipstick stark against her face.

She shouldn't wear that color, I thought. It's too bright for her.

"Karen, do you know what this is?"

"Well, it looks like . . ."

Realization hit me like a blow and I sagged against the car, unmindful of any damage to my beige linen pants.

"Marilee, is that . . . Is that what I think it is?"

She nodded at me, for once speechless.

"What's it doing in there?"

"Karen," she whispered. "We're in big, big trouble."

"But that's not ours."

"No, it's not. But—"

"What's it doing in there?"

"Somebody put it there. Karen, we're in a world of hurt."

"I don't see why, it's not ours. Put it back. We'll call David and tell him about it. He'll take care of it."

"But—"

"Here. Rub it with my hanky and get all your fingerprints off it. Just where your hands are. We don't want to rub them all off."

She took my handkerchief and scrubbed at the surface of the Baggie and then, still using the handkerchief, gingerly deposited it back in the well, tucking it under the folded top. We put the top down and went back into the house to call David Finch.

Using her long, plastic index-fingernail, Marilee began punching in numbers, but halfway through, she put the phone down again and looked at me.

"We can't call Davy," she said slowly. "We can't let the police know about this."

"Are you crazy! Why not?"

"Because if we do, there'll be an investigation."

"So? That's the whole idea, Marilee."

"But remember what we told Davy? Can you *believe* it! And what if Mac *is* mixed up in it?"

"Then he . . . Oh, shit!"

"Exactly. The feds come in and confiscate everything. The house, our cars, the clothes on our back."

"Not *my* clothes!" I said fiercely.

"Well, they *will!* You know how they do it to people who are suspected of dealing cocaine and stuff. Even if Mac is completely innocent, it might not matter. They'll take everything and we . . ."

"And we might wind up in prison ourselves," I finished for her.

We stared at each other.

"Karen, we have to take care of this ourselves."

"What can we do, Marilee? We're just women. These people are dope dealers, criminals—killers—and we're just two women who don't have enough sense to come in out of the rain," I said, using a favorite phrase of Mac's.

"I don't care. We have to do something. We can't let them take our money away. We'll be broke," she pointed out, quite needlessly.

"And something else," I said morosely. "We have to make sure than nothing else happens to Mac, at least until this gets cleared up. If they kill him, or even hurt him, the cops will investigate again and who knows what they'll find."

"Crap!"

"Marilee, I wish I'd never let you talk me into this."

"Oh, shut up," she said.

5

$\mathcal{I}$ can't believe I actually went down to the police station and told Davy Finch I thought Mac was dealing drugs."

Marilee and I stared at each other over the kitchen table, a hefty drink in front of each of us.

"My God, what if they'd actually found something in his car?" I asked, horrified.

"Well, that's water behind the bridge."

"Under."

"What?"

"Under. Under the bridge."

"Whatever. What we have to do is make sure Mac doesn't get killed—at least until we're sure he isn't mixed up in this."

"And can prove it," I added. "Are you sure he's not?"

She frowned, concentrating. "It wouldn't be like Mac. He's always been pretty true-blue Republican, and if President Reagan says dope is bad, Mac wouldn't touch it. But then, he's always been pretty sneaky, too. But I don't think his sneakiness would extend to doing something that illegal. But then, I was wrong about his impotency. I could be wrong about this, too. But . . ."

I stopped her mental oscillation by patting her on the arm. "Don't worry over it now. We just have to find out if he is or isn't. That's the first thing to do."

"How?"

"I don't know. What if we just ask him?"

"Mac! Are you serious?"

"Well, it was a thought. It would be too much to hope it would be that simple," I added bitterly.

"He'd never tell us the truth, Karen. Or he would in such a way so we'd think he was lying. You know Mac."

"I said it was just a thought. Have you got any better idea?"

"Look, it seems to me the very first thing we need to do is take the car in to José. Then, when we get it back, we look to see if . . . it's . . . still there."

"You mean, José . . . ?"

Suddenly, I grabbed her arm. "Marilee! When I was there picking up my car after the wreck, he was talking to a couple of goons, big, rough-looking guys. I was prowling around in the garage, looking for a cloth to wipe off my car while I was waiting for them to finish and I got into the wrong room. There was a briefcase in there, a really nice one, and it was full of money. And, Marilee! There were some scales in it, too."

"Scales?"

"You know the kind they use in chem labs."

"I'm not real familiar with chem labs, Karen."

"Neither am I but I know what lab scales look like and those were."

"Well, hell. That's the story on José, is it? I hate that. He has all those kids and that sweet little wife who—"

"We don't know for sure, Marilee. It could be something totally innocent, you know."

"Wanna bet? Thousands of dollars and a set of scales to boot? Come on!" She suddenly peered at me, squinting. "Why didn't you mention this before?"

"I forgot about it," I said, as casually as possible. My guilt over my near theft was not something that I wanted to admit, not to myself and certainly not to Marilee.

"You forgot about a shitload of money and a set of scales in a briefcase you found in the back of a dirty, junky garage?"

"Yes." I stared at her defensively. "I did."

"Well, that's kinda hard to believe." She grinned suddenly. "What did you do, steal some of it?"

"No! I certainly did not steal any of it!" I looked away and then, in spite of myself, matched her grin. "I nearly did though. I came within an inch of it."

She laughed, patted my arm approvingly and then, serious again, said, "Well, let's find out for sure about José. Come on, let's take my car down and see if that stuff is still there when we get it back."

"Who would have thought José..." I let the sentence trail off, thinking about his friendly, gold-plated smile.

"He's always calling for me to bring it down there for him to work on, Karen. And I thought he was just joyriding around in it." Marilee continued as we got in the Cadillac. "He's probably been storing stuff in it for months. Or maybe even hauling dope all over the state in it!"

"The dope-mobile."

"Yeah. And what would have happened to me if I'd gotten caught with it? After all the times I've let him drive it, too! That really pisses me off."

I looked at her with some interest. I hadn't realized she could get angry about anything; she'd always been so laid-back I'd merely assumed she was incapable of anger. She looked no different from any other time that we'd talked, however, and I suddenly wondered how many other times she'd been angry and I hadn't realized it.

From somewhere in the back of my mind came the memory of our car accident all those months ago. She'd certainly been angry then; it hadn't lasted long, but at that time, she'd definitely been angry.

"Then," she added, "if it's still there, we need to start worrying."

"And we're not now?"

"I mean, really, really worrying!"

We drove the Cadillac down to José's garage carefully, so as to minimize the risk of being stopped and searched, our guilt and fear making us rabidly paranoid. Once there, however, Marilee smiled and chatted with José exactly as she'd always done before, and I had to admire her ability to throw herself into that role of a mindless, feckless airhead with such realism, given her true state of mind.

We left the car there, running down the street for a quick drink, and then, when we picked it up again, José said brightly, "I feexed the top for you, Miz Wallace. It was jost slipped off the cog a little."

"Oh, thank you, darlin'. And not a moment too soon, either. It looks like it's gonna rain any second. Can we put it up now?"

"Sure. No problem, man."

He watched, beaming, as the top slid smoothly up and we latched it over our heads.

"See," he called. "Good as new."

"Thanks."

Marilee waved her fingernails at him as I drove carefully out of the shop.

"And fuck you very much," she muttered, still smiling brightly.

"Do you think it's gone?" I whispered, my own smile flat on my face.

"What do *you* think?"

"Well, he sure wouldn't have let us raise the top if—"

"Right. So now we know about our friend José. Problem is, who put it in there?"

"Maybe he did it. Maybe it's a storage thing to him."

"Or Mac could have."

"Oh, shit," I said. "We're right back where we started!"

"Not exactly. We found out that José is definitely in on it. Tell you what. Drive me over to Mac's office. He's supposed to get his car out of the body shop today or tomorrow. We can say we were in town and thought we'd see if he needed a lift over there. And then one of us can ride home with him."

"To keep him safe?"

"Right. We can't let him be alone for a minute until we get this cleared up."

"If somebody tries to get him and one of us is in the car, do you think for a minute they're going to back off, just because we're in the car?"

It was sarcastically said, but she replied earnestly, "Well, I for one don't want to live if the feds take all our money away. Do you?"

"Marilee, I still think we ought to go to the police with this. It's too much for us to handle. Maybe we can be witnesses or something. Maybe they'll give us immunity."

"You're too smart to believe that, aren't you? You know how they are. Personally, I'd trust Gorbachev before I'd trust anyone in our federal government with a promise."

I had no answer for that; she was probably right. We drove over to Mac's office silently, each trying to think of something to do to clear Mac's name before the bottom fell out of everything.

The next morning, when I forced myself out of bed and staggered into the kitchen, I found that, not only was Mac already gone, which

I'd expected, but that Marilee was gone as well. I circled through the rooms, looking for her, but the house was empty. Sitting down at the breakfast table with a cup of coffee, I worried with an uncharacteristic alertness. Before I'd finished the cup and formulated any plans, however, I heard the roar of the Cadillac's engine, the scream of tortured brakes, the skittering sound of gravel, and finally, a car door slam. Marilee came though the back door, saw me sitting at the table, and smiled triumphantly.

"Well, he made it to work all right," she said, taking off her glasses and squinting at me. "I followed him."

"In the Cadillac?" I asked, aghast.

"Sure. Don't worry. I didn't get too close."

"Marilee, ten miles would have been too close. If you could see him, he could see you. That car isn't the apex of camouflage technology, you know."

"Give me credit for *some* sense. When he left, I told him I had to run down to the market and followed him into town. He knew I was back there, but it was all right."

Mollified, I addressed my coffee cup again, falling back gratefully into my aborted waking-up ritual. Marilee poured herself a cup and sat across the table from me.

"Look," she said. "Here's the deal. We know someone is stashing coke in my car and that José knows about it. We know Mac has been the target of attempted murder, not once, but twice. We know he tried to hire someone to do something for him and that someone was killed that very night, so we can assume it was to do something dangerous, right?"

She looked at me and I nodded stupidly, my hands wrapped around the coffee mug.

"Well, then," she said with a good deal of determination, "now we have to find out whether Mac is actually mixed up in this business or is just behaving like Mac would do if he thought someone was trying to kill him."

"What?"

"Never mind, honey." She patted my arm. "The question is, how?"

"How, what?"

"How do we find out if Mac is mixed up in this thing?"

"You're the Mac expert. You tell me."

We both stared out the breakfast room window, not seeing the

Cerrillos Hills, which floated in sporadic lumps above the shimmering desert to the south. Suddenly, we both looked at each other again.

"Let's check out his closet," she said.

"Right, and check out his desk in the den, too."

We went through everything in the house and garage where Mac might have hidden something, but at the end of the search, we'd found nothing that was unusual.

"Well," Marilee said, "an entire morning wasted. We're right back where we started."

"Not exactly. We know nothing's hidden here."

"There's that," she agreed. "Now what?"

"Well, we should probably check his office, too. How do we do that?"

"Do it when he's not there."

"I know that. But when?"

"Sometime between the time he goes to sleep and when he gets up the next morning."

I was horrified. "You mean, in the wee hours?"

"You don't have to. I can do it without you."

A sense of fairness made me remonstrate with her. "No, Marilee." I sighed. "I'll go with you."

"It might be better if you stayed here, honey. What if he wakes up and finds you gone?"

"Mac? You know better than that. Once he's asleep, he's out. All I have to do is wait until he's down for the night and we could have a parade with a brass band through the bedroom for all he'd know. I think we should do it together."

"Okay. Let's do it tonight and then check the house again in the morning."

"Search the house again tomorrow?"

"Sure. So if he is sneaking shit around, we won't miss it."

"This is getting out of hand, Marilee."

"No, it's not, Karen. All we're doing is searching your husband's office. What harm is that? What could happen?"

At two the next morning, Marilee and I got in my car and drove through the quiet streets of Santa Fe to Mac's office. The parking lot was bare, and on impulse, I veered away from the entrance and parked behind some bushes, halfway down the block.

"What are you doing?" Marilee asked.

I killed the lights and looked back at the parking lot in my rearview mirror.

"I don't want to park in the parking lot. It's all lit up and bare. My car would stand out like a boil there."

"Oh, right. So you're going to park someplace where it's dark so someone can come by and loot it while we're in there, digging through Mac's things. I think we ought to—"

I grabbed her arm, stopping her just before she opened the door and illuminated the car interior.

"Look! Someone's coming out of the door. Marilee! Put your glasses on! Who does that look like to you?"

She fumbled in her monstrous bag, found her glasses, but even before she put them on, I already knew.

"Ricky!"

"What's he doing there?" I asked stupidly.

"I don't know, but he's coming this way. Get down!"

Marilee slid onto the floor and I lay across the console. When we heard the Porsche pass us, we warily peered over the dashboard at the taillights fading down the street in front of us.

"Well!" Marilee said. A great deal of emotion was crammed into that single word.

"What was he doing there?" I asked again.

"Who knows? Maybe he wasn't at Mac's office at all. There are other offices in there. Maybe he was at one of them."

"At two in the morning? Marilee, I don't like this."

"Well, we aren't getting anything done sitting here. Let's go check it out. Did you remember to get his keys?"

We made a thorough, but hurried, search of Mac's offices, but at the end, we hadn't found anything that shouldn't have been there. Driving back home in the chilly darkness, we didn't speak, each worrying over Richard's unexpected presence in the dark hours of the night in the building where Mac had his offices.

As I slipped back into bed next to the viciously snoring Mac, I couldn't help but wonder again what I'd gotten myself into by listening to Marilee. Those kinds of thoughts were becoming a habit, but then, just as I was slipping off into sleep, came longing, the kind of longing I could keep pushed down during the daytime, but without conscious effort to keep it controlled on my part, would slip out of the shadowy corners of my mind and leap at me. I knew it for what it was, who had triggered it, and helplessly, I allowed it to settle over me while I fell asleep next to Mac.

"All right, so we know Mac didn't have anything last night at his office or this morning here at the house."

Marilee put the coffeepot back on the warming plate and sat across the table from me. It was early in the afternoon and we'd already turned the house upside down again, looking for something Mac might have hidden.

"I think it's pretty safe to say Mac isn't involved," she added.

"Well, maybe and maybe not. All we know, Marilee, is he didn't have anything last night or this morning. Or here yesterday morning. So what else do we know?"

She toyed with the handle of her cup, not looking at me. "We know Ricky is involved in this some way."

"We don't know that, Marilee! We only know we saw him coming out of Mac's office building at two . . ."

The argument sounded stupid even to me and I let my voice trail off uncertainly. Marilee patted my arm.

"Look, honey. It's a safe bet he was in Mac's office . . . or there because of Mac. There are only two other people in that building besides Mac, and unless Ricky is into the New Age crystal mail-order business or has something to do with the Women's Alternative Lifestyle Center of Santa Fe, it was Mac's office he was there for."

"Well, we don't know whether or not he was actually in there, Marilee. He might have been just . . ."

Again my voice trailed off.

"Well, he wasn't just waiting around for the trolley. For some reason, he's interested in checking out Mac's offices in the middle of the night. Now, why?"

"Maybe for the same reason we were."

"Because he thought Mac was dealing coke? I don't think so, Karen. That's too weird."

"It wasn't too weird for us to think so, Marilee."

"No, but then we found that stuff in my car, remember? Ricky couldn't have known about that." She looked up at me. "Could he?"

I stared back at her.

"And if he did," she continued slowly, "how did he know about it?"

I got up and refilled both our coffee mugs. It didn't take long; both were still almost full.

"How long has Richard been in business here, Marilee?"

"Ten or twelve years that I know of. Ever since I've been in Santa Fe."

I was more relieved than I cared to admit.

"Why?" she asked.

"So he's not some fly-by-night who's come in here and set up an office overnight to use as a cover."

"No! You don't think that Ricky . . ."

"Don't you?"

"Well, I admit it did cross my mind, but Karen, Ricky isn't a drug dealer. I'd bet my douche bag on it. He's not the type."

"What is the type? Tell me what a drug dealer looks like, acts like?"

"Well, he's probably someone from Latin America, rough looking, blubbery, with a Panama hat and a big cigar in his face, seedy, nasty, and brutal. Nothing like Ricky at all."

"And I always thought drug dealers were sophisticated, rode around in a chauffeured white Rolls Corniche, and flashed a lot of very big jewelry. So you see, almost anyone could be a big-time dope peddler."

"Well, this isn't getting us anywhere. What we have to do now is find out who José's boss is."

"How?"

"Do I have to do all the thinking?" she asked irritably. "I don't know how."

I was surprised. Marilee had not demonstrated irritation very often and certainly never at me. I started to give her one of Mother's stares, but she wasn't wearing her glasses and I knew the effect would be lost. Instead, I sighed and patted her arm.

"I haven't the foggiest idea, Marilee. Don't snap my head off. We ought to work together on this."

But even though we sat there for the better part of the afternoon, nothing came to us, and finally, we tabled it for the rest of the day.

Mac and I were alone that night—Marilee had a date. As before, I marveled at her ability to get dates in Santa Fe regularly when hundreds of single girls half her age were unable to do so. Not only could she count on being taken out at least once a week, but they were real dates, "r.d.'s" as she called them, dates in which the man picked the woman up, fed her a real meal, took her to something nice in the way of entertainment, brought her home when it was over— and paid for everything. R.d.'s in Santa Fe were rare, rarer than pitched roofs. True to form, her date for the evening was in his late thirties or early forties, very good-looking, and successful in his field, which was computers or something.

Mac was in a vile mood because of it.

"What the fuck does she see in those little jerks anyway?" he demanded.

I sipped my sherry, knowing by now the dialogue was rhetorical and he wasn't expecting any kind of an answer from me; in fact, he wouldn't welcome one at all.

"Just because they got stiff dicks—"

I tuned him out at that, knowing pretty much what was coming and how it would grate on what few sensitivities I had left after having been married to Mac Carpenter for four months. Instead, I focused on the problem Marilee and I had unearthed: the fact we'd seen Richard Sommerfrught coming out of Mac's office at two in the morning and the ramifications of that fact. I worried with it for a while and then traded it for my second-worst worry—my having told Mac I was pregnant and having to tell him that I'd lied in a few short months when he became suspicious because I wasn't showing, if I didn't before. How did women disguise their periods? I wondered. I couldn't think of any instance in history where a woman tried to hide her periods from her husband no matter how hard I tried. I got nowhere on either problem and suddenly, realized Mac had stopped talking.

Guiltily, I refocused my attention on him. He'd stopped at the glass wall of the living room and was staring pensively down at the lights of the city below. I knew by then that, when he did that, he was truly worried about something and was usually drunk. Quickly I tallied his booze input for the night and realized he was nowhere near drunk. That told me something about his state of mind.

"Honey," I ventured. "Is something wrong?"

"Nothing I cain't handle. You just take care of your shit and let me take care of the important things, okay?"

I set my drink down and stood up. Before I could leave the room, however, he'd bounded across it and taken me in his arms. I suffered the embrace, and then, when he released me, I allowed him to paw me and slurp my face with conciliatory kisses.

"Queen Karen. You're my baby, ain'tcha? You ain't mad at ole Mac, now are ya?"

Hastily I assured him I wasn't angry, knowing that when I convinced him of that fact, and only then, would he stop the painful kneading of my rear and leave me alone again.

"I'm just all upset tonight," he said. "I don't know what she's thinking of."

I picked up my ears at that. This was a new tone in his voice, genuine bewilderment, something foreign added to his usual display of outraged ire when Marilee left the house with another man.

"Who? Marilee?"

He walked back to the window. Casually, too casually, he asked, "How much time do you girls spend together? I mean, does she leave the house very much by herself?"

"No," I answered carefully, trying to catch on to what he was getting at. "She doesn't go out very much, and when she does, we're usually together."

"What about you?"

"Me?"

"Do you leave the house and go places by yourself?"

It dawned on me that he was getting at something specific, but lacking Marilee's insights into his mental workings, I had no idea what it could be. With his back turned away from me, I couldn't tell what expression was on his face, what emotion I should play to.

"Sure," I said. "Occasionally. But most of the time I'm with Marilee. Why?"

He was silent for a few long seconds and then turned to look at me.

"It ain't no problem for you, her bein' here and all?"

"Why, no. Marilee and I get along fine. Well," I amended, not wanting to make it sound as if we conspired against him, "the house is pretty big and we don't see much of each other."

"You're stayin' in bed and takin' care of yourself, ain'tcha? I wouldn't want nothin' to happen to you now."

I assured him I was taking care of myself, I was fine, and tried to lead the conversation back to whatever he'd been fishing for, but the perverse creature refused to be led and the effort was wasted.

The next day passed uneventfully. Marilee and I spent a great deal of effort trying to decide what course of action we should take, how we might find out just exactly who, if anyone, was behind José's using her car as a coke stash, how we might prove Mac was involved, or better, how he was not. Nothing reasonable occurred to us, however, and it wasn't until the following morning, over coffee, that Marilee said, with some measure of triumph, "I know what we can do. I thought of it last night."

"What?"

As usual, I was not at my peak functionability, having only gotten up a few minutes before.

"I'm going to take my car back into José's this afternoon, tell him something minor is wrong with it, and then we'll see."

"See what?"

Even in my befogged state of mind, her plan made no sense to me. Either we would or we wouldn't find another Baggie full of coke in her car when we got it home, and what would that prove? We already knew of José's involvement.

"We'll just take care of it then."

"Take care of it?"

"We'll just take it out of the car, and when José can't find it, something will happen."

"Well, sure, I guess so! He'll come hunting for it with a big gun or something!"

"Maybe, and maybe not. Maybe someone else will get upset if it's gone and tip their hand to us. Then we'll know."

"Marilee, that's crazy! We're not talking about a catfight at the

Laundromat or something, you know. We're talking about people who deal drugs for a living and whose sideline is killing people. Remember that ex-con Mac tried to hire?"

"Sure, I remember."

"Listen, Marilee. We're going to the police. We've fooled around with this long enough."

"Who are we going to tell, Karen? We sure can't go to the feds, and we can't go to the cops because they'll go to the feds. It's my car they're stashing their junk in. Mine, Karen! You know what that makes me?"

"I know what it makes you if you don't report it! Listen, Marilee, we're just two women. People—drug investigators, undercover people, even judges, Marilee!—get killed by these people all the time and you want us to just go out and find out who's stashing dope in your car. I'm telling you, we've gone far enough. I say we take our chances with the feds."

Marilee patted my arm. "Now, listen, Karen. Let's just stop and think about this. You're going off half-cocked again. You know how you are, honey. Now let's think about this thing calmly, look at everything and make a rational decision. There's no sense in getting all excited—"

"Oh, right! There's really nothing to get excited about, sure! We find cocaine in your car, Mac may or may not be involved in heavy-duty drug traffic, the feds may or may not take all our assets because of it, and—"

"Exactly! The feds may take all our assets and we'll wind up being bag ladies, without even enough spending money to buy these Dragon Lady nails." She wiggled her artificial nails at me. "You remember what it's like being broke? You remember what dealing with the IRS was like? They're kittens compared with the drug enforcement people, Karen. Do you seriously want to go through that again?"

I hesitated. She had me there, and realizing my hesitation and the cause, she patted my arm again, pressing her point.

"Now, listen. What's it going to hurt if we just take the dope out of the car and see what happens. Then, if things get too crazy, then we call Davy and let them take care of it."

It took her several more minutes of earnest talk, but in the end, I agreed—as I had known all along that I would.

"All right, Marilee. But just that far. We take the coke out of the car, and then, if things get out of hand, and they will, we call the police and tell them everything. Agreed?"

"Sure."

"I mean it, Marilee!"

"Sure, darlin'. You know I don't lie to a girlfriend."

"Yeah, right," I said sourly.

We took Marilee's car into José's shop that afternoon, and I waited in my car while Marilee, with a great deal of creativity, described to José the nonexistent noises that were supposed to have precipitated her concern about the Cadillac. I watched as he nodded soberly, flashed his gold teeth at her, patted the Caddy's hood benevolently, and took the keys from her hand. She smiled brightly at him and walking back to my car, turned and waved at him, but when she'd slid into the front seat with me, she muttered, "There. All we have to do is wait until he's finished with it and calls us."

"This is stupid, Marilee."

"You're probably right, honey, but it's too late now."

Early the next afternoon, I took her back down to the garage to pick it up, and when we'd gotten it back home, I watched as she lowered and raised the ragtop. It went down and up again smoothly, without effort. Marilee shut off the engine and dug around in the well where the top was stored when it was down.

"Oh, fuzzy!" she said, pulling her hands out again and staring intently at the end of a finger.

"What is it?"

"I popped one of these nails off. Now I've got to dig until I find it and—"

"Is there anything else there?" I asked impatiently.

She felt around again and pulled out the errant fingernail, which she tucked into the pocket of her jeans.

"No, not a thing," she said.

I was more relieved than I cared to admit, even to myself.

"Well, that's that," I said. "Now, maybe you'll . . . What are you doing?"

She'd opened the trunk and was going through it, carefully, feeling under the matting and around the spare tire.

"It could be hidden somewhere else. He doesn't have to hide it the same place each time. Here, help me with this tire."

We went through the car thoroughly, examining any place that might hide something, and eventually, behind the rear seat, we found it. As before, it was a quart-size Baggie partially filled with a white powder.

We stared at it for some seconds, Marilee with a healthy show of triumph, and me, ruefully.

"Well, well, well," she said, grinning up at me. I stared at her, suddenly realizing something I should have caught on to long before.

"You're actually enjoying this, aren't you?" I asked, somewhat stunned.

"Honey, this is better than sitting in the Pink, hustling cookie bandits. Now, where can we hide this stuff?"

"This is just a game to you, isn't it? Do you realize we could die? Do you have any concept at all of your own mortality?"

"We're not going to die. We're just stupid little housewives, Karen. Who's going to think we have enough sense even to find this in the first place, much less figure out what's going on here? As long as we don't do anything flat out, no one's going to think we're involved. Right?"

"I don't know, Marilee. That's pretty shaky reasoning—"

"Don't worry about it. We're already into it up to our armpits anyway. Now, where can we hide this?"

"It has to be someplace no one would think to look, Marilee. If we get caught by the feds with it—and those guys will look everywhere, you know—we'll die in prison of old age."

"Well, cheer up. Maybe it'll be the other bad guys who find it and we just die."

"This isn't funny, Marilee."

"Probably not, but fut the whuck, darlin', what is?" She suddenly peered at me brightly and said, "I know!"

"What?"

"Where we can hide this and no one will ever find it."

"Where?"

She turned and marched into the house, carrying the Baggie. I followed her, curious, and in the powder room, she flipped up the ring on the commode and before I could stop her, carefully dumped the contents of the Baggie into the water and flushed it. She rinsed the Baggie two or three times in the sink, and taking it into the kitchen, she opened a can of tomatoes and dumped them into it. She rinsed them around and dumped most of the tomatoes into the disposal, put the Baggie in the trash compactor, and dumped the coffee grounds from that morning's coffee on top of it.

"There," she said, rinsing the sink and running the disposal. "All we have to do now is take some damp toilet paper and go over every inch of the powder room, just to make sure I didn't drop anything."

"Consuela comes in this afternoon. She'll get it when she cleans."

"No, we don't want to take a chance of any of that stuff in the house. If the feds come in with a search warrant and dogs, I don't want there to be even a grain of it here for them to sniff out."

"You realize you've just destroyed several thousands of dollars' worth of coke, don't you? Maybe hundreds of thousands. Maybe even millions! That's going to make someone very, very upset."

"That's what we want, darlin'," she said, grinning at me. "Now, we'll just wait and see what happens."

Shaking my head, I said, "You're crazy, you know. You really are crazy! All that hair color has oozed into your brain over the years and rusted it."

She laughed. "Better to be rusted out than bleached white."

"Screw you."

"I'd settle for that. Now let's go put my seat back in place before Consuela gets here."

We didn't hear from José for a couple of days, and then, just as we were about to pull out our hair, both red and ash blond, he called and casually offered to tighten up the brakes on the Cadillac.

"Do they need tightening, darlin'?" Marilee asked innocently, and looking at me, added after a pause, "Well, can it wait until I get back from Albuquerque tomorrow afternoon? I thought I'd run down there and spend the day shopping. You know how I am."

I could have kicked her but she said, "Well, okay, José. You're probably right. What would I do without you, darlin', to take care of my car?"

I drove the Cadillac down to the shop and we stood around, chattering, until José told us it would be a few minutes before he could get to it and suggested we leave it with him for an hour or so.

"Oh, that'll be fine, darlin'," Marilee said. "Mrs. Carpenter and I'll just run and get us a late lunch."

I smiled at him with what I hoped was my usual cool smile, and Marilee and I trundled down the street toward the plaza. When we were seated at Pasqual's, she said to me, "You did fine, Karen. Now, we'll just see how things are when we go back. Be real careful not to act any different than you usually do. He's liable to be pretty upset when he can't find . . . you know."

"I think that's a pretty safe thing to say. I hope he doesn't pull a gun on us or something. Maybe we should take someone back with us."

"You're overreacting now. He's not the big boss. He won't do anything but what he's told to do, and nobody with any sense would shoot us in broad daylight on Cerrillos Road."

"What if he kidnaps us? He could make us go with him to talk to whoever—"

"No, I don't think so. He'll be too freaked out to think straight right away, and besides, he wouldn't think we had enough sense to find it behind the seat of the car. He won't want us to know anything, anyway. No, it'll be okay for us to pick it up. Just make sure you act the way you always do around him. And let me do all the talking."

"Fine with me," I said with sincere emphasis.

José was not smiling when we went back for the car. There was not the usual gold flash as he talked to Marilee, nor was there any of the kidding that he usually did. Marilee pretended not to notice, and as I usually did, I stood off to one side and examined the Sangres in the distance while she talked to him.

"You been lettin' anybody drive your car, Miz Wallace?"

"Why no, José. It's just been sitting in front of the house like it usually does. Why?"

"The . . . the brakes're just about to go out on you. Somebody's been ridin' 'em real hard, man. You take it anywhere?"

"No, José. If I go anywhere, I usually go with Mrs. Carpenter, here."

Thus cued, I cut my eyes around to him, a distant expression on my face. I was anxious to see how he was taking what she was telling him, but true to Marilee's warning, I hadn't given him any more attention than I usually did during one of their conversations. I needn't have bothered; he wasn't paying any attention to me. He was tight-lipped and there was a slightly wild look in his eyes, which he'd focused on Marilee's face.

"You didn't let nobody drive your car, man?"

"José," she said with just the right amount of anxiety, "I just can't afford to have them fixed right now. Isn't there something you can do and maybe, put it on Mr. Carpenter's bill somehow?"

It was her usual remedy for taking care of what ailed the Cadillac and her acting was flawless. I began my minute examination of the mountains again.

"Don' *worry* about it, man." Every drop of the sweat on his forehead was in José's voice. "Are you sure you didn' have your car somewhere that somebody could get into it? To drive it, I mean?"

"No, José. It's just been parked in the driveway like it usually is. Do you think you could fix it and bill Mr. Carpenter again? Like we did last time?"

"Yeah, yeah, man. Don' worry about it! Have you been home most of the time?"

"Oh, God, darlin'." She laughed, obviously relieved that the Cadillac would be fixed at no cost to her. "You know how I am. I'm gone every minute of the day I can be gone. Mrs. Carpenter and I are hardly ever at home."

Thanks for taking me off the hook, I thought, and began walking toward the Cadillac, suggesting a termination to the conversation as I usually did. Marilee chatted a few more minutes and then joined me in the front seat.

"Well," she whispered, smiling and waving at him, "now we'll see."

"Yeah, right. I wish we hadn't done this, Marilee."

"Well, at least we've done something. We're not just waiting around for something else to happen to us. This'll sure force the rats out into the open, betcher boots."

During dinner that night, Mac received a telephone call and without any explanation whatsoever to us, left the house, got in his car, and drove away. Marilee and I sat at the table and stared at each other for a few moments, and then, echoing my thoughts, she said, "I wonder what that was all about?"

I could only shrug, and we spent the next couple of hours pacing around the living room, miserable with anxiety until we heard Mac's car again. Throwing ourselves into chairs, we snatched up something to read and pretended casual interest when he came back into the room.

"Hello, honey," I said. "Everything all right?"

"Sure. I forgot something at the office."

It was then I noticed that the left side of his face, which he was trying to keep away from us, was red and slightly swollen.

"Oh, Mac. Your face! Are you—"

"Don't worry about it!"

He stood at the bar, pouring himself a drink. I looked over at Marilee, but she was watching him intently. It was then I heard the rattle of the bottle against the glass and realized his hand was shaking. Something had upset Mac very much.

"Mac . . ."

"You girls go on to bed. I'm gonna have a little drink or two before I turn in."

Thus dismissed, Marilee and I obediently got up and left the room. In the hall, I paused to raise my eyebrows at her, but she briefly shook her head, warning me, before she turned to go on down the hall toward her own room.

It was hours before Mac came to bed, and when he did, he was almost too drunk to walk.

I awoke earlier than usual, realizing something was wrong, that I was waking to that same sense of constant dread I'd lived with for three years as an incompetent single woman—a sense of impending doom that was uncontrollable, unmanageable, at least by me. I staggered into the kitchen, accepted a cup of coffee from Marilee, and sat at the table. Before I'd even taken the first sip, however, Marilee was speaking urgently to me, and staring up at her, I concentrated fiercely, trying to make my brain function, to understand what she was saying to me.

"Marilee, wait until I've had some coffee," I begged.

"No, this can't wait. Look!"

She shoved the morning edition of The New Mexican at me, tapping at a news story with one of her plastic fingernails. I picked up the paper and worked my eyelids, trying to focus my eyes on the printing, pushed out of my usual stupidity by the urgency in her voice.

When I'd read it, I said, "This is just about some guy who died last night, Marilee. What . . ."

I paused, allowing the niggling at the back of my brain to grow, form itself into understanding.

"You don't think José . . . ?" I began, my eyes wide with the shock of it. I couldn't finish the question; it was simply too awful to contemplate.

Marilee's face was pale, shocky itself. I was surprised to see she had freckles, extremely faint ones, which now seemed stark against the skin of her face.

"I called down at the shop," she said, "and he hasn't come in yet. No one's answering the phone and it's already ten. I haven't got the guts to call his house. You do it!"

"Maybe we ought to wait."

"No! I have to know, Karen! Just call and ask for José Gonzales. Here's the number."

Dutifully, I got up, went to the wall phone, punched out the number, and was intensely relieved when a man's voice answered the phone.

"José?" I asked.

"Who's calling please?"

I realized then something was wrong; it was an Anglo voice that had asked the question and had asked it crisply, with a good deal of authority. I almost answered out of habit, but then, recognizing the voice, I pushed down the cutoff button, abruptly terminating the call. I replaced the phone in the cradle and looked at Marilee.

"Well?"

"David Finch answered the phone, Marilee."

"Oh, shit! Oh, shit!"

"Yes, indeed, shit! Marilee, why would David Finch be at José's house?"

It was pretty much a useless question; we both were fairly sure why.

I snatched up the folded newspaper and reread the article aloud. It was short, a back-page piece of news that merely stated a Hispanic male in his middle or late thirties had been found on the side of the highway to Galisteo, shot once in the head, execution style. He'd been killed sometime between seven and ten the previous evening. Identification of the body was pending.

"What do we do now?" she asked me.

"You're the one with all the answers! You tell me!"

She was silent for a few seconds, and finally I asked, "Mac . . . ?"

I couldn't finish the question. With no grace whatsoever, I sat back down in my chair. My legs were suddenly too weak to hold me up. Marilee patted my arm, a gesture made from habit rather than from any particular concern for me. Her mind was focused elsewhere.

"He was awake when I got up, but then, that's not real unusual," she said. "He left for the office at the regular time."

"Did he read this?" I held out the newspaper to her.

"I don't know. Probably. He reads every inch of it as a rule. He probably did. Do you think . . . ?"

"Well, he was gone from the house last night for a couple of hours. He would have had time to . . ."

When I still hesitated over the verbalization of the thought, Marilee got up and refilled our coffee cups. Sitting back down at the table, she said, "Karen, this has gone too far. We have to tell the police what we know."

"We can't *do* that now! You know we can't! Not now! They'll think Mac did it and God only knows what will happen then. We got ourselves into this mess and we have to work it out ourselves, Marilee. And we have to do it before the police catch on to Mac."

"You're acting like you think Mac killed José."

"Don't you?"

"Well, it could have been perfectly innocent, his leaving the house like that."

"Oh, sure, Marilee. He gets a call in the middle of dinner, leaves the house immediately without bothering to finish—very un-Mac-like, by the way—and comes back home a couple of hours later with a swollen face. What did his face look like this morning?"

"He's got a black eye."

"So someone hit him."

"We don't know that!"

"Marilee, I think it's pretty safe to say he didn't get it from some girl, and he wasn't drunk enough to have had an accident. Someone probably hit him. Maybe José put up a fight. Was he roughed up any?"

"The paper didn't say."

"So, the big question is, is Mac capable of murder?"

She screwed up her face with concentration.

"I don't know, Karen. He's done some pretty rough things. He's pretty ruthless. You know he started out as a roughneck on a drilling rig. You know what those guys are like."

I didn't but I could imagine.

"But could he *kill* someone, Marilee? Execute someone?"

"I don't know. I just don't know, Karen."

"Well, for the sake of the argument, let's say he can. And did. Then, we have to understand he's into something bad enough he would kill over it. If he thought José had lost or kept that Baggie of stuff, and he killed him, then you know where that puts us? If he gets caught, the drug enforcement guys will say everything we have was bought with drug proceeds and confiscate it all."

"Karen, what if it wasn't Mac? What if it was someone else?"

"Do you really believe it was someone else? Really?"

"It could have been!"

"Sure."

"Well, it could have been. And anyway, there's something else you haven't realized. Maybe Mac did kill José, or had him killed, but we're just as guilty, Karen. We're the ones who took that Baggie of coke. You saw what José was like yesterday afternoon when we picked up the car. It was us who got him in this situation. We were just playing a game and it was real-time stuff for him."

I didn't say anything. She was right.

"So Mac might have actually pulled the trigger but we really murdered José, Karen."

"He was dealing coke, Marilee. Think of all the people he's probably killed with that stuff."

"That's his problem. That doesn't excuse what we did."

I toyed with the handle of my coffee cup. Marilee fiddled with hers.

"I keep thinking of María and all those kids," she finally said.

"Who?"

"His wife."

"I don't suppose he had a whole lot of insurance."

"Probably not. And even if he did, I don't guess the insurance companies are all that keen on paying off drug dealers' families when they're killed."

"Same thing with murderers' policies," I pointed out.

"I don't think Mac did it," she said, her jaw set.

"Why are you being so stubborn! You said yourself he's pretty ruthless!"

"I don't care. I just don't think he did it."

I pointed out what was obvious to me, had been for some time. "You still love him, don't you? You really care about him, what happens to him?"

"Well, shit, Karen. Damn it! We were married for all those years. I've been with that asshole for thirty years all told, and in thirty years, you can't help but have some feeling for the fucker. Sure, I care about him, but even if I didn't, I just don't believe he did it."

"Why not?"

"Because, if he did and he gets caught, and he will if he did, we lose it all anyway. We have to believe he's innocent. It's the only thing we have."

We drove down to José's shop early that afternoon, ostensibly to find out when José could repair Marilee's brakes, but really to gather any information we could. The place was closed and there was a uniformed policeman guarding it. Marilee chatted familiarly with him, calling him by his first name, Carlos, expressing surprise that the garage was closed, shock when Carlos told her José had been killed, and all the while, she pumped him adroitly for details. I, conforming to my usual custom, pretended great disinterest in the whole conversation. Over lunch, we discussed the few things she'd found out.

"So José was beaten up first," I said.

"Well, that would make sense. They would be trying to find out whether or not he'd ripped off the stuff himself."

"Maybe he got in a lucky blow and Mac got a shiner."

"Don't count on it. I'm sure he was pretty well held down."

"What do you think about the fact he had a record?"

"José didn't seem that kind," she said slowly.

"Are you surprised? Really?"

"Well, sure. He seemed pretty down-to-earth and responsible. He ran that garage. Who would have thought he was an ex-con. Wonder what other secrets he had."

"Apparently quite a few. Does Mac own a three fifty . . . whatever?"

"A .357 magnum. Like champagne. And three five seven are the first numbers of my social security number. That's how I remembered it when Carlos told me that's what José'd been shot with."

I wasn't surprised anymore at the mental capacities coming from that seemly empty head, having had them demonstrated to me so many times. Now, I merely noted it, congratulated her briefly but sincerely, and asked again, "Does he have one?"

"I don't know. He's got several guns, but I wouldn't know a .357 magnum if it fell on me."

"How do we find out? We can't ask him. Or anyone else for that matter."

"We could find out what one looks like and then look at his."

"The library!"

"What?"

"We can go to the library and do some research. There's bound to be a book with pictures of guns in it there."

"Where is it?"

"Over by the Museum Shop where I used to work."

"We can do it after lunch. There's no way I'm leaving this plate of pasta for . . . Karen, look!"

I looked up from my plate, saw she was staring out the window of the restaurant, and looked that way, just in time to see Richard passing. I felt the familiar lurch of my stomach I always felt when I saw him unexpectedly, and then felt it drop to my feet as I saw the condition of his face. Even from the distance of several feet it was obvious to me his mouth was swollen, and there was fresh adhesive tape across the bridge of his nose, stark against his tan. I half-rose to my feet, clutching my napkin.

"Oh, Marilee. Look at his face! He's been hurt. Someone . . . Oh, shit!"

I sat back down and stared at her. I knew without asking what she was thinking; it was the same thought that was going through my mind—that it was past coincidence that Mac and Richard would suffer facial injuries during the same time. The adhesive tape on Richard's nose had been brand-new, the cut on his lip was recently done. The injury couldn't have been very old, perhaps done the night before, certainly no earlier.

Had it been done the same time as Mac's? And if so, had they been together? Santa Fe was too small a town for there to have been two unrelated fights on the same weeknight, statistically speaking.

There was only one conclusion to be made. It would seem, whatever Mac was into, Richard might well be involved in, too.

The understanding that Richard might well be mixed up in whatever mess Mac had gotten himself into, which probably wasn't anything very good, was appalling to me, surprisingly so, but I knew any speculation on it would have been, in any case, fairly useless. I was, moreover, unable to eat any more of the lunch before me, and Marilee, seeing I had lost my appetite, suggested we leave it and go on to the library. It made a welcome diversion, and I was able to push my worry over Richard to the back of my mind while Marilee and I hunted up a picture book on guns. We found one, looked up a .357 magnum, and were surprised to see that a .357 could be either a revolver or an automatic, that the term was merely a designation of bullet size. We photocopied the picture of them both and left. Once back at the house, we looked through Mac's accumulation of handguns, comparing each of them with our pictures, and were finally able to conclude that, if he did, indeed, possess one, it was not in that collection.

"Where else would he have a gun?" I asked. Even though I had been his lawful wife for four months, it was still easy to defer to Marilee's knowledge of Mac.

"Well, there might be one in his car. Or at the office. Or in his briefcase. You know . . ."

Her voice trailed off, and holding the paper close to her face, she stared at the photocopy of one of the pictures pensively.

"What's the matter, Marilee?"

"I could swear I've seen a gun like this one before. But where?"

"Maybe Mac—"

"No, I don't think it was Mac's, but I tell you, I've seen this kind of gun before. Someone I know has one like it."

"Who?"

"Damn it! I can't remember. I just hate it when something sticks to the edge of my mind like this! It must be the onset of old-timer's disease or something; I didn't use to be like this."

"More likely it's thirty years of Mac telling you you're stupid that's done it. You hear something like that often enough and you start believing it yourself, and when you start believing it, then you manifest it and—"

"Well, it'll come to me sooner or later." She grinned at me. "In the meantime, let's go look in the garage for that gun."

A thorough search of the garage turned up nothing, and finally, back in the living room with a glass of wine in hand, I said, "This really doesn't mean anything, Marilee. If we don't find the gun, it just means there isn't one now. He might have tossed it after . . . He would be a fool to keep something like that around if he used it for . . . like we think he did. It would really be incriminating and stupid. Whatever you say about Mac, you can't call him stupid. He may have already gotten rid of it."

"Well, if we do find one like that, then we know for certain he—"

"What? Might have done it? Without any ballistics tests, we wouldn't know if it was the murder weapon or not. It seems to me this is pretty much a wasted effort."

"Maybe so. But it doesn't hurt to look for it, and besides, I can't think of anything else to do. Can you?"

I didn't answer and instead, sipped my wine. Finally, she asked, "What do you think about Ricky?"

She had known I was thinking about him, but having known her for these several months, I was no longer surprised at her perceptiveness, even recognizing the fact that she was almost blind.

"I don't know what to think, Marilee. He'd obviously been in a fight."

"It's really funny both he and Mac got their faces busted in the same night, isn't it?"

I didn't answer, and finally, she said, "You see? It's not so easy believing someone you care about might be guilty of something awful."

I stood up and began pacing the floor. It was a habit that I'd picked up from Mac, and when I realized what I was doing, I sat back down again. Irritably, I said, "Well, what could he have gotten into with Mac? It's pretty safe to say there's no love lost between them. Maybe they just ran into each other on the street and duked it out. Neither one of them is shy about his feelings for the other. Both of them are pretty volatile."

"Karen, Mac gets a telephone call in the middle of dinner, gets up and leaves, is gone two hours, and then comes home with the makings of a black eye. That tells us that the encounter wasn't mere chance.

Then, the next day, Ricky is sporting a split lip and a sore nose. That tells us they were together somewhere and the encounter wasn't altogether friendly, right?"

She peered at me and I nodded, curtly.

"Neither one of them are into fighting over nothing. So then," she continued, "we have to assume that someone, probably Ricky, called Mac—"

"Why, 'probably Ricky'? It could have been anyone! We have absolutely no proof that it was Richard who called here last night."

"All right, all right! So it may not have been Ricky who called, but you can not tell me the two of them weren't into some kind of fracas last night together. I'm telling you that they were. But why?"

"I wish we knew for sure whether or not they'd hit each other. If we knew that, we—"

"Wait a minute! If they hit each other, their hands would show it."

"Their hands?"

"Sure. Their knuckles would be skinned or something. At least, Mac's would. The mouth and nose are pretty hard parts of the body. You hit someone on the mouth or nose and your knuckles are going to be scraped or swollen or something."

I could see the sense of that.

"Well, okay. We'll check Mac's hands tonight when he comes in, and after he's asleep, we can run up to his office and look for the gun. All right?"

"Sure."

Having some plan of action cheered us both somewhat, but for the rest of the afternoon, I worried about Richard's injuries and what they might mean. I knew better than to talk my fears over with Marilee, however. I knew she would read all sorts of inappropriate things into my anxieties, and for once, I didn't particularly welcome having to deal with her pattering through my feelings.

Marilee had already started dinner when the phone rang. I could hear her answer it from my bathroom, where I was indulging in a bubble bath that should have been relaxing but wasn't. I had been in the tub for almost an hour by then, not from any desire for cleanliness or relaxation, but because it was one place in the house I could be assured that Marilee wouldn't intrude.

It was a day for surprises. Marilee tapped at the bathroom door and came in without waiting for an answer. Flipping down the lid on the commode and sitting on it, she blew out her breath and gave me a meaningful look.

"What's the matter," I asked, lowering the book I'd been pretending to read.

"That was Davy. He's pretty upset with us."

"Why is that?"

"He wants to know all over again about the stuff we were supposed to have found in Mac's car. He thinks there may be some connection to it and 'another crime' they're investigating."

I sat upright in the tub. "What's this 'we' business? Have you got a mouse in your pocket or something? That was your story, your lie, remember?"

"Well, anyway, he's wanting to know exactly who we were talking about, although he thinks he already knows. Why did I ever tell him such a thing in the first place?"

"You're going to have to tell him the truth, Marilee."

"Which truth? Which part? How much of it do I tell?"

"I say we just tell him the whole thing. All of it. Make a deal with him and then let them worry with it, it's their job in the first place."

"And risk getting Ricky involved, too?" she asked slyly.

"Richard?"

"Sure. If Ricky's involved in this, too, and we tell all we know to Davy, they'll find out sooner or later. We won't be able to keep him out of it, now will we? Do you want that?"

I didn't answer, thinking. She was right, but before I could say anything further, she added, "And they'll be on him like chickens after a grasshopper. He may be perfectly innocent, you know."

"Of course I know," I answered her crossly. "I have no doubt in my mind Richard is just some innocent bystander who's gotten hooked up in this whole crazy mess."

Like me, I could have mentioned. I could have also added, *And because of you, Marilee.*

But I didn't. Accusing Marilee of anything would have been useless, and there were certainly more important things to worry about.

"What did you tell him?" I asked.

"Well, I sort of put him off and talked all around Robin Hood's barn and finally he got pissed off and hung up. I have a feeling we're going to hear from him again though, real soon."

When Mac got home that night, Marilee and I were both wary until we'd ascertained his mood. I realized suddenly that we were always like that; that, until we knew what kind of mood he'd come home in, we were careful to maintain a low profile.

What kind of a life is this? I wondered. How could Marilee do this for thirty years? How could other women put up with this every afternoon for years and years? And years?

But then, I realized I had been like that with Jack, that it was probably something all wives did and merely shrugged off as part of the job.

Mac was in the kind of mood that, if not destroyed before he'd had his first drink of the evening, would mellow into a fairly pleasant, slightly avuncular attitude toward Marilee and me. If not angered or set off on some little thing, he would relax, begin to tease Marilee in his caustic, unflattering way, and paw me. It was certainly better than the alternative.

Quickly, I poured Mac a drink and sat next to him on the couch. He took a healthy swig and I could almost feel him relax, feel the tension draining from his body. Carefully, I picked up his right hand and held it in my lap, chatting all the while to divert him. Casually, I turned it over and looked down at it. Mac, seeing I'd glanced down at his hand, jerked it back, but I'd seen enough. His knuckles were scraped and scabbing over, puffy and red in the first stages of festering. It was that hand which had hit Richard in the face, destroying his looks, however temporarily, hurting him.

Mac looked at me with an expression that almost dared me to comment, and perversely, I said, "You've hurt your hand, Mac. How did it happen?"

"Don't worry about it, darlin'. It's okay."

"Did you do it at the same time you hurt your eye?"

"I said don't worry about it!"

His mood was deteriorating, rapidly. Marilee shot me a glance, warning me, but I persisted, angered at the memory of Richard's bruised face, suddenly unable to be the sweet little woman who allowed herself to be bullied and pushed around while she manipulated like hell from the background. Nastily, I asked, "Have you been in a fight, Mac?"

"It don't matter what I been doin', little gal. You just don't worry about me, okay? I kin take care of myself."

Marilee sat in her chair across the room, gaping at me. I realized that, for once, she was unable to think of anything to say that might smooth things over. I seemed to be unable to stop and heard myself speak again, leaning on him even more.

"What did the other guy look like, Mac?"

"I don' wanna talk about it!"

He threw himself to his feet and stalked to the bar, freshening his almost full drink. I noticed he didn't bother to add any water to the bourbon he poured in.

"Whatever you say, Mac."

Having made my point, whatever it was, to my satisfaction, I got up and strolled through the living room, through the house into my dressing room, where I sat at the vanity and began leisurely brushing my hair. The woman who looked out from the mirror at me smiled, a smug smile that had a rare sparkle in it. There was something else in the look on my face, too.

If you touch Richard again, I threatened Mac silently, I'll kill you myself.

Marilee and I adjourned to the plaza the next day for lunch at Pasqual's. We'd made another moonlight foray to Mac's office the night before, searching for the pistol, this time without incident, and for good measure, we searched his car when we got home. There was no gun in either place, .357 magnum or otherwise.

"Are you sure you saw a gun like that," I asked Marilee the next day when we'd been served our lunch.

"I'm telling you I remember a gun exactly like that Dirty Harry gun there. I've seen it somewhere. If it's not Mac's, then someone else owns one like it."

"David Finch?" I prompted. It was a logical choice, I thought, given the fact that he was a policeman.

"No, Davy's service pistol is a revolver. You know, with the little thingy that holds the bullets that goes round and round. He said you could always count on a revolver, that a . . . well, whatever that Dirty Harry kind is—"

"An automatic." I, at least, knew that much.

Marilee wasn't impressed by my knowledge. "Yeah, right, an automatic, can jam on you. It wasn't Davy's, I know that. Where else could I have . . ."

"Well, don't worry about it right now," I said when her voice trailed off.

"I just hate it when I can't think of something like that."

"Don't worry about it," I repeated. "What do we do now?"

"Well . . . I know one thing we don't want to do again and that's antagonize Mac. It took me hours to get him calmed down again last night. What were you thinking about when you set him off like that?"

"I was pissed off."

"About what?"

"I was upset he'd hit Richard, and sitting there and holding the hand that had done it, I suddenly wanted to hit him."

"Shit, Karen."

"I just got tired of playing games, Marilee. Why the hell do we have to tiptoe around and placate him all the time? He's worse than a spoiled little boy, and we might as well be in slavery as to put up with his moods and tempers."

"It's just easier this way, Karen. He's too old to change now and I know I am. This is the way we've always handled things. Look, Karen, it's not for much longer. Just hang in there until we can get this thing settled."

I didn't answer her. She was so positive Mac wasn't a dealer, but I wasn't so sure myself. Having learned something of Mac's personality over the time since I'd first met him, I personally had some real doubts about his innocence. I kept them to myself, however. Discussing them with Marilee would only have been a wasted effort. If she took someone under her wing, then her loyalty toward that person was absolute, rock hard, everlasting. Idly, I wondered what she would do if she ever had to choose between two of her friends. It was an unresolvable question to my mind and I gave over, putting my attention to better use, toward the chorizo burrito on the plate in front of me.

• • •

When we got back home, however, the discussion was forgotten—immediately. From the condition of the living room, someone had been there while we were out and had gone through the house, completely, without a thought for replacing anything or worrying about destruction. The couches had been overturned, cushions and pillows ripped open, books pulled out of the shelves and tossed on the floor, plants uprooted and the potting soil dumped on the tiles and Navajo rugs. It had been a systematic search, a thorough, wantonless looking for something that had left nothing unexamined.

"Jesus Christ in heaven!" Marilee whispered, standing just inside the foyer door.

I stood behind her, looking over her head at the mess, speechless. It was almost beyond my comprehension that someone should have come into a space I considered private and created such havoc. I literally doubted my eyes at first and then felt violated, as if someone had actually harmed my body.

"What happened?" I asked stupidly.

"What do you think happened?" She flew into the living room and began setting it to rights, putting a great deal of energy into it. "Come on and help me. We have to get this house put back together before Mac gets home."

"Marilee, I'm calling the police. You know what they were looking for. What if one of us had been here? I'm telling you this is too much. We're playing with people who have absolutely no compunctions about breaking into someone's house and ripping it to shreds. If they do that, they'll hurt us, too. They won't care. We're just a cog in the machinery to them."

"Are you ready to let the feds—"

"Bullshit, Marilee! I don't want to die or get tortured or anything. That's what these people do, you know."

She straightened up and placed the cushion she'd been restuffing back on the couch. For the first time, I saw her irresolute. Without saying anything else, knowing that to do so would give her fuel for further argument, I walked to the living room phone and began punching out numbers. I was through arguing, and something of my determination must have shown because, when she walked up to me and took the receiver out of my hand, I could tell by the look on her face I'd won.

"I'll do it," she said. "Davy knows me and it's him I want handling this. I can trust him not to get all excited and go bananas on us."

"What in Christ's sweet name were you *thinking* of, doing a stupid thing like that!"

I had watched David Finch's face while Marilee filled him in on everything that had happened, had watched it take on an interesting shade of puce, and with the disclosure that we'd flushed what was probably a bag of cocaine down the john, it had become outright purple. I suddenly recognized a slight resemblance to Mac Carpenter and then dismissed it when Marilee answered, "We were afraid the feds would come and confiscate everything, Davy, and we weren't sure just how deep Mac was in it. We were just going to hold off calling you until we knew for sure he wasn't mixed up in this."

He stared at her, speechless. It sounded insane, even to me, and maybe it did to Marilee, too, because she shrugged and stared at him helplessly.

"Do you realize you've destroyed evidence?" he finally said, almost whispering it. It was obvious he was keeping himself under control only with a great deal of effort.

The way he said it—"destroyed evidence"—it sounded as if it should have been capitalized, underlined, put in boldface type. It sounded unutterably idiotic, horrendous and unforgivable, final. I began to realize how serious our predicament was, and realizing that, the pitiful picture of myself behind bars, living out what was left of a miserable life in prison, followed immediately. It was all I could do to keep my teeth from chattering.

"But Davy"—she patted his arm—"we didn't know what it was."

I suddenly recognized the helpless look for what it was, realized what she was doing. The realization heartened me somewhat and I was able to say with some degree of credibility, "It was only after we'd done it that we began to put two and two together. And by then, it was too late."

"Jesus!" he said, obviously awestruck by our stupidity.

"And now," I continued, "Mac is going to come home and have a stroke over the condition of this house. You know what he's like."

I waved my arm around, and David, thus distracted, said, "Yeah. Look, I'm going to get someone out here to guard the place. You two, by doing what you did, probably aren't safe, and I'd feel a lot better if I had a couple of men out here."

Both of us were silent. I was thinking about what Mac would be like, seeing the destruction of his house. Who knew what Marilee was thinking.

As it turned out, we didn't have to worry about a tantrum from Mac. He didn't come home that night, and the next morning, David came out to the house again to inform us his car had been found on the road to Clines Corner, empty, abandoned, and completely ripped apart.

Mac was missing.

6

I put my hand on Marilee's arm, to steady her, give her support, but she shook it off.

"Where is he?" she demanded. "Is he okay?"

"We don't know, Marilee. There wasn't any blood in the car so he might be all right. We just don't know. We're doing everything we can, but in the meantime, you stay here. Don't leave. Put your cars in the garage and lock the doors. Keep all the doors and windows locked and don't open them for any reason. Keep the alarm system turned on and let me know immediately if something else happens. I'll have men posted out here constantly. You should be pretty safe if you don't do anything stupid."

His attitude was that, given the chance, we'd do just that, but Marilee and I nodded, for once too frightened to argue.

After he left, she sat down on the couch suddenly and I realized her face was extremely pale, had lost all its tan so that it was yellow. The lines in her face stood out, making her look old. I went into the kitchen and got her a cup of coffee, and bringing it back to the living room, I tipped some brandy into it. Handing it to her, I told her firmly, "Drink this, Marilee. You can't get weird on me now. We have to keep our heads straight, for Mac's sake."

She took the coffee and sipped it, curling her hands around the mug as if she were drawing strength from its warmth. I went to get a cup for myself, and by the time I'd returned to the living room, some of the color had come back to her face.

"God damn them if they've hurt that stupid son of a bitch!" she said, and I ignored the obvious contradiction.

"Marilee, what did you think would happen when we started fooling around with dope dealers? They play for real, you know."

"Don't start on me, Karen! I'm not in the mood for it."

"Well, you'd better *get* in the mood! I don't know what you're so upset about anyway. You *wanted* him dead, remember? It was *your* idea to have me marry him and then give him another heart attack. It's the same thing."

"It's not the same thing, damn it! I didn't want him to get murdered."

I suddenly lost patience with her. "What the hell is the difference? You mindless idiot, *he's going to be just as dead!*"

She started crying at that, and instantly contrite, I sat beside her on the couch and gathered her up into my arms.

Sobbing into my shoulder, she said, "But dying of a heart attack was what he chose. He didn't choose being beat up and then killed like José was. If they're hurting him . . . Right now they could be—"

At that instant, the phone rang. Making a face at the interruption, she stopped crying, and waving me back on the couch when I started to reach around her to answer it, she picked it up. I watched the anguish on her face change into something else, an expression I was not familiar with, at least not from her. I'd seen it on men's faces, however, and recognized it immediately. It was not the expression of a victim.

"Who is this?" she demanded at one point, but then was silent, staring at me, until she slowly lowered the receiver.

"It was the bastards who have Mac," she said tonelessly.

"Who has him? Where is he? Is he all right?"

"I don't know. To all questions. They want the dope we took out of my car or they say they'll kill him."

"They *said* that!"

"In so many words. We're not supposed to call the police and they'll call us back later today."

"Marilee, what do we do now? Call David?"

"We can't do that. They said they'll kill him, remember?"

"But we don't have the coke. How can we give it to them? We have to call the police, Marilee."

"They said they'd kill him," she repeated, and at that display of stubbornness, it was all I could do to keep from grabbing her and shaking her until her head fell off her shoulders. With a great deal of effort, I controlled myself and asked, as gently as possible, "How do we know he's still alive, Marilee? You have to face the fact that he may already be dead. They may have already killed him, and even if they didn't, his nitro pills are here, in his bathroom. You know any kind of rough handling is going to set him off. Even if he has some extra pills with him, do you really think they're going to stop torturing him long enough to let him take any if he needs them? It's you and me now. We have to take care of ourselves. We have to call David. It's the sensible, rational, intelligent thing to do."

"How would you feel if it were Ricky?"

"What?"

"Would you say the same thing if they had Richard Sommerfrught? Probably not, Karen. Admit it."

Everything I had said to her had been like talking to a stone wall. I took another grip on my patience and said, with as much emphasis as I could muster up, "Marilee, that's irrelevant. It's not the same thing at all," I said, but in spite of my reasoning, I was confused, more so than I wanted to admit to her.

She picked up on it immediately.

"If there's any chance in hell, Karen, I have to try. Don't you see? If I let something happen to him now, his death will be my fault."

I stared at her, almost speechless with disbelief. "And it wouldn't have been all those years when you wanted him to die of a heart attack? What about all those high-calorie meals? What about all that cholesterol? What about all your spite marriages? Marilee, forgive me if I'm being stupid, but I just don't see—"

"It doesn't matter. I have to try."

"Well, you can do what you want to. I'm not going to let myself get killed, or put in jail either, because of your crazy, harebrained guilt trips—that you've put on yourself, by the way. I'm calling David."

"Karen, you can't! They said—"

"They said! These people are big-time coke dealers, Marilee. Just how much do you believe they'll keep their word? Look," I said, trying to keep my own fear from building into something I couldn't handle, "Marilee, let's do this: Let's call David and tell him what they said, and then, if they call again, if there's any clue at all, I'll help you hunt him up. Okay?"

She hesitated, and seeing that, I pressed my point.

"Besides, if we tell David what they said, maybe it will help them find him. You never know."

I was gratified to see that, at last, I'd said something that made sense to her. She hesitated, and before she could argue with me further, I picked up the phone and called David Finch.

When the phone rang again, it was well into the later part of the evening. Marilee was out of her chair, across the room, and answering the phone before its second ring. She looked at me with a significant look and said, "Oh, hi, Ricky. What're you doing, honey?" She paused and then said, "Great. Karen's right here. Do you want to talk to her?"

I stood up to take the phone from her, but she refocused her attention on it and then said, "Well, we had a burglary out here. Somebody broke in the house." Another pause. "Oh, honey, we'd love to but we're staying in today. We can't get out of here until the insurance adjuster comes out, and then we have to get stuff put back together. It'll probably be an all-day effort, from the looks of things. But thanks anyway. Can we have a rain check? . . . Oh, thanks, darling. . . . Well, I suppose. . . . Sure. 'Bye."

She put the phone down and said, "Ricky wanted to take us to dinner."

"Oh?"

"Yeah. And when I said we couldn't, he asked if he could come out here."

"Why?"

"He didn't say."

We looked at each other for a few seconds, unable to make any sense of this new development, and then Marilee went outside to tell the man dozing in the police car to expect a cream-colored Porsche.

Richard, when he entered, gave the house a quick appraisal, more in the way of checking it out rather than noting the mess that Marilee and I, with Consuela's help, had been trying to right all afternoon, and I remembered it was he who'd decorated it several years before.

It would make sense he'd be interested in a professional way. By the time Marilee had handed him a drink, however, his attention had refocused itself on us.

"Where's Mac?" he asked casually.

Too casually? I asked myself this question, hating myself for my suspicions, and hating Marilee for putting them there.

"Oh, God, darlin'. Who knows? You know how he is."

"What happened to your face?" I asked.

"I got in a fight."

"You *did?*" Marilee made owl eyes at him. "Why, darlin', that's not like you. What happened?"

He grinned at her. "What do you mean, that's not like me? I was in the Crotch, you know. Just because I'm a decorator doesn't mean I don't know how to fight."

"The Crotch?" I asked.

"Nam. I was a Marine in Vietnam."

Somehow, I wasn't surprised, but the way he said it told me that he didn't want to go into it any further. I also realized he was pulling one of Marilee's tricks, that of refocusing attention away from an unacceptable question.

"Mac was in a fight, too," I informed him. "What happened, Richard?"

He stared at me for a few seconds and then put his drink down on the table in front of him.

"All right, Mac and I had some words. Where is he, girls?"

"About what?" I persisted.

"What do you think?"

"I don't know. You tell me."

"You and I were seen leaving the plaza in my car. He was pretty upset about it."

Marilee stared at me, eyes wide and eyebrows raised, but I ignored her.

"Were you the one who called him a couple of nights ago?"

He looked at me blankly.

"Called him? No."

Either he was a *very* good liar or it was someone else who'd telephoned Mac and caused him to leave the house and his dinner abruptly.

Marilee spoke up, telling him about the call and Mac's departure.

"Well," Richard said, "he caught me coming out of a restaurant and we had some words, and then he followed me to my car and we finished it there. He caught me off guard and I only got one blow in before everybody stopped us. I guess you might say"—he grinned suddenly, wincing as it affected his split lip—"that I lost the fight. If you were counting, that is. Who would have thought that old man could move so fast? And there I was, trying to hold back out of respect for his age."

"Well, Ricky, that's a mistake you won't make again."

"You're sure right about that! You don't have any idea where he is?"

"Why do you want to know?" I asked. "That sounds contradictory to me."

"If you want me to help you," he said quietly, "you'll have to tell me what you know."

At this surprising turn of the conversation, Marilee and I looked at each other and then, realizing how guilty we probably looked, glanced away again.

"What do you mean, Ricky?"

"Mac got himself into some stuff he shouldn't have. Tell me what you know."

"We don't know what you're talking about, Richard." I looked at Marilee meaningfully. "What kind of stuff?"

He stared at me for a few seconds, and then conversationally, he said, "That's something I really dislike about you and Marilee. You both pretend you're some kind of frivolous, eyelash-batting twits, and it's really beginning to grate on my nerves."

"Why, Ricky!"

"And while you're at it, you might as well stop pretending this is some kind of happy little nest and that you two and Mac are a nice little family. It doesn't wash. What's going on here? I've watched you both and I just can't figure it out. What are you up to anyway?"

"I don't know what you're talking about, Richard."

"I would expect something like this from Marilee. That's how she gets her kicks, doing crazy things. But you didn't strike me as being crazy, Karen. At least, not after I got to know you."

"Really?"

I gave him the full benefit of Mother's stare, and after a few moments, he looked away. Picking up his drink, he took a sip and said lightly, "Well, I've made mistakes before. Now, where is old Mac?"

I was infuriated, and Marilee, seeing the dangerous set of my jaw, hurried to smooth things over.

"Darlin', we aren't sure. He hasn't come home yet and we don't know where he is."

That much, at least, was true. Richard stared at her pensively for a few seconds and then, abruptly, excused himself and left the house. It was all I could do to keep from throwing something heavy at the door by which he'd exited, and even before the sound of disturbed gravel had settled, Marilee was patting my arm, peering up anxiously at my face.

"Karen, calm down. What *is* it with you two that you fight like that? I've never seen anything like it. Put the two of you in the same room and it's like cats at the animal shelter."

I transferred my anger to her.

"He's an unmitigated asshole! I've never met anyone who's a bigger jerk, not even Mac! What gives him the right to come in here and . . ."

I stopped, took a deep breath and a deeper swig of my drink, and then sat down on the couch, but before I could say anything else, the phone rang again.

From the look on her face when she answered, I knew who'd called. My anger at Richard was suddenly forgotten completely.

"How do I know he's okay?" she asked. "Let me talk to him."

I waited, but the fixed expression didn't leave her face. Finally, she said, "I'm not going to do anything until you let me talk to him, and if you've hurt him, you fucker, you're in some big trouble . . ."

She held the phone out away from her face, looked at it as if she could read something written on it, and then slowly replaced it in its cradle, watching it as if it might suddenly jump up again and bite her.

"They hung up on me," she said needlessly.

"They wouldn't let you talk to him?"

"No."

I crossed the room and put my arms around her, patting her on the back. She leaned against me momentarily and then pushed away and walked to the window, where the sunset had turned the western sky into a riot of warm colors. I joined her and we stood there, staring at the scene before us.

We stood there a long time, and then, finally, not knowing what else to do, we began straightening the room again.

Sometime in the night, I thought I heard a phone ringing somewhere far away, but before I could wake enough to answer it, it stopped. Even as I tried to wake enough to check, knowing something somehow was very wrong but not remembering what it was, I sank back into oblivion. Several times, I thought I heard it ring, but I could never quite awaken enough to go answer it.

When I got up late the next morning, Marilee was gone and there was a note on the kitchen table. I stared at it blearily some minutes before I could make any sense of the words:

"Karen—I'm going to pick up Mac, but I should be back before you wake up. Don't worry. I'm okay. Everything's okay. It was all just a mix-up. I'll explain everything in the morning."

I looked up at the kitchen clock. It was eleven forty-two.

"Marilee," I called, suddenly very nervous. "Marilee, are you here?"

I went through the house quickly, calling her, and then ran to the garage, looking for the Cadillac. It was gone.

I ran outside, thinking she might have left it in front of the house, but the gravel drive was empty. The policeman, sitting in his car, looked up, startled, but before he could say anything to me, I ran back inside the house and called David Finch.

"She's gone," I told him. "Marilee's gone! There was a phone call in the middle of the night and I guess that's when she left. I'm going to look for her."

"No! Don't leave that house! Do you hear me! Wait right there. I'll be there in a few minutes! Don't leave!"

While I waited for him, I dressed, brushed my hair and my teeth, and then, with nothing else to do but worry, I paced the floor, wringing my hands uselessly. I reread the note, confused at the upbeatness of it, given the situation.

It was as if she'd been assured that everything was all right, I told myself. But she had more sense than to trust the people who had Mac. Why would she do something so stupid? Why hadn't she wakened me? What had they told her that made her think everything was all right, to make her so relieved?

I had no answers for any of the questions, and it was with a great deal of relief myself that I saw David's car skid to a stop in the driveway. He got out and approached the other cop, who'd also gotten out of his car. Jerking open the door, I ran out to meet him, thrusting the note out at him.

When he'd read it, he said, "What did she mean, 'everything's okay'?"

"I don't know, David."

I quickly filled him in on the details and he read the note again, frowning.

From inside the house, I heard the phone ringing. I ran back in to answer, leaving David to talk with the cop.

"Miz Carpenter?"

It was a rough voice and I was instantly on guard.

"Yes? Who is this?"

"Lissen . . ."

"Karen." It was Marilee's voice, breathless, talking very fast. "I remembered where I saw the gun. It was—"

The phone was suddenly silent.

"Marilee? Marilee, where are you? Who—"

"Don't call the cops." It was the other voice, tough, menacing. "Get that bag you took. Bring it with you and go to the plaza in an hour from now. Stand on the north side, across the street, in front of the museum. Somebody'll meet you there. Understand?"

"Yes, but you listen to me! If you hurt her . . ."

I stopped speaking because the phone was dead.

"Who was that?"

I whirled, and seeing David in the doorway, I replaced the receiver, guiltily.

"No one," I said, trying for the right amount of nonchalance and cursing myself because I lacked Marilee's ability to dissemble.

"Bullshit! Do you want me to arrest you? I can do that, you know! I can take you out to the detention center for questioning as a material witness, not to mention the evidence you destroyed. Don't even think about withholding—"

Thus appealed to, I dropped the pretense.

"They've got Marilee. They want me to take the bag of coke to the plaza in an hour."

"Who?"

"I don't know. I talked to Marilee briefly. They definitely have her."

"*Shit!*"

I went to the kitchen, rummaged through the drawers until I found the box of plastic bags, and taking one, I blew it up halfway and sealed it. I put it in a small brown-paper sack and rolled the top down. David watched me.

"What are you doing?"

"I have to meet them on the plaza and I have to have something in my hands."

"No! Absolutely not!"

"Are you *crazy!* If I'm not there in an hour, there's no telling what they'll do to Marilee! I'm going and that's that!"

He stared at me for a few seconds and I stared back, letting him think. Finally, he blew out his breath in a short burst and said, "All right. All *right!* But you hear me good. You stand on that street and you hold that bag in both hands against your body. Don't let anyone walk up or drive by and take it away from you. You hold it tight. And whatever you do, you don't get into anybody's car. Do you understand me?"

"What are you going to do?"

"I'm going to be right there and we'll grab that guy so fast he'll never know what hit him."

"You can't do that! If you arrest him and he doesn't show up again, they'll know you have him. They'll do something to Marilee then. Damn it! You can't..." I took a breath, willing myself patience. "They said for me not to call the cops, David. They really mean business. They'll kill her. Do you want that on your conscience?"

"No, but I sure as hell don't want two of you dead, either. And that's what'll happen if you get in a car with them."

"What if I refuse? What if I..."

"Then, god damn it, call your lawyer!"

"All right. Let me get my handbag."

"Forget it. You won't need it. You're riding with me. I'm not going to let you out of my sight for a minute until this is over. You can just consider me part of your wardrobe or something."

At ten minutes to one, I was standing on the portal of the Palace of the Governors exactly in front of the entrance to the museum, my brown bag clutched to my chest with both hands. As David had instructed me, I stood near the curb but not close enough so that someone could drag me into a car. The tourists swirled around and behind me slowly, their attention fixed on the wares the Indians had displayed on blankets spread on the bricks. I was unaccustomed to standing around on a street, and even though I pretended great non-chalance, I felt that I stood out from the rest of the crowd so that anyone with a lick of sense would know I was there to meet someone.

So what? I asked myself. People meet each other all the time. Why be so paranoid about this? I'm just standing here, waiting, for God's sake. People do that all the time.

Vaguely, I glanced around the crowd, checked my watch as surreptitiously as possible, and then looked across the street as if trying to make up my mind about something. I still felt foolish, however, and concentrated on that feeling rather than the fear that something was happening to Marilee at that very moment, that I was probably in danger myself.

I turned slightly and looked into the crowd to my left, trying to see if there was someone who didn't fit in with the rest of the tourists. People were examining jewelry and pottery, haggling with the vendors, who, with true Indian stoicism, ignored any rudenesses or overt fawning and, between customers, chatted among themselves about such mundane things as softball games and baby colic.

No one looked unusual. No one looked as if he or she didn't belong.

I looked across the street again and then casually looked to my right. The crowd sifted slowly around David, who leaned against a pole a few feet away, ostensibly checking a map of the plaza area and looking around as if he were trying to orient himself. He ignored me and I, him. Everyone's attention was focused on the things on the blankets; no one was paying any attention to me at all. No one stood out from the crowd, and suddenly, I wondered if David was the only cop around. I looked up, glancing through the plaza for the cop who usually walked that beat, and saw him, clear across the plaza and down San Francisco a little way, talking to a woman in front of the Häagen-Dazs shop. His back was to me and he was pointing to something down San Francisco. The woman looked in the direction he was pointing and then back in my direction, but the distance was too great for me to see her face clearly.

A lot of help he's gonna be, I thought to myself. So it's going to be just me and David.

With a surprising amount of effort, I refrained from looking in David's direction again. The sun beamed down through the thin mountain air. A bearded young man dozed, prone on a bench on the near side of the plaza. Pigeons waddled to and fro, busy with whatever business pigeons deal with. A large dog, who could name several species of setter among its near ancestors, licked the ice cream off a toddler's face while her parents watched, laughing. Casually, I glanced down at my watch again.

It was now two minutes after one. The call had come at exactly noon by my watch. Slowly, I shifted from one foot to the other, beginning to perspire in the hot sun.

"Karen. Karen!"

From the familiar lurch of my stomach, I knew who was calling to me even before I looked up and saw Richard angling across the plaza toward me.

Oh, no, I thought. Not now. Go away. Please, just go away.

My dismay must have been evident on my face because as he waited for the traffic in order to cross the street to join me, his face fell into a grim look. I had time to reflect that the look was beginning to become a habit with him every time he saw me, then dismissed the thought when he approached me.

"You doing lunch on the plaza?" he asked me.

"What?"

"I didn't think you had to do that anymore now that you're Mrs. Carpenter."

"What?"

"Your lunch . . ."

He reached out and touched the bag clutched against my chest and all hell broke loose.

David yelled something at me and then something at Richard, pulled a gun, and with his other hand, jerked me behind him. The bearded youth who'd been asleep on the bench was halfway across the street, leaping over the hoods of cars, his own gun drawn. The woman who'd been talking to the cop sprinted across the plaza, leaving the cop to stare and then belatedly, to run after her. To my left, one of the Indian vendors had jumped up from his blanket and pushed roughly through the crowd, a pistol in his hand, too. All of the guns were pointing at Richard.

David's back blocked my view of Richard's face, but when I had regained my balance and moved so I could see him again, he'd raised his hands, cowboy style, and crouched a little, an expression of extreme wariness on his face.

"Wait," I said urgently, jerking at David's arm from behind. "This is a mistake!"

David relaxed, reholstered his pistol under his jacket. "Oh," he said to Richard, obviously disgusted. "It's you."

At that, the other cops relaxed and Richard lowered his arms. I remembered, irreverently, that they were both Marilee's ex-husbands. Was there any residual friction between them? I wondered, and then forgot it as not being important.

"Yeah. It's me. What the hell's going on?"

"What are you doing here," I demanded. "Go away. You're screwing everything up."

He looked at me, confused. "What?"

"Go away. Right now. I can't talk to you now, Richard. I'm busy. Later. I'll call you later this afternoon and explain everything. Please, just go away now. Please."

David grimaced. "It doesn't matter now. We probably scared him off. We might as well pack it in. Shit!"

"David," I said urgently. "We can't give up. We have to try. Marilee—"

"Karen, after all this craziness, you think he's gonna be here, just walk up and start talking to you now? Forget it!"

He turned away and the other cops gathered around him briefly, then dispersed into the crowd. I realized people were standing well back, wadded up into knots, staring at us with gaping faces, and not wanting to be the center of such offensive public scrutiny, I turned and walked quickly down the portal. The crowd opened for me as if I'd been Moses with a magic wand.

"Karen, wait."

I realized Richard had followed me.

"Go away."

"What's going on? Where's Marilee? Please, Karen, talk to me. Where are you going?"

"To call a cab and go home. Leave me alone."

"I'll take you home."

"No, leave me alone."

"My car's right down the street, Karen. Let me—"

I turned and faced him. "Will you just leave me the fuck alone!"

There, I thought. I've done it. I've said "fuck" on a crowded street. I'm no better than Mac Carpenter ever was.

At the thought of Mac, an unbidden mental image of him, probably beaten and maybe already dead, and then the sequential thought that Marilee would be treated the same way, maybe worse, that she had counted on me and I had ruined any chance of obtaining her release, I felt my face crumpling. He reached for me, took me in his arms.

"Karen, please. Tell me what's going on. Let me help."

I relaxed against his strong body, smelling the fragrance I always associated with him, breathing it in, feeling it soothe and quiet my fears. His strength and caring were reassuring, and I let my mind run through the jumbled events, trying to put them in some kind of order for the telling.

Suddenly, the memory of his walking across the street toward me, picking me out of the crowd, hailing me, jumped into my mind, activating a small, wary voice in my head. What a coincidence, the voice said to me, silkily. What a fluke that he should be walking on the plaza at that very moment, a busy man like Richard. Too coincidental? And the note from Marilee—it had sounded as if she'd gone to pick up Mac, completely unsuspecting of anything wrong. Marilee was smart. She wouldn't have believed just anyone. It had to be someone she felt to be trustworthy. An ex-husband, perhaps? Richard?

I stepped away from him, making my face blank. "Help me, Richard? Help me with what?"

His eyes flickered, a slight shifting away and back, very faint, but I was watching for it and I saw it.

"I can help, Karen. I know Mac is missing. Tell me what you know."

"I don't know anything, Richard."

"Where is Marilee?"

"Where do you think! Excuse me, Richard. I have to talk to David again about something."

I pushed past him, reversing my direction through the crowd of tourists, who were beginning to break up, and approached David. When I turned around again, I was glad to see Richard had disappeared.

"David, can somebody give me a ride home. I don't have my money with me, remember?"

"Yeah, but first, you're coming down to the station with me."

"What for?"

"I want a statement from you. I want—"

"David, listen to me! I have to be at home. Don't you understand? If they try to call me again, I have to be there to take the call."

He hesitated and then said, "Yeah, that's probably a pretty good idea. Come on, I'll wait there with you."

I tried to convince him that I would call him the minute I heard anything, but no amount of argument on my part, however, could change his mind. It was with some resignation that I followed him to his car.

The next few hours passed slowly, dragging us along with them. David and I paced the floor, sometimes separately and sometimes in tandem, stopping only when we were physically tired, and then, after resting, one or both of us began it again, doggedly, as if by pacing we could hurry the action along.

"Damn! I hate this!" he exploded at one point. "I don't know why I ever thought police work would be exciting. Ninety-five percent is standing around, waiting for something to happen."

I couldn't think of anything to say to that and we fell back into an uneasy silence, each busy with his own worries.

I couldn't get Marilee's breathless voice out of my mind, coming over the telephone, talking fast, trying to get her message across quickly, before they stopped her. *Karen! I remembered where I saw the gun. It was—*

She was obviously talking about the .357 magnum with which José had been executed, but why tell me that at such a time? I would have expected almost anything from Marilee except that, and my mind kept repeating itself, playing her voice over and over like a cassette player, hung on auto-reverse.

Karen! I remembered where I saw the gun. It was—

It had to be significant, I told myself, but no matter how I took the words apart and put them back together, I couldn't pick up anything from it at all.

Finally, late in the afternoon, more to have something to do than from any real hunger, I went into the kitchen and prepared something for David and me to eat. We sat in the breakfast nook, pushing the food around on our plates. Abruptly, I pushed the plate back and looked up at David.

"Marilee taught me to cook," I told him. "I keep wondering if they're feeding her. She likes to eat and . . . You know."

"Yeah." He pushed his own plate away and added, "I remember."

To keep him talking, I asked, "Why did you divorce her?"

He looked up at me, surprised. "I didn't. She was the one who wanted out."

Now I was the one to register surprise. From our conversations, I had always assumed each of Marilee's marriages had ended because the man she was married to at the time got tired of it, of her. She'd never said that; it had merely been an assumption on my part.

"Why?" Then, realizing I might be prying, I added, "But perhaps that's too personal a question."

"No, I don't mind. When I married Marilee, I was just a cop, floating along, having fun with the other guys, chasing women, hiding from all the crap I'd grown up with, stuff I didn't want to face or deal with. She was like a whirlwind, kind of. You know the kind of thing that picks you up and dances you around, and then—bang!—leaves you. But you're in a higher place than you were before and you're changed. You think to yourself, 'Jesus Christ! What was *that?*' but you're different. You can't ever be the goof-off you were before. She talked me into taking the sergeant's exam, and from there, it was easy for me to work my way up. No matter what happened, I could always see Marilee's face, telling me how smart I was, how good I did, how wonderful, how terrific, how much I deserved out of life, that it was just mine for the reaching out and taking. And the damn thing was, she believed it all. She really did, you could tell. You can tell when somebody's shitting you and she wasn't. She believed it all. After a while, you get to believing things like that, too. You get to thinking you can do anything."

"I know. She probably saved my life," I said, realizing suddenly that it was very likely so—that, if she hadn't come along when she did with her effervescent approach to life, I might very well have killed myself in despair of ever having anything halfway wonderful in my life again.

"David," I said urgently, clasping the hand that lay beside his abandoned plate. "We have to find her! We have to—"

The phone rang and I froze, looking at him. He jumped to his feet and sprinted into the hall toward the living room, saying, "Wait! Don't answer it yet. Let me get the other phone."

He reappeared in the hall, telephone in hand, the cord stretched out behind him. The phone jangled again.

"Put your hand on the receiver but don't pick it up yet. On three, okay?"

I nodded and touched the receiver in the kitchen, watching him. When he'd counted to three, I picked it up, watching him simultaneously pick up his own receiver.

"Hello," I said, fighting the quiver in my voice.

"Detective Finch there?" asked a male voice.

"Yeah?" David said.

I leaned against the counter and hung up the phone.

"Yeah? Where? . . . Yeah, I know it. Anything else there . . . ? Tell those apes not to touch *anything*. I'll be right there."

"What is it?" I asked him. He hung up the phone and headed toward the front door, not looking at me. I ran after him.

"David, what is it?"

"They found the pink Cadillac."

"Marilee's car? Where?"

"Same place they found Mac's."

"Is she . . . Did they find . . ." I couldn't finish the sentence.

"No sign of her."

"I'm going with you."

"No, you're not! You're staying right here."

"David, I'm going."

He stopped and looked at me. I stared back at him, determined and defiant.

"I don't suppose I could count on you not to do anything stupid, could I? Like running off somewhere if you get another phone call?"

I stared at him.

"Shit! Well, come on then. But you stay out of the way. I don't want to have to baby-sit you while we're out there."

"You won't," I said grimly.

The road to Clines Corner wound around mesas and up and over geological formations that I had no name for. It was a bleak, lonely road but not without its own sort of beauty. I had no eyes for it, however—not that night.

The Caddy sat in the fading light, on the shoulder about twenty miles from Santa Fe, nosed down toward the ditch, its tail fins poking obscenely up into the sky. Two state trooper cruisers sat on the shoulder, parenthesizing the Cadillac, blue and red lights flashing. David slid to a stop behind the first and got out, approaching the group of troopers who'd been standing around, smoking and talking. I scrambled out of the car after him. The troopers looked at me curiously and then focused on David.

"What's up?" he said, and listened as they filled him in.

I started to walk around him to approach the car, but without taking his eyes off the other men or interrupting them, David reached out and grabbed my arm, detaining me. I didn't argue.

When they'd finished talking, David led them toward the car and I followed after, trying not to stumble in my pumps over the loose rocks along the shoulder.

The car had been systematically taken apart. There were no other words for it. It had been ripped up, torn down, dismantled as much as it possibly could be and still remain drivable. There was no sign of Marilee, no evidence she could ever have been in the car.

"Anything on the ground around it?" David asked, looking.

"Naw," one of the troopers said with some degree of disgust. "Not even a footprint. They knew what they were doin', all right."

We began a circle of the car, David helping me over the rough ground by the same grip on my arm he'd used when we first got there.

"What's this?"

He was staring intently at the front bumper and I looked where he'd pointed. There, under the double headlights, was a word rubbed into the road dirt. The troopers crowded around, blocking my view.

"What is it?" I said. "What does it say?"

"Shine that flashlight on it. Looks like K-A-R . . . something, something. The last two letters are pretty sloppy, like they were made in a hurry."

"Karen," I said, pushing through the troopers to see. "It's my name! She tried to write my name!"

"I don't know. Doesn't look much like E-N to me. Doesn't look like much of anything, just two squiggles."

"Yeah," one of the troopers said. "Looks to me like they tried to write N-E."

"Naw. Looks more like W-R," another said.

"It's my name," I insisted. "She tried to write my name!"

"Why?"

I looked at David, thinking. Why indeed?

He asked it again. "Why would your name be on the car?"

"Maybe she wanted to tell me something."

"And she wrote your name?"

"Well, maybe she started to write a lot but they interrupted her."

"That's not a big enough space for a lot of words."

"No . . . I don't suppose it is."

"Why would she write your name? Why *your* name? Why not someone else's name? Why not some kind of a hint or something. It doesn't make sense."

It didn't make sense to me, either, but I was positive it was my name, that she'd tried to tell me something.

"We don't even know that Marilee wrote that, Karen."

"She wrote it. I know she did."

David looked up at my stubborn insistence that it was Marilee who'd written the letters in the dirt on the car. "Don't keep anything from me, Karen. Marilee's life may depend on it."

"David, I swear. I know that's my name and that Marilee wrote it there. But I don't understand. Not any more than you do."

"All right." He turned to the troopers. "You looked through the car good?"

"We didn't open the trunk."

"Open it. You have a key, Karen?"

"No, it's Marilee's car."

One of the troopers went back to his car and got a crowbar and forced the trunk. David moved around to watch, but I stood there at the front of the car, staring down at the letters that Marilee had scratched in the road dirt with one of her fingernails, trying to understand why she might have written my name and not someone else's.

The trunk went up and one of the men said, "Shit!"

"Shine a light over here," David said, and at the expression in his voice, I started around the car to the back. David met me and pulled me back to the front.

"Karen, don't go to pieces on me now."

"What is it? Is it . . ."

I couldn't finish the question, but he knew whom I meant.

"No, it's Mac. It doesn't look good."

As if by confirmation, one of the troopers at the trunk said, "He's bought it. Looks like he got roughed up some first."

"This is his wife," David said at the expression on my face. "Come on, Karen. Let's go back to my car."

He led me past Marilee's car, effectively blocking my seeing inside the trunk with his body as he did so. He needn't have bothered. I couldn't have looked in the trunk if I'd had to. When I was seated in the front seat, he closed the door and said to the others, "Get an ambulance and a tow truck out here, and one of you stay here with it and make damn sure that writing doesn't get rubbed off until we get a chance to look at it in better light." And then to me, "Come on, Karen. I'm taking you home."

David, after posting another cop outside the house and lecturing me sternly concerning what I should do when they called again, if they did, had gone home.

"Call me immediately," he'd said, fixing me with a glare that was meant to be intimidating.

"All right."

"Don't get smart or heroic."

"I won't."

And leaving his home number on the sofa table, he departed.

That night, I lay fully clothed on the large bed I'd shared with Mac, waiting for a phone call from the people who had Marilee, trying not to think of Mac's body, crammed into the trunk of the pink Cadillac that he'd hated so much. I distracted myself by using the hours to mull over and over the word Marilee had tried to write on her car, the fact that Richard hadn't been honest with me and his likely guilt or lack of it, where Marilee might have seen the .357 magnum. I pulled each problem out, one at a time, trying to make some sense of it and then, as I became frustrated with each one, let it go again. I missed Marilee's input, missed talking problems over with her, hearing her crazy reasoning that, in the end, usually wound up making sense. The house was empty for the first time since I'd come there as the bride of Mac Carpenter, and without the energies he and Marilee had invested into it, it seemed dead, flat.

As the hours wore on, it became harder and harder to push memories of Mac back, and finally, I let them come, seeing him as he'd been, warts and all. I remembered my fervent appreciation of his handling of all my financial problems, and just as quickly, remembered him stubbornly insisting we "party" with that little hooker in Vegas. I remembered his little cruelties toward Marilee and the fact that he worried about her apparent inability to take care of herself. I realized that, whether he'd cared to admit it or not, he'd still loved her, as much as he could love anyone, and that any feeling he'd had for me was anemic by comparison.

Suddenly, I was very, very glad Marilee and I hadn't given him a fatal heart attack. It was my understanding then what real guilt would have been.

The phone remained silent, and twice I picked it up to make sure it was working.

"Please call," I whispered, sending out a subliminal thoughtwave, trying to connect to whoever was responsible for Marilee's abduction in order to initiate some action, however awful. I realized then what was worse than outright fear and confusion, and that was the soul-killing waiting, coupled with the kind of anxiety that built slowly in the small hours of the night into something monstrous.

Please call. Please.

I concentrated on the problems at hand, forcing my mind away from the pictures it kept wanting to build of Marilee in the hands of the kind of men who executed people, who'd killed Mac, men I'd angered by not following their instructions. José's face, sweating with fear after he'd found the bag of coke missing, loomed up, wouldn't go away, and then, without warning, transformed itself into Marilee's, equally frightened.

Please call.

The phone remained silent, accusingly so.

You made a mistake by telling David, Marilee's face accused me. *They know you told them. Whatever happens to me now will be your fault. I told you so. I told you we should just take care of it ourselves.*

And I had nothing with which I could defend myself. As usual, she'd been right.

Sometime in the middle of the night, I must have dozed because I was dreaming. Marilee and I were walking down Galisteo Street together, talking and laughing, and we came to a large building, not one that actually existed anywhere on Galisteo.

"I have to go in here," she said, looking at me strangely.

"Why?" I asked. "There's nothing here that's interesting."

"I have to."

"Why?" I insisted.

"Because I have karma with this place."

Suddenly, I sat upright in bed, staring at the far wall as if I were seeing a movie played on it. Carefully, I went through the dream before I forgot it, knowing something about it had awakened me, and then I remembered David's voice.

"It looks like K-A-R-something-something."

It was the word Marilee had written in the road dirt on her car. I had assumed it to be my name and that assumption had thrown me off.

"Karma." I said it aloud, as if to test it. "K-A-R-M-A, karma!"

I called up the memory of the word, trying to see if the last two letters could have been an M and an A.

It doesn't matter, I told myself. I know it. It has to be. Karma.

My excitement at having discovered what Marilee had written for me dissolved when I realized it still made no sense to me. I lay back on the bed, thinking about the word, trying to remember where I'd heard it, trying to figure out what Marilee had meant for me to know.

Why did she write such an inane word? I told myself it wasn't a word she would use, not something that would ordinarily be in her vocabulary, not something that was consistent with her lifestyle. It would be more like the women she'd said Richard had been dating, women who were into the New Age thing, who had hairy armpits and . . .

Richard again, I thought. It's always Richard. He keeps coming up again and again.

The thought of the New Age women made me think of Harvey

Wallace. What had Marilee said about him—that he'd told her they had unfinished karma together, that he slept with his women patients because they had karma with him.

I sat up on the bed again, slowly this time.

Harvey Wallace, M.D., Santa Fe's local dope peddler? No, I told myself. That's too, too crazy.

I got up and went into the living room and without turning on any lights, walked to the window and stared out, past the cop car, down toward the lights of the city below. I remembered the house Marilee had pointed out to me as belonging to Harvey, the sprawling adobe crown on its own private hill. A very expensive property, a very remote one, I remembered her saying. It even had its own landing strip. And, I asked myself, during their short marriage, they lived in a condo in town? How strange when he had such an opulent place only thirty minutes or so away!

The clock in the hall chimed once and was silent. I went back into my bedroom and turned the lamp on my vanity on. My porcelain clock, a gift from Mac that Marilee had obviously picked out, said twelve-thirty. I sat on the edge of the bed, picked up the phone, and began punching out David's home number from the piece of paper he'd given me. Halfway through, I paused and then hung it up again.

"You screwed up," Marilee's face in my mind accused me again. "You shouldn't have told David. They bungled everything. I knew they would. I told you so."

"So what am I supposed to do?" I asked her, exactly as if she were in the room with me, but her face faded and I was left alone with the question.

It occurred to me I should perhaps make sure Harvey was our man before I started pointing fingers. I could imagine Mac's dead face, purple at the lawsuit I might cause by running to the police, blabbing that Dr. Harvey Wallace, a respected local psychiatrist, was a coke king, a kidnapper, and a murderer. If they jumped on Mac like they did just because of something Marilee had merely hinted to them, what would they do to Harvey?

Even then, it was hard for me to think of Mac as being dead and incapable of anger.

I gave some consideration to the fact that, if I left, someone might call with new instructions and I wouldn't be there to take the call. But then, I told myself, they might not either. I could wait all night without a call, hours wasted that might be crucial to Marilee's safety and well-being. And what if they did call to set up another meeting? What would I take them? An empty bag? That wouldn't get me anywhere and sure as hell wouldn't help Marilee. I would have to take them something because I wouldn't have David backing me up this time. I'd learned about that.

Perhaps I should just go over to Harvey's office, I told myself. Maybe there's something there that would tell me. It would only take me a few minutes to drive into the city and back, and it would be something to do besides sit by the phone, waiting and worrying.

Leaving the phone off its cradle so that anyone who called would think that I was still at home, I changed into slacks and a sweater, got a pair of court shoes from my closet, and put them on. Grabbing my bag, I went into the garage to my car but stopped before I raised the door, remembering the cop who watched from the front of the house. When I drove past him, I realized he would see I was leaving and follow me or worse, call David. I remembered then that Marilee had managed somehow to get away the night before without being detected. I gave some thought to the problem and then activated the button that raised the door. Without starting my car, I took it out of gear and using the slope of the driveway, let it roll backward silently, past the police cruiser where the cop dozed, fighting the dead power steering, down the hill to the road out of sight and sound. Once there, I started the car, turned on the lights, and drove toward the city.

I'd gotten all the way to the building where Harvey had his office before I realized I had done a very stupid thing. I had gone tearing off without once remembering I had no access to his office, that it would be locked up tight and I certainly would not have a key. I parked on a side street and sat in my car for some minutes, thinking. No plan of action occurred to me, but not wanting to call the trip wasted, I got out and made my way down the street to the front of the building. The building itself was built around a courtyard with an iron picket gate giving access to the offices, which opened, Santa Fe–style, off the courtyard. I eyed the gate speculatively and decided that, even if I stooped to such antics, it would be too high for my forty-five-year-old legs to climb. Helplessly, I shook it slightly, thinking it might be unlocked, but it held firm and I started to turn away in despair. The pickets caught my eye, giving me the idea that, as stick-figured as I was, I might be able to squeeze through them. It wasn't easy but I managed it, and thanked whatever god was in charge of physical appearances for my flat chest. I pulled my bag through after me and skulked happily through the shadows of the open courtyard to the front door of Harvey's office.

It, too, was locked, and I stood there, staring at it, waiting for another idea. Finally, I pulled my wallet out of my purse and went through my credit cards in the dim light, choosing the one I used least, my Neiman-Marcus card since there was no Neiman's store in Santa Fe. I dug and scraped at the bolt in the crack between the doorframe and the lock, and finally, after completely ruining my card, I realized that, contrary to what one sees on television, a credit card does not open all doors. Checking the windows didn't help—they were all shut tight and bolted from inside. Frustrated, I stared at them. An idea began to grow in my head, and along with it, Mother's face, puckered with disapproval. Not ladylike, she told me, not something consistent with Buchanan behavior, tawdry and hoydenish—illegal. I had learned from Mac, however, that there were few things a good lawyer couldn't get you out of, and from Marilee, that being too prissy kept you from getting anywhere. I picked up a good-size rock from the flowerbed border and smashed it against one of the windows. The noise seemed to go on forever, loud and irrevocable. It never occurred to me that breaking glass might make so much noise, and I crouched back against the wall, terrified it had been heard. The courtyard was isolated, however, and the noise was contained within it. A soft, seductive scent of incense, patchouli, wafted out to greet me.

When I was sure no one had heard, I reached carefully through the broken glass, unlatched the window, opened it, and levered myself and my bag through it.

Once inside, I was forced to turn on a lamp, cursing my stupidity again, this time, for not thinking to bring a flashlight with me. Quickly, I glanced through the waiting room, looking for something that might tell me I'd been right about Harvey Wallace. The lush, cloud-blue room was sparing of anything I could recognize as a clue, and turning off the lamp, I felt my way into Harvey's office. By the light of his desk lamp, I went through the stuff on it, moving the crystals and bundles of smudging-grasses, hunting for anything that would tell me that I hadn't made a terrible mistake. I pawed through the drawers, beginning to become a little frantic at the thought I might have broken into a perfectly innocent doctor's office, when, in the bottom drawer, I found a leather shoulder holster. It was empty. Without knowing exactly how big a .357 magnum might be, I was sure the holster belonged to one.

Karen! I remembered where I saw the gun. It was—

Marilee's words haunted the room but it was still not proof that Harvey had done anything except buy a holster for a .357 magnum. I put the holster back in the drawer, closed it, and when I reached over the desk to turn out the light, I saw it—a tiny slash of orange on the blue carpet in the waiting room, against the far wall, partially hidden by a chair. When I picked it up, I recognized it immediately. It was one of Marilee's fake fingernails, the Dragon Lady kind that she waved around at people so promiscuously. She'd worked it off and left it as proof she'd been there, in that office, and I realized that, in the middle of the night before, she'd gotten a call from Harvey, an ex-husband whom she trusted, not remembering until she got to his office where she'd seen the gun. And by then, it would have been too late.

I let myself out the back way, hurried to my car, and sat there for a few minutes, thinking. I was torn between calling David, turning over the fingernail to him and telling him everything I knew, or driving out to Harvey's place and—doing what? Crashing in on armed, dangerous men, criminals who had already killed at least once and who had nothing to lose and a lot to preserve by offing me as well?

Not too bright, Karen, I told myself, but without warning, I saw the fiasco on the plaza and knew I couldn't risk Marilee's life by telling the police anything.

SWAT teams aren't known for their subtlety, I remembered. The second that Harvey Wallace heard a weird noise, he'd kill her. He'd have to.

Besides, I'd committed a crime. I could just imagine David's face when I told him the reason I knew about Harvey was that I'd broken into his office.

I refused to let myself think about the fact that Marilee might already be dead. I could only hope that, whatever had been between them, it was enough that Harvey had put off her execution for a while.

I remembered Marilee's voice, talking to me, soothing me, her hand patting my arm, comforting me. I remembered her crazinesses and the crazy things that had happened to me, Karen Buchanan Travis, a genuine ramrod-spined, pursed-lip, tight-assed Texas princess, since I had known her. I realized that, except for Marilee, I had never had a friend, never had anyone to whom I could confide, who really cared what happened to me. All the people I had known, including my mother and Jack Travis, had merely been acquaintances, people whom I had held at arm's length, who hadn't been able to penetrate my barriers, or who hadn't cared enough even to try. I remembered the innumerable lunches in which Marilee and I had laughed over some trifle she'd seen humor in, more laughter than I'd done in all the years before I'd met her. I remembered her knack for taking other people's discards and making something special from them, something useful and pretty. She'd done that with me, too, I realized, and done it gently, pulling me along, easing me out of my hurt, making me experience life assertively rather than merely waiting to react to whatever happened to me as I'd always done. I remembered her Tang-colored hair, the fake eyelashes that kept coming unstuck in the corners, the Dragon Lady nails, the pink monstrosity that she drove with such feckless abandon around the streets of hapless Santa Fe.

I realized I loved her, that what I felt for her was more than friendship. It was the feeling I should have had for my sisters and didn't.

"Damn!" I said aloud, hitting the steering wheel in desperation. "What am I supposed to do now? What?"

The smart thing to do would be to call David, I told myself, dump it all on him, let him handle it. He was her ex-husband, he obviously still had some feeling for her, he would take care of it. That's what I'd been trained to do—let some man take care of any problems. After all, he was a cop, a professional, and I was merely a woman, someone who'd pretty well demonstrated she could only make a mess of her own life. David would handle it better than I could, I told myself; he did things like that all the time. It was his job.

I remembered the fiasco on the plaza that afternoon. Sure, I thought. David, if left alone, might handle it fine. But what about the others with him? What if they screwed up? Could he guarantee they would act appropriately in any emergency? Could he guarantee Marilee would come out of this with nothing worse than a hair-raising story to tell?

Suddenly, I sat upright in the car, staring sightlessly through the windshield. Something had occurred to me. If Harvey was the one who had Marilee, who'd killed Mac, if Harvey was king of the dope runners, if it was Harvey Wallace who'd killed José with his .357 magnum, then it wasn't Richard who'd done all those things!

Richard, I thought. I could trust Richard, after all. Richard would help me, would know what to do.

My relief was almost a tangible thing inside the car with me. I saw his face, smiling, thoughtful, handsome, rugged, angry. My relief was enormous, the same relief that I'd felt when Mac cleaned up my financial worries.

"If you want me to help you, you'll have to tell me what you know," he'd said. "Mac got himself mixed up in something he shouldn't have."

"Let me help, Karen," he'd said after the plaza thing, and suddenly, remembering his arms around me, I knew what I wanted to do.

I started the car and drove through the small hours of the night to Richard's house and parked in the driveway. There were lights on in several rooms and I gave some thought to the fact that he might be entertaining, but there were no cars parked around, nothing to indicate he was having a party.

Maybe he has a woman in there, I thought. What an ass I would be to blunder in on them.

Marilee's voice, the permission-giving one, spoke up in my mind indignantly, "So what if he has a woman in there? This is a good reason to disturb them, get her out of there. What's he doing with another woman anyway? He could have had you. Take your pinafore off and get in there!"

By the weak moonlight, I made my way firmly to the front door. Just as I was going to press the doorbell, however, something made me pause, suddenly wary, suddenly very alert. The door was slightly ajar, not something that was particularly consistent with life in burglary-prone Santa Fe. Carefully, I pushed on the door, calling Richard's name softly as I did so.

The door swung wide, silently, and I stood there, bewildered by the havoc I saw. Someone had been there before me and had done the same thing to Richard's house as had been done to mine. Someone had wrecked it, looking for something.

"Richard," I called, suddenly frightened out of any anxiety over someone hearing me. "Richard, are you here?"

I went through the rest of the house, frantically, wading through the wreckage, calling him. The house was empty, but as I stood in the living room again, a smudge of something on the cream-colored carpet leaped out at me. I knelt and touched it. It was blood, still wet.

"Oh, Jesus!" I whispered, my mouth suddenly very dry. "Not Richard. Please."

I realized, without having to think about it, that whoever had searched the house had done something to him, probably wounded him and either took him away or he'd dragged himself away. Quickly, I ran outside, looking for him, looking for any sign he'd crawled across the yard. There was nothing. I had to assume he'd been taken away and was now a hostage like Marilee, or worse, that he was dead and they'd taken him to dump his body beside the road—apparently their usual method of getting rid of unwanted bodies.

No, I told myself firmly, trying to keep some measure of control. If they killed him, they'd have left him here. Why would they bother taking him if he were dead and risk being stopped by the police or something. No, he's alive and they've taken him with them.

There was no confusion in my mind then about whether I should tell David what had happened. There was no more mulling things over in my mind, no more mental oscillation. My only thought then was to find Richard and make sure he was all right.

I ran back to my car, leaving the house as I'd found it, and drove out of the city toward Harvey Wallace's place, hoping I could remember how to get to it, hoping I could think of something to do before I got there, praying I wouldn't be too late.

As it happened, I had no trouble finding Harvey's rancho in the dark. As I drove along the highway, hunting the turnoff, I heard a buzzing overhead, and just as I recognized it as being from a light aircraft, its landing lights switched on and it dropped immediately down into the space between two *cerrillitos*. I realized I'd stumbled onto the landing strip, and without doing more than congratulating myself, I drove on past, exactly as if I were out for a moonlight drive or was someone heading home after a late night in Santa Fe.

A mile or so down the road, however, I turned off my lights, turned around, and drove precariously back by the feeble light of the moon. Pulling off the road near the landing strip, I parked behind the only protection in sight, a lone cedar shrub, got out, ran across the road, and with a great deal of difficulty, negotiated the Cyclone fence that surrounded the property. Once on the other side, however, it occurred to me the fence might have been electrified, that, in my naïveté, I had taken the awful chance of electrocuting myself—and then I forgot it. Skirting the open areas between the cedars, I made my way up the hill, pausing several times to get my breath in the thin mountain air. Halfway up, I looked back down at the landing strip and saw there was some movement around the plane, but without any more light than they were using, I couldn't tell if they were loading or unloading.

Please, I thought, hurrying on. Please let them be unloading coke or something. Please don't let them be putting Marilee and Richard in. Please . . .

It seemed I climbed forever. Finally, however, I reached the wall that enclosed the buildings that sat on the top of the *cerrillito*. From the road, the complex had looked impressive, but I now realized it was even larger than I had thought. The adobe wall was probably six feet tall, judging from the relationship to my own height, and it seemed to go on, unbroken by any gate, forever. I tried a practice leap, trying to see over it, and then began looking around for something I could climb on. Nothing presented itself and I followed the wall for some distance before I found any help that I could use—a place in the wall where the mud stucco had flaked off and the adobe bricks had melted, making it a little lower than the rest of the wall. I peered over it cautiously. The expanse of swept yard and most of the buildings that sat in it were quiet, dark. Only in the main house were there any lights, and those were few and blocked somewhat by the smaller outbuildings that sat in the yard between the house and me.

"You should have had this bad spot fixed, Harve," I muttered, and leaping again, I caught the top of the low place, stiffened my arms, and scrambled over. Sprinting for the closest building, I paused by the doorway to open it, poke my head in, and whisper, "Marilee?" There was no answer, and I shut the door and ran for the next building. I was almost certain that Marilee and Richard would be in the main house, but there was always the chance that my luck would hold and I'd find them in one of the outbuildings. I repeated the question at the next building, with the same results, and turned to run to the next building. As I did so, I realized I had stepped in a massive dog pile. I scraped the side of my foot along the ground, and then, realizing that, where there was dog shit, there would also be dogs, and large ones from the size of the pile, I forgot my shoe and ran, with a large loss of aplomb, to the next building. When I tried to open the door, however, I realized it was locked.

"Marilee," I whispered, so close to the door that I felt the splinters on my lips.

"Karen?"

My relief was so great I almost had to sit down. Leaning against the door, I whispered, "Shh! Open the door."

"I can't. It's locked from the outside and I'm tied up."

I looked around without much hope for the key, and realizing that, if it was there, I couldn't see it in the moonlight anyway, I slipped around the building, hunting for a window. There was one on the far wall from the door, a hingeless thing that was designed not to open but merely to let in light. I'd learned about windows, however, and when I'd found a hand-size rock and checked the area again for people, I smacked it sharply against the pane, heard the glass crack, and then, gritting my teeth at the noise, I hit it harder and the glass fell away, leaving a small hole. I rimmed the frame with the rock to knock out the rest of the glass, hauled myself up, and dropped into the darkness of the shed, crouching on the floor, trying to see in the flat blackness.

From somewhere in the distance, I heard a dog begin to bark.

"You asshole! What are you doing here?"

"It's good to see you, too," I whispered, grinning into the darkness. "Where are you?"

"Over here. Did you think to bring the cops or anything with you?"

"No. You told me they'd just screw things up, remember?"

"I changed my mind. What's that terrible smell?"

"Dog shit. I stepped in it on the way over."

She giggled. "Don't tell me Queen Karen actually has dog shit on her shoe!"

I found her and hugged her briefly. "Are you all right?"

"Yeah, but untie me quick. I think my fingers are turning black. I don't suppose you thought to bring anything to eat with you, either?"

"They haven't fed you!"

"This isn't Bishop's Lodge, Karen. No, that son of a bitch Harve is too busy hauling dope in here to even remember to throw us some seaweed once in a while. The fucker!"

"Honey," I whispered, as gently as possible. "Mac . . ."

"I know," she said when I paused, hunting the right words. "I was there. He jumped all over them when they started pushing me around. You should have seen him, Karen. He was magnificent. They never laid a finger on him. It was his heart. Finally. It was the way he wanted to go."

I put my arms around her and we hugged briefly, the second Mrs. Carpenter consoling the first.

"Where's Richard?"

"I don't know. I've been in here most of the day. I didn't think you'd ever get here. Is Ricky here, too?"

Still whispering, I quickly filled her in on the condition that I'd found Richard's house in, working frantically with the knots that held her wrists and ankles together. Finally, she was free, and when she could stand again, I led her to the window.

"Karen, I can't climb up there! It's too high."

"It's either climb up there or stay here. Come on, I'll give you a boost."

I got under the window, and by groping each other, we situated ourselves so she could put one of her feet into my cupped hands. Laboriously, she crawled up me, and my body sagged against the wall with the added weight.

"Marilee," I grunted. "When this is over, you have seriously got to give some thought to losing weight."

"Fuck you."

"Well, a friend would tell you. Be careful of that glass. I may not have gotten it all out of the frame."

With some effort, we poked her through, and thanking my hours on the tennis court, I levered myself up and scrambled through after her. She was already at the corner of the small building, peering around it, preparing to run for the outer wall and freedom. I caught up with her.

"My car's behind some cedars along the road," I told her. "Here are the keys. Go back and get some help."

"What are you going to do?"

"I have to find Richard."

She clutched me. "You can't stay here, Karen!"

"I have to find Richard! I can't leave him here. There's no telling what they'll do to him."

"Karen—"

The dog, which had stopped barking while I was in the building with Marilee, now began again, a different kind of bark, a bark that had a heavy undertone of growling and snarling in it. I pushed at Marilee, impatiently.

"Go on. I'm going to find Richard."

Turning, I sprinted for the main house, hoping he was there, not allowing myself to think of the condition in which I might find him.

I skulked around the perimeter of the main house, drawn to the lighted windows like some great, feckless moth. The house had been designed for passive solar and most of the windows were undraped, so it was easy for me to peer in and see that the house appeared to be deserted.

Perhaps they're all down at the landing strip with the plane, I thought. Of course, if it had come in with a load, it would make sense they were there, taking care of it. Had they taken Richard with them?

I began to search the house for an entrance, realizing the dog's barking was bound to alert somebody sooner or later. It seemed the dog was tied up or fenced or otherwise restrained because his barking got no closer, however much it had intensified. The sound of it did more to frighten me than anything else I'd experienced in a long time. It was an atavistic fear, not something that was produced by any rational thinking on my part, and it was with a great deal of relief that I finally found a sliding door that was unlatched. Opening it, I slipped into the house and shut it again, making a flimsy barrier between me and the dog.

I stood there for a few seconds, getting my breathing under control again and looking around me. I'd entered into the dining room, and by the dim light of the moon through the door and the lighted portions of the house, I made my way carefully through the rooms, avoiding the furniture as much as possible, checking for any sign of Richard.

Just as I'd decided he wasn't there, I heard voices, a door open and shut, and Harvey Wallace said, "It doesn't matter. Turn him loose. He doesn't bark like that for fun."

Oh, Marilee, I thought. I hope to hell you're clear of this place.

The door opened and closed again, and after a minute or two, the dog's barking and snarling became just snarling, low, vicious sounding, dangerous, and growing closer fast. I mentally traced my path up the hill, trying to decide if Marilee had had time to make it back to the car, and decided that, even with the downhill slope, she probably hadn't.

But she'd have a good head start on him, I assured myself, and maybe he'd be confused at first by our diverging trails in the yard.

I forgot the dog, realizing that, with Harvey in the house, I was now in some danger myself. I looked around for some place to hide, but before I could find anything suitable, the dog began to throw himself against the dining room door by which I'd entered. I suddenly realized I was trapped inside the house with a man who killed people, or caused them to be killed, who would have no problem with killing me, and my search for a hiding place took on an added impetus. I slipped down the hall, found the laundry room, and entering, I closed the door to a crack. Holding it that way, I listened. Even on the other side of the house as I was, I could still hear the dog as it slammed itself repeatedly against the dining room door.

God, is he *on* something? I wondered, awed a little by his single-minded attack on the door, and then I forgot the dog as Harvey's voice grew louder down the hall by which I'd come. Frantically, I threw my head around, looking for a place to hide. The laundry room was bare of closets or low cabinets and except for the washer and dryer, it had no furniture to hide behind or under. There was an outside door, but even as badly as I wanted to hide from Harvey, there was no way that I was going outside. The dog was out there.

Quickly I jerked open the dryer and with some difficulty, wadded myself inside it and pulled the door to.

"It doesn't *matter*," Harvey was saying. "The dog will take care of it. Get down to the plane and get Sommerfrught loaded on it. I'll get the other one. We'll kill two birds with one stone."

The other man laughed.

They were right in the laundry room and then I heard the outside door open and close. Someone's, Harvey's, footsteps turned and went back into the hallway.

It was all I could do to stay in the dryer while he walked away, knowing Richard was at the plane, that he'd be out of reach of any help from me soon, that I was trapped uselessly in the house by a demented dog. I heard a door slam and then another, an outside door, and unmindful of my own safety, I unfolded myself from the dryer and gritting my teeth, let myself out of the house by the laundry room door. I ran flat out for the corner of the house, ignoring all discretion in my anxiety over Richard, and rounding it, I smashed right into Harvey. He grabbed me reflexively, and before I could get away from him, he'd latched onto my wrist with an industrial-strength grip.

"Who . . . Why, it's the second Mrs. Carpenter. How odd!"

"Let me go, asshole!"

I jerked uselessly, trying to free myself. He tightened his grip and led me back into the house, closing the door behind us. Turning, he enveloped me in his arms and I smelled the sweet incense smell that permeated his clothing. His embrace was strong, insistent, and with my ear against his chest, I heard it rumble. Amazingly, he was chuckling.

"I've had the oddest feeling that you and I might run into each other again, so to speak. Unresolved karma, don't you know? We've had lifetimes and lifetimes together, Karen. Did you get a sense of it, too?"

"Listen, if you hurt Richard—"

"Who, Sommerfrught? Well, that's out of my hands, you know. We all make choices, darling, and his was to meddle. Now, who am I to deny him his destiny?"

"What?"

"It's really humbling to be a part of someone's life choices and to know we're not responsible for his, or her, lessons. All we can do is try to make his, or her, path a little straighter, give them a hand over the roughest parts."

He made no sense to me and I placed my hands flat against his chest and firmly pushed him away from me, breaking his hug. He grabbed my wrist again and frowned.

"I'm seeing a great deal of negativity in your aura," he said with mock sternness. "We need to work on that."

"Some other time," I muttered, trying to twist away from him.

The barking and snarling outside changed somehow, and then after a short silence, the barking resumed. It was different somehow, slightly frantic and hollow, as if he'd gone into an echo chamber. Harvey, sensing the difference, turned his head and then, dragging me behind him by his grip on my wrist, walked through the house to his bedroom.

Oh, shit, I thought, suddenly frightened by a new anxiety. Surely, he doesn't mean right now?

He ignored the bed, however, walked to the bureau, and opening the drawer, took out a handgun. Without anyone's having to tell me, I knew it was a .357 magnum, *the* .357 magnum. He checked the clip, pointed it in my direction, and released me. I rubbed my aching wrist and watched him, wondering how I could get away from him, or failing that, how I could stall him until Marilee could get back with David and his boys.

The gun was huge and I stared at it, mesmerized a little, much as a bird is mesmerized by a snake. With a surprising amount of effort, I pulled my eyes away from it, refocusing on his smiling, charming face.

"Of course," he was saying, "we may have only a little karma together, quickly resolved, or one of us may choose not to resolve it this lifetime. We always have that free will, you know. So don't try anything foolish. I'm running out of time and I would hate to have to make a destiny decision on the spot. You'll be a good girl, won't you?" he pleaded.

"A good girl? You're telling me to be a good girl? At least, I don't go around smuggling in dope or killing people . . ."

Too late, I realized my mistake and clenched my jaw as I watched his face fall.

"Oh, dear. So that's how it is. How depressing!" His face brightened and he said, "Well, there's always some good in anything, and the good thing here is that I won't have to worry with this too much. You've made the decision yourself, and apparently my karma with you is limited to helping you down your chosen path."

"What!"

"It's not something I'm going to enjoy, but then, a lot of our destiny isn't pleasant, now is it?"

I ignored him, my attention suddenly on the sliding glass door behind him. Very carefully, I called together all the distance I'd learned from Mother, gave him the benefit of her icy remoteness, shuttering my face so he couldn't see any of the horror and consternation that I was feeling. Marilee was standing at the door, her nose against it, cupping her eyes with her hands, peering inside with that nearsighted squint of hers. One sleeve of her blouse was ripped away from the shoulder, and I saw she was missing some more of her fingernails. Seeing us standing there, she jerked herself away from the window, out of sight.

The dog's barking had taken on a pleading note, was getting hoarse.

". . . and then," Harvey was saying, "at the end of each lifetime, we decide if we've completed our lessons correctly or if we'll have to repeat them."

Marilee, you idiot! What are you doing still here? How are we going to get some help? What are they doing to Richard while this idiot's blathering away? And what happened to that dog?

"Tell me more about this destiny business," I said conversationally, moving over to sit on the edge of the bed. Harvey turned to follow me, placing his back to the doorway of the room.

"That's what I've been talking about," he said, a little petulantly.

"I mean, tell me about the drug thing. You're smuggling coke in here. Why?"

"Why not?" He smiled, his good humor apparently restored.

"But you have a good practice. You give seminars all over the West. People respect you. Why would you want to take such a risk?"

"It's lucrative, much more so than listening to neurotics whine about their imagined miseries. Think what good I can do, given enough money. Think of it—the Harvey Wallace Foundation for Spiritual and Psychological Research. Besides"—he shrugged—"I can't seem to resist the challenge. It must be a destiny thing."

"The challenge?"

"Quite a little setup I've made for myself. Someone flies the coke up from Colombia and I take it to my distribution points when I give my little seminars. Never very much, never very often. Just enough to build up a pretty healthy balance in a Swiss bank. I'll be able to retire pretty soon and devote myself to my true calling."

"And to do that, you'd kill people, even Marilee?"

"That would not be my choice, but it's our karma together. The decisions were not mine to make, unfortunately. They were taken out of my hands. As you did when you came here, snooping around. Not very smart, Mrs. Carpenter, and you impressed me as being a very smart lady. I'm disappointed."

He leveled the pistol.

"Well," I said frantically. *Where the hell are you, Marilee?* "I'm not sure I'm understanding what you're saying about destiny."

Patiently, he began again and I nodded occasionally to keep him talking, giving Marilee a chance to get through the house. I could see my face in the mirrored closet door, realized my expression was one of rapt interest, displaying none of the turmoil that was rumbling through my mind.

I heard a tiny clink, somewhere down the hall, then silence.

"Sometimes we get blocked, of course," Harvey was saying. "I feel that's what I've been called here to do, unblock people—"

"Mostly women, I take it?"

I couldn't help the barb but he continued on smoothly, and I realized he was flowing on the sound of his voice, that he was only partially aware of me.

"—give them a sense of their life mission and . . ."

Marilee appeared behind him with a cast-iron skillet in her hand and squinted fiercely, judging her distance. As she brought the skillet down on his head, I jerked sideways to minimize my being shot by reflex action on Harvey's part, but I needn't have worried about it. There was a flat thud and Harvey went limp. The gun fell out of his hand and skittered across the tiles. Before it had stopped, I was on it, picking it up, gingerly.

"Did I get him?"

"You did great. What are you doing here? You're supposed to be—"

"Well, hell, Karen. I couldn't let you go hunting Ricky all alone. No telling what kind of trouble you'd get yourself into, and I was right," she finished triumphantly. Suddenly, savagely, she kicked Harvey's inert form. He made a sound like a blowing whale and I stared at her.

"That's for Mac, you fucking bastard! And this"—she kicked him again—"is for my Cadillac! And this one . . . is for my manicure!"

I was beginning to feel a little sorry for Harvey. He was certainly going to hurt the next day.

"Will you *forget* him? Do you know how to use one of these things?"

"Well," she said, taking a breath, "it's easy enough. You just point it at someone and mash the trigger. My God, Karen, don't you ever watch TV?"

She stepped over Harvey and went into the adjoining bathroom. I heard the sound of running water and then, incredibly, the sound of an electric toothbrush.

"What are you doing?"

"Brushing my teeth," she gurgled.

"Are you crazy!"

"No," she said, rinsing. "I've been sitting in that little house for hours without a toothbrush and I just couldn't stand it any longer. Now I have to pee."

I was already heading for the door. "Catch up when you're through."

"Just wait a minute, will you! It won't take long and you can tie Harve up while you wait. We don't want him waking up and sneaking up on us again, do we?"

It made sense to me and I put the gun down long enough to wrap Harvey pretty thoroughly in some bathrobe cords and ties. Then, for good measure, I roped him to the legs of the bureau. By the time I was satisfied and had picked up the gun again, Marilee was ready to go.

"Good job, Karen. You must have been a Girl Scout once."

"Not in this lifetime. Mother would have cast kittens at the thought of one of her daughters doing something so vulgar."

As she walked past him toward the doorway, she paused to kick him again.

"And what was that one for?" I asked, leading the way down the hall.

"I don't know. Just for fun, I think. I was going to kick him in the balls, but I pulled up at the last second. He was too good in bed. A girl shouldn't work up that kind of karma. No sense in burning bridges behind you."

"Well . . . sure," I said.

I went out the back door warily, Harvey's gun poked out in front of me. I was through fooling around. I was going to shoot the dog the second I saw him. Marilee groped her way after me.

"Do you know where Ricky is?" she asked. "Wait for me."

I paused outside the doorway, looking around. Whispering, I said, "Come on. But be careful of that dog. If we see him, you get out of the way because I'm going to shoot him."

"You won't have to do that. He won't bother us."

"How do you know?"

"Because I took care of him."

I turned to look at her. Her face was merely a blur in the dim moonlight.

"What did you do, for God's sake? He was throwing himself against the door like he was up on something and—"

"There's a little wishing-well thingy over on the other side of the house, can you believe it? Only Harve would have something that corny in his yard. Anyway, it's about ten feet deep. I got the dog in there."

"How did you manage to do that? And if you try to tell me you sweet-talked him into it, I swear to God, I'll shoot *you!*"

"Well, sorta, I did."

I could hear the grin in her voice.

"He jumped for me and I hit him in the face with a shovel. It wasn't real subtle, but it worked fine. It stunned him a little and I just pushed him in. He grabbed for my sleeve as he was going over the edge and tore the hell out of my blouse. This was a Bottalini, too. I got it at the Sally for only—"

"Marilee, they're going to load Richard into the plane! How do we get down to the landing strip?"

"Oh. There's a path that leads down to the hangar. Over here somewhere. Here it is."

I pushed past her and sprinted down the graveled path, turned my ankle in the loose rocks, and fell headlong. I felt the skin on my hands sting, and rolling up to a sitting position, I did a cursory examination of the knees of my slacks. They were ripped, and in the moonlight, I could see a dark patch forming on one of them. Marilee reached past me and picked up the gun.

"Are you all right?"

"Yes, damn it. I'm fine."

She gave me her hand and, grunting, levered me up.

"You shouldn't run on these paths, Karen. They're—"

"Thanks, Mother."

"Well, a friend would tell you. Now, you'd better take the gun because I probably couldn't hit the side of the hangar with it unless I were right up against it."

I took the pistol, and limping, I led the way down the hill again. Running was out of the question anyway since my knees were killing me, and Marilee was right, the path was far too steep and treacherous for anything more than a fast walk.

The hangar was little more than a T-shaped pole barn, airplane size, walled on all the sides except the front, and roofed with tin. The plane was pushed back inside it and three or four men lounged around, leaning on the far wing, the fire from their cigarettes making red dots in the haphazard moonlight. I put my hand out behind me, warning Marilee. Cautiously, I peered around the edge into the hangar, looking for Richard in the gloom.

Please don't let him already be in the plane, I prayed. Please. Give us a break.

I smelled Marilee's perfume before I heard her hiss in my ear, "Over here."

Leaning against the back of the hangar was a good-size shed, and in the light of the moon, I could see the hasp was held shut by a spike slipped through the loop. Marilee was already working on it, swearing under her breath as she lost the last of her fingernails in the effort. I leaned against the door to ease the pressure off the hasp. It slipped out and she opened the door, leaning inside.

"Ricky?" she whispered into the darkness.

There was no answer, but hearing rough breathing, I pushed past her hurriedly, and sweeping my arms out in arcs in front of me, I moved forward, hunting for Richard. My foot hit something solid, producing a groan from the floor, and my hands, reaching down, touched warm cloth. I felt the solid body inside it, felt dampness, stickiness on it.

"Richard," I whispered frantically, gathering him up into my arms. "Richard?"

"Karen?" he said groggily.

"Shh. They're right outside."

His voice obediently dropped to a whisper. "Sweetheart, you shouldn't be . . . Shit! Stop jerking me around like that! You're killing me!"

"Oh, God, Richard! What are you doing here?"

"That goes double for you. Would it be too much to hope for that you and Marilee could just let things the hell alone?"

"Listen! Just how badly are you hurt anyway?"

"I got roughed up some in the scuffle, is all. Somebody hit me with something and my head hurts like hell. This sure hasn't been my week, has it? First that old man punching me out and then this. What are you doing here?"

"You're *welcome*, Richard! I'm sorry Marilee and I came out here and rescued you!"

"I'm not rescued yet, but thanks for the effort. Now how did you get here?"

"I went out to your house and it looked like you'd had a fraternity party in it. Then I saw blood and I figured—"

"I jumped them when those assholes started tearing up my Bakos. God damn them! I don't suppose you thought to bring a gun with you, did you?"

"Well, as a matter of fact, I—"

"Great! Just great! Give it to me! How many rounds do you have?"

"What?"

"Did you bring any extra ammo? Ammunition? The gun *is* loaded, isn't it?"

"Well . . . I'm not sure. We took it away from Harvey."

"Karen," Marilee whispered. "Come over here and look!"

"What is it?"

"Baggies and Baggies of stuff, all neatly stacked up. This must be Harve's stash."

Richard got slowly to his feet and then sagged against me. I grabbed him on his way down, eased him to the floor.

"Oh, Jesus," he whispered, his voice shaking.

"Are you all right?"

"No. I think I'm . . ."

He suddenly went limp, and frantically, I whispered to Marilee. There was no answer.

"Marilee, where are you?"

The only sound was Richard's rasping breathing. I felt on the dirt floor until I found the gun he'd dropped. Holding it in my hands gave me some measure of security, and I crouched on the floor between the open door and Richard's body, trying to decide what to do. A dark form stepped into the comparative light of the doorway. I raised the pistol, aimed it, trying to control my shaking. My jaw was set and I took a deep breath, steadying myself. Nothing, I told myself, no one was going to do anything else to Richard than had already been done to him. I was determined, fiercely so.

"Karen," Marilee's voice whispered. "Where are you?"

"You idiot, I almost shot you!"

"Look what I got!"

She groped toward me, and taking my hand, she placed it on something metallic and cold. I felt along it and realized it was another gun—a rifle or shotgun, something with a long barrel.

"Where did you get this?"

"It was just leaning up against the wall. So I thought, fut the whuck! and took it. We can always use another gun, can't we? I bet I could scare hell out of somebody with this, even without my glasses."

Her excitement and pleasure would have been evident to anyone with the intellect of a stone. Cruelly, I shredded her triumph.

"Richard's passed out again. I think he's lost a lot of blood. How are we going to get him out of here? Neither one of us can carry him. Even if my knees didn't hurt, I don't think I could haul him very far and you sure couldn't carry him. Now what?"

She was silent for a few seconds.

"How far away is your car?"

"Too far. It's parked almost directly at the end of the landing strip, across the road."

She was silent for a few more seconds and I let her think. I was fresh out of ideas myself.

"So if we can get him down to the end of the landing strip, how far would we have to carry him from there?" she asked.

"Across the pasture a little way to the fence, over the fence, and then across the road. Maybe seventy or eighty feet, all told. But Marilee, how can we get him down there? The landing strip has to be at least a mile long."

"You know anything about driving a plane?"

"What! Marilee, I couldn't fly a plane on a bet. I—"

"I didn't say anything about flying it. I said drive it. All we have to do is load Ricky up in the plane and drive it down to the end of the landing strip. I don't have my glasses and Ricky's out of it, so you'll have to do the driving."

"Listen, you idiot! I wouldn't know the first thing about 'driving' a plane. I wouldn't even know how to start it. No, Marilee. No. I'd kill us all."

"And Harve and his boys won't? We don't have anything to lose, Karen. It's our only chance. Unless, of course, you want to leave Ricky here while we go get help."

"No! They'll kill him!"

"Right, so we have to take him with us. The only way we can is for you to drive us. And the only thing out there to drive is that plane."

I sighed. It was a ragged sigh that left me almost limp.

"I wish I'd never met you, Marilee."

"Oh, bullshit! Think of all the fun we've had." I could hear the grin in her voice. "You can't tell me you'd rather be working at the Museum Shop and fighting for money. Just think of these guys as the IRS and all those creditors that Mac . . ."

I patted her arm when she hesitated. In the danger of the last few hours, both of us kept forgetting Mac had died. Marilee took a deep breath.

"What'll it be, Karen? Drive us out or sit here, wailing and wringing our hands, waiting for somebody to go up to the house, find and untie Harve so he can come down here and shoot us all?"

I sighed again. "I guess we don't have a hell of a lot to lose, do we? All right, all right. One question, though: How are we going to get Richard on the plane?"

"Do I have to think of everything? My God, Karen, give me a break!"

"Well, you can get mad if you want to! But whose idea was it to dump that coke in the john in the first place and—"

"Shut up."

We sat there for a few moments, and then remembering, I said, "They're supposed to load Richard in the plane. Let's let them do it. We sneak around and get in first. When they load him in, we take off, right? In a manner of speaking that is. And that'll give me time to look over the instruments and things."

"Great! You're all right, Karen. You get your back to the wall, darlin', you do just fine."

"Thanks. Now come on before they come after Richard and catch us in here."

We left the shed, relocking it behind us, and crept around the back to the other side of the hangar, peering around it. The men were still congregated around the wing, smoking and talking. We were, however, close enough to hear them, and Marilee pulled me back, away from the edge of the wall.

Putting her mouth close to my ear, she whispered, "How are we going to get past them to get in the plane?"

I gave it some thought. Motioning for her to follow me, I went to the back of the hangar and went a little way into the scrub cedars. Crouching behind one, I pulled her down with me and whispered, "Look. Let them load him first. We couldn't hide in the plane anyway. There wouldn't be any place to hide in there, except the baggage compartment in the rear. I think Jack had a plane like this, and if it is the same kind of plane, that baggage compartment is tiny, believe me. I, for one, have had enough of being wadded into a small space. So, they load him up, and when they leave, *then* we get in. All right?"

"But how will you know about the instruments? Did you fly much with Jack?"

"No, only a couple of times when he first got his license. I decided pretty quick he was going to kill us both and I quit riding with him."

"You won't have much time to look anything over."

"Well, maybe I will. They're waiting for Harvey, aren't they? I can personally guarantee you it will take a while for Dr. Harvey Wallace to come down that hill."

She was silent for a few seconds.

"Maybe," she said slowly, "maybe we should divert them some."

"What do you mean?"

"After they load Ricky up, what if we give them something to look at besides the plane. That way we can get in and get gone before they realize what's going on."

"Look at? Like what?"

There was some suspicion in my voice. I had gotten very leery of Marilee's ideas.

"Well, maybe a fire or something. Maybe set the burglar alarm off at the house. It's too bad we didn't think to call Davy while we were up there."

"Yeah, isn't it?" I said sourly.

"Well, that can't be helped now. What do you think of—"

"Shh." I grabbed her arm. There was some activity around the shed in which Richard was locked.

"They're getting Ricky?"

•"And they're not being any too gentle about it, either, are they?"

She was silent, but when I half rose in response to the sight of Richard's inert body being roughly dragged between two of the men, she patted my arm. I was conditioned enough by then to relax again, squat back in the sandy New Mexican soil, unmindful of what was left of my pants, and wait more or less patiently for them to finish loading him in the plane.

After a few minutes, the plane rolled out onto the landing strip, pushed by the men who'd been standing around before.

"Marilee! They're getting ready to go!"

"Don't panic now. They have to wait for Harve, remember?"

"How are we going to get into it, sitting out in the open like that? They'll see us run across the tarmac!"

"Not if they're not there, they won't."

"What are we going to do to chase them away?"

"Not 'we.' I am going to go up to the house, set something on fire, creating great havoc and causing them to leave the plane alone. While I'm doing that, you get into the plane when you can, get it started, and figure out how to drive it. I'll hurry back down, and while they're fighting the fire, we'll hit the road. In a manner of speaking, that is."

In the moonlight, I could see the grin on her face.

"I'm glad you're having so much fun, Marilee. I just wish I could disengage my good sense like you have and party right along with you."

"Well, fut the whuck, darlin'. Did you have anything better to do tonight? Now you sit here and when they leave—"

"I know, I know. Get in the plane."

"Right."

She started to get up, but suddenly, my hand went out and grabbed her shirt, pulling her down again so our faces were level.

"Marilee. Be careful. Okay? Please. I . . ."

She patted my arm. "I know, Karen. We're all we got. You be careful, too, hear? Oh, by the way, don't wait too long. If I'm not back in a few minutes, you go on and send somebody back for me."

"Oh, no, Marilee! I'm not leaving without you. You hurry back and—"

"Why in the hell are you so stubborn? Why do you have to argue with me about everything? Listen! You have to think about Ricky and yourself now. If I see I can't make it back, I'll hole up somewhere and hide until help comes, okay? I'll be all right."

"Marilee . . . Okay! God damn it! Do it your way then! Just be careful, please!"

"You know me. I wouldn't lie to a girlfriend. Here, take care of my gun while I'm gone."

"Wait! Take this one. You might need it."

I handed her Harvey's .357 magnum and she got up to make her way uphill through the cedars while I sat in the dirt, my sore knees stretched out in front of me, watching her go in the weak moonlight.

I sat for hours, it seemed, though it could only have been minutes. During that time, my fatigue, which my body had held in abeyance with adrenaline, hit me, and my knees, which had merely been painful until then, began to ache in earnest. It seemed every bone in my body ached, every muscle, and the tendons in my neck had turned into old, weathered rawhide, had withered up until they were so painful that my entire neck hurt. My brain, responding to my lack of sleep, felt lithified, as if someone had opened the top of my skull and poured in cement. It was too dark to see my watch, but I estimated the time to be around four o'clock, not my favorite time of day in the best of circumstances. My eyes stung and I considered closing them for a few minutes, lying down on the dirt and resting until Marilee did her fire thing and I could sprint for the plane. I realized, however, that if I did that, I might not ever be able to get up again. That realization, and the worse worry that scorpions might crawl on me if I slept, precluded my lying down and closing my eyes, however tempting it was. My thighs quivered, jerking with pain, exhaustion, and tension, and I rubbed them, much as I would have done after a heavy-duty tennis tournament, promising myself that if, when, Marilee and I got through this thing, we would go in and have a deep-tissue massage that would go on for hours. Only that, I told myself, would make me feel halfway decent again.

Marilee, on the other hand, had seemed as alert and energetic as she had hours before, and I wondered where she found that energy. Physically, I was in much better shape since her only form of exercise was flirting, and moreover, I was several years younger than she.

Thinking about Marilee caused me to worry again, and rather than sit and wonder about what might be happening to that half-blind, half-witted woman, I gave some thought to how to "drive the plane." I remembered very little of those few times I had ridden with Jack, except terror and rampant airsickness. Jack had been prone to daredevil acrobatics, and I had come away from my flights with him with two certainties: I would never, never fly again in little planes, and it's not impossible for a person to barf while upside down. Now, I scraped through my memories of those flights, unpleasant as they were, trying to remember what Jack had done to taxi the thing down the tarmac in preparation for takeoff or after landing. I remembered there was a key to start the ignition, like a car, and that, to steer it on the ground, one manipulated foot pedals. Other than those two things, I could remember very little except...

I frowned, thinking, remembering. Jack had taxied down the tarmac and while he was doing so, had talked into the microphone to the tower, getting takeoff clearance.

Abruptly, my head cleared, my lithified brain began to function again. I had forgotten the plane would have a microphone, that, with that microphone, I could contact someone, the police, or failing that, the tower at the Santa Fe airport! Once I got in the plane, I could start trying to contact someone while I was waiting for Marilee to get back. Maybe, with any luck, we could get someone out fast enough that we could have help getting Richard from the plane to my car.

As if cued, the top of the *cerrillo* flamed, much like a small volcano, and I dragged myself up, bending my stiff legs into a painful crouch, so as to be ready when the men left the plane alone.

Everything happened pretty fast after that. In seconds, they had seen the fire and left the plane and hangar to run up the path. Breathing a short prayer that Marilee would have the sense not to use the path coming back down, I legged it toward the hangar as fast as I could, dragging Marilee's gun, praying also the key would be in the ignition. Carefully, I peered around the edge, making sure no one had remained behind to guard the plane, and when I realized it was clear, I limped out from behind the hangar, hurrying as much as my legs would allow, and dragged myself up on the wing and opened the door on the passenger's side. Richard was slumped on one of the backseats and I paused to make sure he was still alive and to buckle him in. Then, I slid into the pilot's seat.

The key was there and I gave some thought to starting it. Did I put it in some kind of gear? I didn't think so but I wasn't sure. Frantically, I went through my memories again. My mind fizzed, spewed. What if it jumped on me and started going? Where were the brakes? I took a deep breath, made myself relax, and mashed tentatively on the foot pedals. Nothing happened that I could tell, and gritting my teeth, I turned the ignition, pushing the pedals all the way down as I did so. The engine coughed, rattled, and died. I felt with my foot for an accelerator and then remembered that, instead of that, there would be a throttle. Groping around in the moonlight, I found it, twisted it savagely, turned the ignition again, and stomped the foot pedals reflexively when the plane coughed, rattled, roared, and lurched forward viciously. Thankfully, it stopped in response to the pedals, and I sat there for a few seconds with the engine roaring and vibrating the plane, causing it to tug back and forth while I got my nerves under control again. My legs were quivering so much by then I could barely keep the pedals down, but I ignored them, trying to adjust the throttle so the engine didn't roar so much. When I'd done that, I realized the plane's tugging against the pedals had eased somewhat, but just as I was about to activate the microphone, I realized my bad knee had completely given out suddenly, that the plane was beginning to rotate on the landing strip, describing a slow, tight circle. Panicked, I tried to force my bad leg to cooperate, but the pain was so intense I had to ease up. Swearing, I waited until the plane was aligned with its nose pointing down the landing strip again, and then I twisted the throttle way down, off. The engine died.

I sat there, sweating for a few seconds, and then, with the ignition key turned on, I tried working the microphone, twisting the knob through the frequencies until I heard conversation. I pressed the microphone button and yelled, interrupting the conversation, "Hello, hello. This is an emergency! Can you hear me?"

"Reading you, emergency. What is your position? Over."

"I'm south of Santa Fe, south and west of Galisteo. Hello? Hello . . . ? Over."

"I'm not picking you up on radar, emergency. Can you give more definite position? Over."

"I'm on the ground. On a landing strip. Dr. Harvey Wallace's landing strip. I can't tell you exactly where, but it's somewhere south of Santa Fe, just after you get to the Galisteo turnoff and east of the highway maybe a couple of miles. . . . Over."

"If you're on the ground, what's the emergency? Over."

Suddenly, I heard gunfire, coming from the top of the *cerrillo*.

"Oh, my God! They're shooting at her!"

I realized I hadn't depressed the mike button and did so, repeating and adding, "They're coke dealers and they're shooting at my friend!

Call the police. The Santa Fe police. Call David Finch. He's a detective with the police. He knows about this. Tell him Karen Carpenter and Marilee Wallace are trying to get away in a plane and we need help! Fast...! Over."

"Marilee Wallace? The woman who drives that pink Cadillac?"

"Yes!"

For the first time, there was a tiny bit of agitation in the voice.

"Roger. Copy. Will do. Do not, repeat, do not take off. Do you copy? Over."

"Are you *serious!* I'd rather be shot dead than get this thing up in the air and barf upside down again! Just get David Finch or somebody out here. Fast!"

"Wilco. Over and out."

The plane suddenly dipped to the side a little, and from the corner of my eye, I saw a dark form scramble up onto the passenger's wing. Marilee jerked open the door.

"Let's go," she yelled, breathing in great panting breaths. "Why aren't you started yet?"

I grabbed her, hugging her, overcome by relief that was almost painful in its intensity.

"Are you all right? I heard shots."

"Yeah, so did I. Who knows what the stupid assholes were shooting at. Probably each other. I hope so, anyway. I took the time to call Davy. Aren't you proud of me?

"What did he say?"

"Later! Let's get going, for God's sake!"

"You're going to have to drive. My knee's out."

"Are you serious! I don't know the first thing about—"

"Weren't you the one who was having such a good time, playing tough lady? If you can drive that stupid Cadillac, then you sure as hell can drive this plane. Get over here!"

"I don't have my glasses," she said. But she traded places with me and fumbling with the steering wheel, said, "I don't know what to do. I don't have my glasses."

"So what else is new? That's never stopped you before. I'll tell you what to do. You just listen. Buckle yourself in first."

I spoke rapidly, telling her how to start it, and whispering to herself, she got the plane started, got it moving slowly down the runway.

"The steering wheel doesn't work!" she yelled. "What do I do now!"

"You steer with those foot pedals while you're on the ground. They're brakes. You mash the one on the side of the direction you want to go."

My instructions were confusing, but Marilee grasped the concept immediately and the plane straightened out on the runway. I increased the throttle a little and we began moving faster. Marilee crouched close to the wheel, squinting intently through the windshield.

"Doesn't this thing have any lights?" she asked through gritted teeth.

"There's landing lights somewhere but I don't know which switch—"

"Find it! I can't see worth shit!"

I fumbled along the dashboard, feeling for a switch, and finally found a set of two toggles. Without letting myself speculate on what they might be for, I flipped them and the lights glared out in front of us.

"Thanks."

"You're doing fine, Marilee."

"Just tell me when we come to the fence. I can't see much farther than the end of this plane."

From somewhere behind us, I heard a shout and then more gunfire. This time very much closer.

"Karen! They're shooting at us!"

I didn't answer her but twisted the throttle instead, and the plane lurched ahead.

"What are you doing!"

"Making us go faster. Just watch the road."

Our speed built rapidly and it was with some satisfaction that I realized we were leaving the men behind us. I looked ahead, hunting for the end of the runway and the fence, which should have been a little farther still. The plane hopped and then hopped again, a longer hop. I felt my body sink a little into the seat.

"Karen, we're taking off! Oh, dear God . . ."

I was already twisting the throttle back and the plane suddenly fell, heavily, hit the ground, and bounced. Marilee twisted the steering wheel frantically.

"Push it forward! Push it away from you!" I yelled at her. She shoved the wheel toward the nose of the plane and it fell again, bounced twice more, and stopped. The engine roared, vibrating the plane.

Marilee sat, statuelike, her arms and legs stiff out in front of her, staring at the landing strip in front of us. I twisted the throttle back again until the engine was nothing more than a purring kitten.

"Shit," I whispered.

Marilee gulped twice and I realized she was swallowing back vomit. She was no longer squinting. Her eyes were bulging, huge, round.

The intensity and decibles of the gunfire behind us increased, suddenly.

"Ready to go again?" I asked. "Marilee?"

"Sure you don't want to drive?"

"You're doing just fine. Just a little farther now. We have to, Marilee. If they get after us in a car..."

"Let's just kind of tootle down the road like a couple of little old ladies in a doodlebug, okay? I forgot to tell you, I get sick when I fly."

"So do I. So we won't. Okay, ready? I'm just turning it up a little now, okay? You're doing great, Marilee."

I increased the throttle a tiny bit and the plane began shuddering.

"Marilee, let off the foot pedals a little."

"I can't. My legs won't work."

"Now, Marilee. I just turned it on a little. We won't be going very fast at all. Come on, Marilee. We have to. They're right behind us. Come *on!*"

She shifted slightly and the plane began inching forward slowly. I turned the throttle up a little more.

"What are you doing?"

"We have to build up a little speed, Marilee, so that we can get through the fence."

"What! What do you mean, get *through* the fence? I'm not driving this thing into that fence."

"Why not? You've hit everything in Santa Fe with that fucking car of yours. Why would this bother—"

"Listen! You hit something with a plane and it explodes! Don't you ever watch the news?"

"It's the only way to get through it. We can't climb over it. I did that, coming in, but it nearly killed me and my knees were fine then. There's no way we could get over it now and we sure couldn't get Richard over it. So we have to go through it with this plane."

I increased the throttle again.

"Karen, listen! That's a Cyclone fence. Planes can't go through Cyclone fences."

"You don't know that! It's all we have, Marilee. We have to try."

The end of the runway loomed ahead, and past that, the fence gleamed in the landing lights of the plane, solid, impenetrable. I increased the throttle.

"Karen, it won't work!"

Marilee jammed her legs stiff. The plane shuddered, slowed.

"Get your feet off those pedals, Marilee! It's our only shot. Get 'em off!"

"We can't do it now!"

The plane slowed, stopped with its nose at the end of the runway, quivering like some huge horse stopped in the act of taking a hurdle. Marilee took a deep breath.

"We can't do it from here. We have to turn around and go back a little way so we can build up some speed again. How do you turn this thing around?"

"Lift one of your feet."

I twisted back the throttle and we rotated slowly, heading back toward the hangar. When we'd gone some distance, she stopped the plane again and took a deep breath. In front of us, coming down the *cerrillo*, car lights vied with the dying light from the fire Marilee had set.

"Here they come," I said quietly.

"I know. I know. You wish you'd never let me talk you into this. Well, so do I. Here we go."

The plane rotated and we started down the runway again. Marilee reached down and twisted the throttle all the way up. The plane jumped.

"Oh, shit," I said, suddenly realizing what she was going to do. "Marilee . . ."

"When I say 'now,' you turn that thingy back off again. All the way. Tell me when we're at the end of the runway. Okay?"

"Oh, shit, ohshit, ohshitohshitohshit!"

"*Shut up!*"

The end of the runway loomed again and behind it the fence. At the very end of the runway I yelled, "*Do it!*" and Marilee, squinting fiercely, jerked back on the steering wheel and then, as the plane cleared the fence, shoved it forward again, hard.

"Now!" she screamed, and I twisted the throttle back all the way. The engine coughed and died and we hit the highway, bounced, skewed sideways, bounced again, rotated end to nose in the air, and fell into the cedar where my car was parked.

I realized I was screaming and shut up.

Marilee blew out her breath and looked at me.

"I wet my pants," she whispered. "God damn old-timer's disease! Harve's gonna have a fit when he finds out."

From the backseat, Richard moaned, and at that, we jerked out of our seat belts and dragged him off the plane. It took some doing to stuff him in the back of the Mercedes, but we managed, and as we roared out onto the highway, the car that had been following us down the runway skidded to a stop hard against the fence. I heard gunfire again, much closer, and the back window of my car crumpled and fell out, showering Richard's inert body with glass granules.

"Oh, my God, Karen! They're shooting at us!"

"Where are our guns, Marilee?"

"Still in the fucking plane, can you believe it!"

"Well, we're not going back after them!"

I floorboarded the accelerator and the powerful engine responded, hurtling the car down the highway. Ahead of us, topping a rise in the road, red and blue lights blinked abruptly.

I hit the brakes so hard the car turned sideways before it stopped, and piling out, we raced toward the sheriff's car. It swerved, fishtailing to a stop, and I saw there were more behind it.

"Go up to the house!" I yelled at the sheriff's deputy who got out. "They have the world's largest coke stash up there. Look in the shed behind the hangar on the runway!"

7

fter a couple of hours at the police station, Marilee and I were excused to go home. My knee was killing me, but nothing, short of murder, would have kept me from falling into bed and sleeping away the entire day. That evening, at Marilee's insistence, I went down to St. Vincent's Hospital, got my knee x-rayed, taped, and braced, and then dragged myself upstairs to visit Richard, who'd come off relatively lightly with a mild concussion and the loss of a lot of blood from his scalp wound. Then I went back home and went back to bed.

The next morning, we spent several hours with David Finch, men from the Santa Fe County Sheriff's office, and some people who looked as if they might be skinheads, but who turned out to work for the federal narcotics-enforcement agencies and who stared at us in absolute disbelief when we explained our involvement in the entire mess. David pretended he'd just learned about our flushing the bag of coke down the john, and to give him credit, he was a pretty good actor. He'd learned a lot from living with Marilee after all.

When it was all over, Marilee and I were free to go, and we dragged our aching bodies over to Pasqual's for brunch to rehash everything.

Richard, it turned out, had been working in a small way for the feds; he'd served in the Crotch with one of them and was merely "keeping an eye on some people" as a grudging favor. Mac, true to his own particular brand of paranoia, apparently thought Richard, having stolen one of his wives, was after the other and was somehow responsible for the attempts on his life, so he had his own little investigation going. He'd apparently jumped to some pretty accurate conclusions, gotten too close to Harvey Wallace, and when Marilee had flushed away the bag of coke, was suspected of it.

"So I really did kill him," Marilee said, twirling pasta on her fork absently.

"Well, I don't think you can say that. You know what Harvey says. Everything's karma. Weren't you the one who said Mac really wanted to die? Didn't you tell me he was living on borrowed time?"

"Well, yeah, but . . ."

"So, you miss him. Admit it."

"Well, I do! He was an asshole, but you know, if someone suddenly removes a boil from your finger, you miss it. And Karen, he wasn't always like you knew him."

I could see that, given any chance at all, she'd pass over from being sad to downright morose. I knew how to cure that, however. Gently, I patted her arm.

"Well, fut the whuck, honey," I said. "What are you going to do with your share of the money?"

She brightened instantly.

"First thing, I'm going to buy a new car and hire a little cookie bandit to drive it for me. Then I'm going to get some contacts. I'm tired of losing my glasses all the time. I guess I'll get a house somewhere—"

"Why don't you continue to live with me?"

She stared at me. "I thought you and Ricky . . . Well, after a decent time, of course, that you and Ricky would get married."

I grinned at her. "Now, why would I do a thing like that?"

"Well, I just assumed . . . You know how you are about him."

"Richard is wonderful and right now I love him, but I don't think I want to get married any more."

"Why not?"

"Why?"

"I asked you first."

"There's no reason to get married, Marilee. I have money. Lots and lots of it, thanks to Mac. After what happened the other night, I sure don't need anyone to take care of me anymore, and from the looks of things, I would be having to take care of him. And as Mac used to say, why buy a cow when milk is so cheap? Besides, what if I got married and Robert Redford came along and wanted me to go to Africa or somewhere with him? No, I don't think I will. Being a serial marrier like some people we know and love doesn't really appeal to me."

"Screw you."

I laughed. "Well, a friend would tell you. Hey, I know what let's do this afternoon. Let's go find us an investment banker and wheel and deal like the big boys."

"I know just the one. You'll *like* him."

"He's not another one of your ex-husbands, is he?"

"No, God, honey, but he's as darlin' a little sweetheart as you'll ever see."

"I'll leave him to you. I can only take care of one man at a time." She sipped her wine.

"You know, Karen. Now that it's all over, it was kinda fun, wasn't it?"

"What! Are you crazy? We nearly died! I've never been so scared in my life and you were, too. Admit it."

"Well, it sure beats sitting around the Pink, drinking and getting old. I wouldn't mind doing something like that again."

"Do me a favor and don't try to talk me into doing it with you."

"Admit it, Karen. You had fun."

"Finish your pasta."

"I'm not hurrying through this. I've rushed too many meals lately. This one I'm enjoying."

"Fut the whuck, right?"

"Right."

Author's Note

Several people were nice enough to take the time to talk to me about things I wasn't sure of.

JON CHACOPULOS, PH.D., my classic car resource person (who I suspect almost had a heart attack when the Caddy got trashed) and who read the finished manuscript for plot logic and a man's viewpoint.

DOUG FLOYD, my gun person, who assures me that, even though a .357 is pretty heavy for an automatic frame, there is a company that makes them.

MIKE GOODSPEED, Public Affairs Officer, Oklahoma City Police Department, who talked to me about police work, drove me around in his cruiser, and showed me what real cops are like.

JENNIFER JASPER GOURLEY, who plotted with me initially, who, during the writing, provided encouragement every time I was sure the stepwives had done something irrevocably stupid, and who dealt with my constant anxiety that they wouldn't be able to handle successfully what they'd gotten themselves into.

DARRELL HARRIS PARKER, who enthusiastically read the manuscript, told me it was wonderful, that I was wonderful for writing it, and who taught me that life can be, and often is, fun for fiftyish women.

CHET WALTER, District Attorney, First Judicial District, Santa Fe, New Mexico, who gave me some helpful insights into the criminal mind.

GINNY WILSON, who proofed the manuscript and was so full of praise that I was encouraged to try and peddle the thing.

These people shared their knowledge with me and/or provided support and for that, I thank them. Any mistakes are my own.